*"After that massage, I will follow you
to the moon and back."*

She stood up, got her foot tangled in a cord and stumbled right into his arms.

"Whoa, there, darlin'. I know I worked the kinks out of your neck but I didn't touch your legs," he teased.

One second she was straightening up; the next he was looking down into her brown eyes and then his lips closed on hers. The kiss set off bells and whistles so loud that he couldn't hear a damn thing but ringing in his ears. Her lips were soft and the way her hands pressed against his chest sent bursts of heat right through his shirt to his skin. Dammit! Dammit! He'd never been so attracted to a woman in his whole life. It wasn't fair that fate had put her in his pathway and then said he couldn't have her.

Merry Cowboy Christmas

Merry Cowboy Christmas

Lucky Penny Ranch, Book 3

Carolyn Brown

FOREVER

NEW YORK BOSTON

Copyright © 2016 by Carolyn Brown

Cover illustration by Blake Morrow
Cover design by Elizabeth Turner
Cover copyright © 2016 by Hachette Book Group, Inc.

Forever
Hachette Book Group
1290 Avenue of the Americas
New York, NY 10104
forever-romance.com
twitter.com/foreverromance

First edition: September 2016

Forever is an imprint of Grand Central Publishing.
The Forever name and logo are trademarks of Hachette Book Group, Inc.

The publisher is not responsible for websites (or their content) that are not owned by the publisher.

The Hachette Speakers Bureau provides a wide range of authors for speaking events. To find out more, go to www.hachettespeakersbureau.com or call (866) 376-6591.

ISBNs: 978-1-4555-3494-4 (mass market), 978-1-4555-3495-1 (ebook)

Printed in the United States of America

OPM

10 9 8 7 6 5 4 3 2 1

In memory of my grandfather,
Herman Gray.
Thank you for all the sweet memories
and for your faith in me.

Dear Readers,

Sometimes a couple of characters come along who just steal an author's heart. Jud and Fiona were like that for me. I loved Allie and Blake in *Wild Cowboy Ways*—who doesn't love a wild cowboy with no intentions of being tamed? And I adored Lizzy and Toby—starting backward sometimes does have its reward. But Fiona, with her wanting to belong, and Jud, with his determination to put down roots, combined with all the magic of the Christmas spirit—it was a story I loved telling. I have to admit, they've become my favorite holiday couple.

As always, there are many people who help me take a book from a two-paragraph idea all the way to the book in your hands. To those I owe my deepest gratitude. First I'm taking a deep bow to my editor, Leah Hultenschmidt. And then another one to the team at Forever—from cover guru Elizabeth Turner to marketing expert Jodi Rosoff and publicist extraordinaire Fareeda Bullert. And one more to Bob Levine and Raylan Davis from the sales team. I'm so blessed to have all these fabulous folks working on my team! Now that my head is dizzy from bobbing up and down, I'll simply raise a cup of coffee to toast everyone at Grand Central. You are all totally amazing and I'm honored to be working with you.

A curtsey to my agent, Erin Niumata, and my agency, Folio Management, Inc., for continuing to support me. And my thanks as well as my love to Mr. B, the man I've been married to for half a century. He's always ready to drop whatever he's doing and take a road trip with me to see the places that I write about. And to my readers, hugs to you all for being the best fans in the whole world.

'Tis the season right now to be jolly, so enjoy your visit in Dry Creek, Texas, over the holiday as you read *Merry Cowboy Christmas*.

Here's wishing all my readers a very Merry Christmas.

Until next time,
Carolyn Brown

Merry Cowboy Christmas

Chapter One

J ud Dawson tapped the brakes and slid a few feet before his big black truck came to a stop. The rusted out old bucket of bolts he'd been following on the slick road wasn't quite so lucky, though. It kept going right through a barbed wire fence, taking out two steel posts before it finally came to a halt, kissing a big scrub oak tree about fifteen feet from the fence line.

Jud had barely scrambled from the cab of his truck to see if the driver was unhurt when a redheaded woman dressed in tight jeans, boots, and a sweater hopped out of the truck, kicked the shit out of her blown-out tire, and tangled both her fists in her hair in anger.

"Are you okay?" he yelled as he ran toward her, phone in hand ready to call 911 if he needed to.

"Hell no! My truck is a wreck. I'm going to be late to dinner and I'm so mad I could spit tacks." She shook her fist at the gray skies. "Damn tires only needed to run for another half a mile. Since when does this part of Texas get snow in November? I should thank you, but I'm too mad to be polite right this second."

"I can take you wherever you need to go," Jud offered.

She stopped ranting and shivered. "Do you know where Audrey's Place is?"

He nodded. "Yes, ma'am, that's actually where I was headed. You must be..."

He hesitated, trying to remember her name. Faith. Fancy. Something that started with an *F*, or was it a *V*? If she was headed to Audrey's, then she had to be the youngest Logan sister, the married one from Houston who everyone said was giving Midas a run when it came to money. So what the hell was she doing driving a ratty old truck?

"I'm Fiona Logan, and I do thank you for stopping and for offering. Let me just get my stuff. The suitcase and box can wait," she said.

Evidently she'd decided he wasn't an ax murderer or a crazy ex-con because she smiled. "Just so you know"—she opened the passenger door of the truck and fished around in the glove compartment—"I do carry a weapon and I have a concealed permit and I can take the eyes out of a rattlesnake at twenty yards."

Damn, but she was cute with that curly red hair, a faint sprinkling of freckles across a pert little nose and all those curves. "Pleased to meet you, Fiona Logan. Good thing I'm not a rattlesnake." Jud grinned. "I'm Jud Dawson, co-owner of the Lucky Penny."

"You're Blake and Toby's cousin?" she asked as she shook his hand.

"Yup, and turns out I'm staying at Audrey's. Your mama 't want me to live in the travel trailer with winter com-

Jud removed an expensive monogrammed suitcase from the passenger seat. It looked as out of place in that old vehicle as a cowboy at an opera.

She nodded toward the fence. "Sorry about the damage to your property."

"I'm just glad you're safe. And I'm sure your family will be eager to see you," he said as he hefted her suitcase into his truck. "What did you pack in this thing? Rocks?"

"Everything I could. What wouldn't fit in there is in the box."

"Lot to bring home for a four-day holiday," he said.

She ignored his remark with a shrug and a shiver.

He whipped off his Sherpa-lined leather coat and handed it to her. "Why don't you get inside the truck and warm up. This will only take a minute."

The box was only slightly lighter than that monster suitcase. As Jud was walking away from her vehicle, he heard a hiss and turned back to see steam escaping from under the hood. Either the steel fence post had punctured the radiator or barbed wire had ripped away hoses and belts.

He shoved the box into the backseat beside the suitcase and slammed the door, circled around the front of the truck, and crawled inside. "Looks like you've made your last voyage in that thing." He started the engine and eased down on the gas. Ice and gravel crunched under the truck's tires as he slowly inched along at ten miles per hour.

"I was hoping that it would get me all the way home."

"At least it got you pretty close." He stole a glance at her. A little shorter than either of her sisters, she was definitely built with curves in all the right places. She sat ramrod straight in the seat in a no-nonsense, take-control posture, but her dark green eyes and the way she kept biting at her lower lip said that Fiona Logan wasn't real sure of herself that Thanksgiving.

Her obvious insecurity didn't jive with the stories he'd been told about the third Logan sister, either. It was shaping up to be an interesting day.

"So what are you doing out on these roads today?" she asked.

"I was sent on an errand. It appears that giblet gravy cannot be made until there is a can of evaporated milk in the house and since Thanksgiving dinner can't be put upon the table unless there is giblet gravy, someone had to go for milk," he drawled.

She nodded and became even more nervous when the old brothel known as Audrey's Place came into view.

* * *

So this was Jud, Fiona thought, the cowboy in the Dawson family that everyone said was the lucky one. His blond hair was a little shaggy, hanging down to the collar of his pearl-snap shirt. An errant strand or two peeked out from under his black cowboy hat and inched down his forehead toward his dark chocolate brown eyes. His face would make a sculptor swoon with all those perfect planes and contours, and his hard, muscular body could turn a holy woman into a hooker.

She was glad that he'd been close by when that damn tire blew out. But sitting with him in the truck, traveling at a snail's pace? The air in the black crew-cab truck was way too thin. She inhaled deeply and let it out slowly and was glad it was only half a mile to her home because his coat around her shoulders suddenly made her hotter than blue blazes.

That he didn't seem to be in a hurry was fine with her. She needed a few minutes to get a grip on her nerves and her racing heart before she arrived. It couldn't be Jud Dawson with the sexy eyes and dreamy body causing her to sweat in the middle of a damn blizzard. It was the fact that she was back in Dry Creek, starting all over from scratch. But when she no longer had money for groceries and rent, she realized she had two choices: either go home or go homeless. And the former, even though she'd have to eat her pride, was better than living in a cardboard box and eating from Dumpsters.

Jud parked beside another big fancy truck and she sat there, staring at the house. She wanted to go in and surprise her family, so why couldn't she make herself open the damn door? Lights shining out through the windows threw rays of yellow onto the snow-covered yard and beckoned her to come on inside where there was comfort and unconditional love. First, she needed something, anything, to calm her shaky nerves. She clasped her hands tightly in her lap and waited.

"You going to get out or sit here and watch it snow all day?" Jud asked.

She frowned, a smartass remark on her lips. But that little voice inside her head reminded her that Jud had been kind enough to help her out.

"Thank you for helping me but don't rush me." She swung the truck door open, stepped out into the blowing snow, and grabbed the suitcase from the backseat. With the driving force of a north wind behind it, the snowflakes felt more like hard sleet pellets when they hit her face, so she walked a little faster, the suitcase thumping along like a miniature snowplow all the way to the porch, where she tugged it up the three steps with both hands. She opened the storm door and hesitated.

"Go on inside and I'll bring the suitcase and the box," Jud said.

He was right behind her, box in hand, with two cans of milk sitting on the top.

She'd vowed she'd never come back to Dry Creek for anything more than a visit. Why would she have to? She'd gotten a fantastic job with a law firm in Houston when she graduated college. Married the son of the firm's senior partner a year later. Her family had no idea he'd divorced her last year and made sure her name was ruined when it came to getting another job. She'd worked at a coffee shop until a week ago when the whole business closed down. Now she was back home. A failure.

"You'll freeze if you don't go inside," Jud said. "Besides, this damn box is heavy and this milk is going to freeze."

She looked over her shoulder. His warm smile melted a few snowflakes but didn't do jack shit when it came to easing her nerves. She took a deep breath, wiped away a tear she hoped he didn't see, and slung open the door.

"Fiona!! Oh. My. God! Allie! Mama! Fiona is home." Lizzy squealed and turned into a bright red blur as she ran from the kitchen. Fiona's eyes barely had time to focus before she was engulfed in a hug that came close to knocking her square on her butt right there in the foyer. Before she could move, her mother and Allie were both there and it became a big group hug that kept them all steady and on their feet.

"Surprise," she said weakly.

Jud stood inside the door, that wickedly sexy smile on

his face as if he were Santa Claus and had just shimmied down the chimney with a big bag of toys. She frowned at him but he didn't budge.

"Jud, where's the milk?" A tall dark-haired cowboy carrying a pink bundle stepped from the kitchen out into the foyer.

"Right here along with the store keys." He headed to the kitchen with both in his hand.

Sweet Jesus!

He'd told her that he lived at Audrey's and that he was Jud Dawson, but it didn't sink in for Fiona until that moment that she would be sharing a house with him.

Chapter Two

When everyone was seated around the table, Katy bowed her head and gave thanks. Fiona's hands got clammy and she felt so faint that she popped her eyes wide open to keep from falling off her chair. The food was going to be stone cold if Katy didn't stop thanking God for everything under the sun pretty soon, so Fiona swiped a hot roll from the bowl right in front of her, hid it in her lap, and ate two bites. She felt the touch of a hand sneaking across her thigh and pinching a corner of her bread and glanced toward Deke, the lifelong friend of the Logan family who had eaten Thanksgiving dinner with them for years. He popped a chunk of her hot roll into his mouth without even opening his eyes.

Then a hand brushed her thigh from the other side and suddenly half the roll disappeared. When she looked up into Jud's brown eyes, he'd already stuffed it into his mouth. Sparks danced around the room like embers from an open fire but Fiona chalked them up to being so damned hungry. Nothing had ever tasted as good to her as that hot bread fresh from her mother's oven. Maybe she'd been a fool to ever leave Dry Creek in the first place.

Finally, Katy finished the grace and handed the carving knife to Deke. Fiona had forgotten just how tall he was until he stood up. He looked down at her and one of his pretty hazel eyes slid shut in a wicked wink. Like she remembered, his sandy brown hair needed to be cut and his upper arms were almost as big as her waist. Deke was a couple of years younger than Fiona and had grown up right down the road. He was in and out of their house all the time. Nowadays he was Allie's right-hand man.

She held up her plate for a thick slice of turkey and glanced across the table at her sister, Allie. Pretty Alora Raine, with her long dark hair and those dark eyes, had learned the carpentry business from their father. She'd married young the first time, and Fiona could have told her it wouldn't work. But in those days she was just the sixteen-year-old younger sister, so what did she know?

Allie sent the mashed potatoes around the table. "I still can't believe you are home, Fiona. Having you here makes it special."

"Yes, it does." Allie's husband, Blake, leaned over and kissed her on the cheek. He'd stolen Allie's heart almost a year ago, and seeing them together, there was no doubt that Allie had gotten the right man this time around.

"You might not think it's so special when you have to fix your fence," Fiona said. "I had a blowout and plowed right through the barbed wire."

"But"—Jud handed off the bowl of green beans to Katy—"no one was hurt and there are no cattle in that pasture, so we don't have to rush out there and fix it right now."

"Are you sure you're okay? Did you walk the rest of the way? Why didn't you call us to come help you?" Lizzy spit out questions faster than bullets coming from an assault rifle.

Fiona held up a finger and finished chewing a bite of turkey.

Lizzy, the middle gorgeous sister with the height, the curves, the temper, and the fire, had been the apple of their grandfather's eye and had inherited the family feed store business right out of high school.

"I'm fine. I did not walk. Jud was driving right behind me and he brought me home. Are you going to hoard that giblet gravy forever, Deke?" Fiona asked.

"He's like that with good food. He's even worse with dessert." Irene giggled at the opposite end of the table from Katy.

Fiona's heart went out to her grandmother. Before the family had sat down, Katy had whispered to Fiona that today was a good day for her grandmother.

Irene's dementia had gotten worse in the past year and now she lived in a facility for people with Alzheimer's in Wichita Falls. Today, though, she was home for the holiday and she was at least semi-lucid.

Lipstick ran into the wrinkles around her mouth and her jet-black eyebrows penciled in a lopsided arch did not match her short, kinky gray hair. But her smile was bright and there was life in her eyes and Fiona thought she was beautiful.

Deke handed the gravy boat to Fiona. "Go easy on that now. I like leftover sandwiches with a little of that poured between the turkey and dressing."

Fiona nudged him with an elbow. "I bet you had a big breakfast. All I had was a stale cheese cracker. Besides, you are not my boss, right, Granny?"

"No, but I am. And cheese crackers are not a decent breakfast." Irene pointed a long skinny finger at Fiona. "You might as well eat sawdust. I taught you better than that. I bet you ain't been eatin' right since you left. You're too skinny, isn't she, Jud?"

Fiona raised an eyebrow at the sexy cowboy beside her.

"Man, I wouldn't touch that question with a ten-foot pole," Toby chuckled.

Lizzy put a piping hot yeast roll on her plate and sent the last item around the table. "Me neither. Darlin', you'd better have two rolls right to start with." She set a couple of rolls on the edge of his plate. "We might need to get you some sideboards."

"Maybe," Toby said.

Slightly taller than his brother, Blake, Toby looked at his wife sitting beside him, his blue eyes twinkling. Yes, they were every bit as in love as Blake and Allie. Brothers had married sisters. That made any of their children double cousins to Allie's new baby, Audrey, who had inherited Fiona's red hair.

"Back to the ten-foot pole," Fiona said.

"She is too skinny, isn't she, Jud?" Irene shot a look down the table at the newest Dawson cowboy, who'd come to the Lucky Penny a few weeks ago.

"I believe that Miz Fiona looks real pretty today and so do you, Miz Irene. That blue shirt brings out your eyes. Would you like some more cranberry sauce, darlin'?" Jud asked.

"You be careful around that one, Fiona. He's a slick talker for sure," Irene said, and went back to eating.

Deke poked her on the arm. "Was it snowing in Houston?"

She smiled. "It never snows in Houston."

"That's why she left Dry Creek. She wanted to live where they never had a good hard winter," Irene said. "I bet the roaches and flies are big as buzzards in that place without a good freeze to kill them off."

"Granny! I don't want to hear about bugs at the dinner table." Fiona smiled, despite her words. She'd forgotten how much she'd missed her family and their crazy ways. A peace settled over—a sense of belonging—that was every bit as important to her soul as the food was to her body.

Irene smiled. "There's my fiery girl."

"Just how long are you staying?" Lizzy asked.

Before Fiona could answer, Allie chimed in with another question. "Can you stay all weekend?"

"Or a week?" Lizzy piped up.

"She's here for good," Katy said. "She brought a cardboard box. That means she's moving back home and it's about damn time."

Fiona's sense of peace fled as she took a drink of sweet tea and swallowed another huge chunk of her pride. She wouldn't tell them the part about being so hungry she was dizzy or how little money was in her billfold. If she did that, her mother might drop with a heart attack right there on the dining room floor.

She straightened her back, put her hands in her lap, and began. "There's something I need to tell you all." She took a deep breath. "A little more than a year ago, Kyle and I divorced. There was a prenup, of course, so all I got was ten thousand dollars, which went fast while I looked for a job.

It didn't take long to figure out that I'd been blackballed in my line of work."

Time stood still.

Fiona was sure if she'd been outside, snowflakes would hang suspended in the air and the wind would cease to blow.

"Fiona Deann!" Katy finally gasped. "What have you been living on? And why would Kyle make trouble for you?"

One shoulder rose in a half shrug. "I guess it upset him when I punched his girlfriend and tried to yank out all her hair."

"He cheated on you?" Lizzy asked indignantly.

"Don't know if he cheated, but she came with him when he told me he was divorcing me. Idiot."

Admitting all that felt so good! Now she could eat dinner without a single worry.

"What did you do?" Allie asked.

"I used the last of my divorce settlement to buy that old truck after my car was repossessed. I put all my fancy clothes in a consignment shop, and some weeks I made enough for groceries from those sales but that ran out after six months. They closed the coffee shop where I worked and I couldn't find anything else and my money ran out. So here I am. Broke and needing a job. You need help at the feed store, Lizzy?"

That was about as short a version as she could make it, but it did the trick. The moment was pregnant with sheer awkwardness. Allie stared at her like she had an extra eye right in the middle of her forehead, but then Fiona remembered a time when she'd looked at her sister the same way when she moved back home after a divorce.

Katy shook her head. "I get first dibs on you. You are the answer to my prayer. I'm run ragged trying to take care of the convenience store by myself. So you, young lady, will go to work with me starting in the morning."

"Mama, I'm happy to help at the store in exchange for room and board here, but I'm also going to need a job that pays me."

"Bullshit!" Irene said loudly. "Living here is your right as family. The job at the store will give you minimum wage just like it would pay anyone else. Right, Katy?"

"Right," Katy said. "How about it, Fiona? There aren't many jobs in Dry Creek. You could probably waitress at Nadine's new café, but I need you worse than she does."

"That's settled," Irene said.

Fiona wasn't sure that it was, but she wasn't going to argue at the Thanksgiving table. Later, when everyone had left, she and her mama would have a long talk and that's when Fiona would tell her that she was not planning to live in Dry Creek forever.

"Sounds like we all have a lot to be grateful for this year. I'm thankful that Toby and I finally found a sofa we could agree on and now our living room has one piece of decent furniture," Lizzy said.

"I'd forgotten about our tradition," Deke said. "I'm thankful for the Logan family and all the good times I've had in this house."

Fiona hadn't forgotten, not on the way home, not in the awkward silence, not even with having to live with Jud Dawson in the house. After the prayer and while they were eating, everyone around the table shared something they were grateful for. She searched for a single thing that she could say because they'd be here until eternity dawned if she shared everything she was thankful for that cold winter day.

"I'm thankful beyond words that Fiona is home," Katy said.

Allie nodded. "I'm grateful for my amazing husband and my daughter."

"I'm thankful that this beautiful woman is both my best friend and my wife and that we have a gorgeous daughter," Blake said.

"Hey, she can be your wife, but she's my best friend," Deke argued. "Fiona, you are going to have to be my best friend since Allie has deserted me."

"I'm thankful to be home and that Deke is my new best friend," Fiona said with a smile.

"For the Lucky Penny and my wife." Toby grinned at Lizzy.

"I'm thankful for Walter," Irene giggled.

"Who?" Lizzy, Allie, and Fiona said in unison.

Katy sighed. "She's taking a trip into the past."

"Hell, if I am," Irene said. "I'm not going anywhere. I am thankful for Walter. He lived over on the Lucky Penny when Katy was getting married. I guess your grandpa got to feeling old since his daughter was old enough to get married, so he found himself a younger woman."

"No!" Lizzy slapped a hand over her mouth.

Well, that damn sure had to hurt, Fiona thought. Lizzy had always had the idea that Grandpa could walk on water.

"Oh, yes," Irene said. "So I started flirting with Walter to get back at him."

"Granny!" Allie said.

Why is Allie so surprised? Fiona held her breath and

hoped that Granny kept explaining because they'd all wanted to hear the story of Walter ever since Blake moved in next door. Granny's dementia was getting out of hand and she kept thinking that Blake was Walter.

"Why are you thankful for Walter?" Fiona asked.

"He made your grandpa realize that I wasn't an old shoe that he could toss in the garbage. He broke it off with that other woman and came home."

"And you forgave him?" Katy asked.

"Course I did. I had no right to judge him when I'd done the same thing with Walter. Besides, Walter wasn't nearly as good in bed as your grandpa," Irene said bluntly. "Now pass me those potatoes and, Deke, carve me off another piece of turkey. I'd like dark meat this time."

And there it was, the truth according to Granny when she was lucid. Fiona was amazed that no one was asking a million questions.

"Where is Walter now?" She finally broke the awkward silence.

"Walter?" The light went out of Irene's eyes in an instant. "Is he a new boy in town? I'm ready for dessert."

"I thought you wanted more potatoes," Katy said gently.

"I want cherry pie with ice cream on top and then I want a piece of pumpkin pie with whipped cream on top. Then I want to go outside and play in the snow." Irene crossed her bony arms over her chest and glared down the table. "I do not want potatoes."

"Miz Irene, how old are you? You told me but I forgot," Deke asked.

"I am thirteen," she said defiantly.

"Well, I think you should have pie," Fiona said. "I will

bring it to the table and we won't wait for everyone to finish before we have dessert."

Irene cocked her head to one side. "I like you. You can stay and talk to me after dinner, right? Is that new boy named Walter cute? Will I like him?"

"I don't know but I'll stay and we can talk about him," Fiona said.

"Who are you?" Irene frowned.

"She's Fiona, your granddaughter," Allie said gently.

Irene ran a hand across her forehead, smudging the dark eyebrows. "I forget things sometimes. Can I take a nap now? Would you take me to my room, Nurse?"

Katy pushed back her chair and laid her napkin beside her plate. "Yes, you can take a nap. I'll show you to your room and sit with you while you fall asleep."

Fiona swallowed hard but the lump in her throat wouldn't go away.

"It's okay." Deke patted her on the shoulder. "We've seen this happen so often that it doesn't surprise us. We're just grateful for the times when she does have it all together."

"But not when she admits to having an affair," Allie protested.

"Why not? We'd figured out that Walter lived on the Lucky Penny at one time. Now we know what happened," Fiona said.

"But Grandpa?" Lizzy groaned.

Fiona smiled. "Made a mistake and I bet he paid for it for a long time, knowing Granny."

"She did the same," Allie said.

"I bet she never told him that and I bet that's why she still feels guilty and keeps revisiting that part of her life,"

Deke said. "Hey, Blake, if she ever comes back over to the Lucky Penny and thinks you are Walter, you should break up with her or make her so mad she'll break up with you. Maybe that would bring closure to her."

Fiona threw an arm around Deke and hugged him. "Great idea. I might like being your best friend."

Chapter Three

There's nothing as empty as a big house after the family all goes home in the middle of the afternoon after Thanksgiving dinner. Katy had invited Fiona to ride with her to take Irene back to the facility in Wichita Falls. Allie had insisted that she go home with her, and Fiona had been tempted to go over to the Lucky Penny and hold that precious baby all afternoon. Lizzy had wanted Fiona to go see her new house, which was now part of the Lucky Penny also. But Fiona begged off every offer, saying she wanted to put her things away.

She stood in the middle of her old room, where not one thing had changed since she graduated from high school. She opened a few drawers to find them still organized with scarves in one, pajama pants and knit shirts in another one. Things that she'd left behind when she went to college. The closet was the same—jeans, shirts, boots, and a couple of heavy, warm coats.

"A fresh start," she murmured.

She'd left everything behind for a purpose: so she wouldn't be reminded of home. It had worked. She hadn't been homesick like the other girls—not one time. She'd lost herself in classes, in the social life, in living on a shoe-string budget and working as a waitress at a steak house. And now here she was back, with the same old third-wheel attitude that had made her want to leave Dry Creek.

She sighed and stretched out on the bed. Allie had been the smart one. She'd always been Daddy's girl because of her love for carpentry. Lizzy was the pretty one and had been Grandpa's favorite because she liked the feed store business. It wasn't that Fiona didn't feel loved; God, no! Her mama and granny loved all three girls as equally as humanly possible. And it wasn't that she was jealous of her sisters and their ambition or their inheritance.

Lacing her hands behind her head, she stared at the ceiling. "It was the belonging that I had trouble with," she whispered.

While Allie and Lizzy put down deep roots, Fiona had grown wings. And now she was right back in the same place with the same feelings as she'd had then. She popped up to a sitting position and shook her head. She wasn't eighteen anymore. She'd flown the coop and even if she was back in it temporarily, that did not mean she had to clip her wings and settle down in Dry Creek.

"Hey, anybody home?" a deep voice yelled right before someone started up the steps.

She hopped off the bed and opened her bedroom door. "Deke?"

"No, Jud. We got that old rattle trap of a truck hauled out behind the barn on the Lucky Penny and fixed the fence." He stopped at the top of the stairs and hiked a hip on the railing. "Hey, it looks like my bedroom is right across the hall from yours. That going to be a problem?" he asked.

"Not one bit. I forgot that you were staying here. Everyone coming back over for supper after a while?"

"Wild horses couldn't keep them away. I'm going out to check on one of the heifers before they get here, though." He smiled.

Blake was the wild cowboy and Toby had been dubbed the hot cowboy, but Jud had gotten the reputation of being the lucky one. Did that mean fortunate in ranching, oil, or women? Or maybe all three? Probably it had to do with that crooked little grin and that swagger.

* * *

Katy had barely gotten her coat off that evening when the family started to arrive for leftover supper. Allie, Blake, and Deke came through the door with baby Audrey all bundled up inside a carrier. As soon as Allie took her out, Deke reached for her.

"Give me that baby, Allie. I haven't held her yet today. I'm sure she's grown a foot since this afternoon," he said.

"Not quite but she's working on it." Blake removed her little pink hat and kissed the baby on the top of her red curls.

Fiona slipped past Deke and took the baby from Allie's arms. "Not so fast, cowboy. You got to hold her a whole bunch of times already."

She sat down in the nearest rocker with the baby in her arms and all her anxiety disappeared. It didn't matter if she had to start all over. She'd made it home, where no one cared if she was penniless or had a million bucks in the bank.

"She looks like Allie, has your hair, and is already showing signs of my temper," Fiona said.

"Hey." Lizzy and Toby pushed into the house, stomped the snow from their boots, and hung their coats on the hooks on the hall tree. "You are hogging the baby. I haven't held her at all today."

Lizzy was the outspoken one for sure. She might look all sweet with those pecan-colored eyes and dishwater-blond hair, but folks around Dry Creek knew better than to cross her. The only time Fiona had ever worried about her was last year when she had been engaged. It was downright scary to see the feisty Lizzy turn into a submissive prim-and-proper woman who was going to be a preacher's wife. Thank God that didn't work out.

"Yes, I am and I don't intend to stop. I can't believe you named her Audrey." Fiona kissed Audrey on the top of her head and inhaled the sweet smell of baby shampoo and lotion. "I'm going to rock this baby until dinner is ready. I'm already falling in love with her, Allie."

"Enjoy it because we'll be eating in five minutes. We just have to pull it all out of the refrigerator. Anyone wants their food hot can stick it in the microwave," Katy said.

"How was Granny when you left her?" Fiona asked.

"You don't want to know." Katy blushed.

"Why?"

"Let's just say she was on another Walter kick and thought I was her best friend. She went into explicit detail and comparison between him and my father. I thought I'd burn up with shame." Katy fanned her face with the back of her hand.

"Just remember that she's not herself and what she's

talking about might have happened or it might be something in her imagination," Blake said.

When Fiona first saw pictures of Blake with his dark hair and green eyes, she'd thought he was the handsomest cowboy she'd ever laid eyes on. Then Lizzy sent pictures of Blake's brother, Toby, and Blake took a backseat.

She chanced a sideways glance toward Jud. With that mop of blond hair and those pretty eyes and quick smile, why on earth wasn't he married?

"Hey, Lizzy, I need some help out here," Katy called from the kitchen.

The cowboys and her sister moved toward the kitchen, leaving Fiona alone in the corner of the dining room with Audrey, which was fine with her. Fiona rocked the baby and sang a lullaby. So what if she couldn't carry a tune. Audrey didn't care one bit.

Her stomach growled loudly, reminding her that the last meal, as big as it was, had long since been digested. Two huge meals a day was pure luxury, especially when she'd arrived in Dry Creek with exactly two dollars and thirty-nine cents in her purse. She'd been afraid to buy coffee or food with it in case she needed to put a tiny bit more gas in the truck. She'd been running on fumes and luck for the last ten miles.

Throw in a prayer and a bit of cussing to that mixture, she thought.

Audrey wiggled around until she was looking up at Fiona with big blue inquisitive eyes. Fiona put her finger in the baby's hand and Audrey quickly closed her tiny fist around it.

"She's pretty special, isn't she?" Katy asked.

Her mother's voice startled her. "You snuck up on me."

"Supper is on the bar. Want me to hold her so you can eat?"

"I hate to give her up, Mama. I'd forgotten what it's like to hold a baby," Fiona answered.

"Then you've been gone too long. Maybe you should volunteer to do nursery duty at church."

"If Allie lets Audrey go to the nursery, I just might do that." She handed the baby up to her mother and went straight to the kitchen. As luck would have it, she fell in right behind Jud. Wide shoulders stretched the knit of his shirt and the remnants of his aftershave, mixed with the outdoorsy scent that he'd picked up doing evening chores, smelled heavenly. Probably because she'd been too busy keeping body and soul together to notice men at all, but dammit, why did he have to look so good?

* * *

That night, Fiona slipped downstairs right after her shower for another piece of pumpkin pie. Standing in front of a full refrigerator loaded with Thanksgiving leftovers was right up there next to having the pearly gates swing open for her to enter heaven. She removed a whole pie and set it on the countertop along with a container of whipped cream, but she held the door open with a toe. Next she took out the pitcher of sweet tea and the plastic container with the turkey leftovers.

Light flashed bright in her eyes and startled her so badly that she almost dropped the tea.

"Mama," she gasped. "You scared the hell out of me."

Katy sat down at the table. "Then you're an angel now, right?"

Fiona smiled and then laughed. "It'd take more than that much of a fright to make an angel out of me. Couldn't you sleep, either?"

"I heard someone out here. Didn't know if it was you or Jud, but since I wasn't asleep, I came out to talk," she answered. "Sit down and tell me the whole story. You've lost at least ten pounds from when we saw you at the homecoming in July."

Fiona fished a fork from the drawer and set the pie in front of her mother. "I love your pumpkin pie. Sometimes I craved it so bad, especially when they made pumpkin lattes at the coffee shop and the aroma filled the whole place."

"You brought one suitcase and one box home. Where are the rest of your things?" Katy asked.

"That's all I have left. I was serious when I said I'd taken them to a consignment shop. I didn't need them and I did need money. I'm glad my room is still the same and I have a closet full of clothing up there. Some of it is a little loose but believe me with this kind of food, I'll put the weight back on," Fiona said.

"Did you go hungry?"

Fiona carried her pie to the table. "Let's just say I ate a lot of ramen noodles. It's amazing what you can do with those things."

"I could kick your butt for not calling me. Not wanting to come back to Dry Creek was one thing. Doing without necessities is another," Katy said.

"Pride." Fiona said one word and then shoveled a forkful of pie into her mouth.

"That's a dangerous thing."

"But it's stuck in my heart with something stronger than superglue."

Katy nodded. "Comes from your grandmother and the

Miller side of the family."

"Finally I reached the end of my rope and came home."

"Well, thank God for the end of the rope. What caused the divorce?"

Fiona nodded. "He wanted to climb the ladder to the top. I wanted to stay home and cuddle a few nights a week." Fiona shoveled more pie into her mouth. "I hated all the dinners and parties. I think once Kyle saw Dry Creek after we were engaged, he realized I didn't have the 'breeding' of a high-society corporate wife."

"That son of a bitch," Katy said.

"I know. I could feel him slipping away and knew deep down we were probably heading for divorce."

"What was the final straw?"

"His old girlfriend came home from Philadelphia to join the firm. Sparks were relit. We were already fighting more than loving, and then he came home one night with his arm around her and told me he was divorcing me. He handed me the prenup, which I'd signed without even reading. After all"—Fiona pushed out of her chair and poured two glasses of sweet tea—"we were in love and the vows said until death parted us."

"And?" Katy asked.

"And it said that I could take out of the house what I'd brought into it, which amounted to my clothes and personal things. My car was in my name, so that was mine for a little while. And I got a ten-thousand-dollar check. The end." She sighed and sipped at the tea. "I started a checking account, paid for some therapy lessons, rented a cheap apartment, finally found a minimum wage job, and you know the rest."

Katy wiped a tear from her eyes. "You went through all

that alone. Fiona, I was here. Your sisters were here and we would have done anything for you."

"I know, Mama, but..." Fiona paused.

"That independent streak that you got from your granny is a mile wide." Katy picked up a paper napkin and wiped at more tears. "Now you've made me cry and I don't cry, so I still may kick your butt."

Fiona cut another piece of pie while she was up and topped it off with a layer of whipped cream. "I'll be round as Santa Claus before I get full again."

"You could use a little weight." Her mother finally smiled.

"Let's talk about the store. Why haven't you hired some help or better yet someone to manage it for you since Granny got so bad?" Fiona asked.

"I must've been waiting on you. I still can't believe you are here, Fiona." She reached across the table and laid a hand on her daughter's arm.

"Still using the bank in Throckmorton and going down there on Sunday afternoon to make a night deposit?" Fiona asked.

Katy nodded. "You remembered?"

"Sure I did. We always loved going there with you when we were kids. We got ice cream and you took us to the park." Fiona smiled. "Memories kept me going, Mama."

Katy pulled her hand back and shook her head slowly.

Fiona patted her on the shoulder. "Everything works out like it should. I'll do whatever I can to help. I should have come back a year ago so I could have spent more time with Granny before things got like this."

"Things do work out and at the right time for the most part," Katy said stoically. "Now let's go to bed and get some sleep."

"I'm going to finish this pie and then put things away. You go on and I'll see you at breakfast. Pancakes and sausage?" Fiona asked.

"Sausage gravy, biscuits, and bacon and eggs," Katy declared.

"Yum!" Fiona smiled.

"Good night, sweetheart. I'll see you at six-thirty in the kitchen. You can make the biscuits. You always could make them just like Mama."

Fiona nodded and kept eating the pie. When her plate was scraped clean, she seriously contemplated another small slice. But then the turkey looked good and the only thing better than pumpkin pie was a turkey sandwich with a thin layer of leftover dressing between the layers of meat.

* * *

Everything in the world could turn around on a dime. Jud didn't remember who said that. It could have been someone famous, infamous, or even one of his grandparents, but it came to his mind that night as he stretched out on his bed. The room was spacious with a queen-sized bed, a nice reclining chair, a small desk, and a big closet. It beat the hell out of living in a thirteen-foot cramped travel trailer.

The snow had finally quit falling and now a cradle moon surrounded by stars hung in the sky outside his window. It was the same as it had been last night and would be tomorrow night if it didn't snow or rain. It took a while for the moon to go from full bright to nothing more than a sliver and then make its way back to a big round lover's moon. But then most things took a while. Like getting used to a different bed or getting to know the squeaks and sounds of an old house. Or hearing another person on the second floor of Audrey's Place. The sounds were faint but that was definitely Fiona in the shower; then the door hinges whined and she padded across the floor to her bedroom across the landing from his.

A vision of her naked in the shower tightened his chest and jacked up his pulse. He quickly adjusted the picture in his mind to include a towel wrapped around her body, but that didn't help a hell of a lot. That vision was even sexier than the first one when he slowly let himself pull the towel away and bring her close to his chest, wet red hair flowing down her back, that tiny waist beneath his fingertips.

"God almighty!" He groaned as he jumped out of bed and paced from one end of the floor to the other. Just because they had bedrooms on the same floor did not mean he could go lusting after her. Katy would send him packing out to the trailer or shoot him graveyard dead if she knew what he'd been thinking.

He fought insomnia for half an hour before peeking out the door and tiptoeing down to the kitchen. If he couldn't sleep, then he might as well make himself a turkey sandwich. A full stomach always made him sleepy.

"So you couldn't sleep, either?" Jud asked Fiona when he found her in the kitchen. "You want a turkey sandwich with me?" He stepped into the light and started for the cabinet. "Where's the leftover gravy?"

"What do you need that for?" she asked.

"I make a mean leftover sandwich. A piece of bread with mayonnaise of course—your mama has a loaf that she made at the same time she did the hot rolls. Then a layer of turkey, a layer of leftover dressing, a spoonful of gravy that I'll heat up in the microwave beforehand, and another layer of turkey. I'll be glad to make you one. If you don't like it, I'll eat yours and mine." He reached into the cabinet for a small bowl to heat the gravy.

"Dressing is in the red plastic container on the bottom shelf of the refrigerator and, yes, I will try your famous sandwich," Fiona said.

He nuked the gravy and then made two sandwiches, cutting each of them diagonally before putting them on the same plate. "No use in dirtying up extra dishes. Do you cook?"

"No one grew up in this house without learning their way around the kitchen. Is this your only specialty or do you make other things as well?" she asked.

"I can make a delicious bologna sandwich and a fair grilled cheese."

She bit into the sandwich. "Sweet Jesus! The gravy adds a whole new dimension. I might even like this better than served hot for dinner."

"Me too." Jud nodded. "Fiona, if you're uncomfortable with me being in the house or if you want time with your mama without a third wheel being around, I can move into the travel trailer."

"Don't be so nice. We'll share a house but we won't share stories and start bonding like *my* sisters did with *your* cousins."

He chuckled and bit into his sandwich. "Well, I'm sure glad we cleared that up."

He glanced across the table at her and Lord have mercy, in his mind she was wearing nothing but a towel. He blinked twice to delete the picture and focused on the sandwich. What he needed was a Saturday night in a country music bar with loud music, women coming on to him, and lots of beers. That would take care of his overactive imagination for sure.

They finished their sandwiches and he put the plate in the dishwasher before heading up to bed with her right behind him.

"I'm going to watch television but I'll keep it turned down," she said.

"Honey, don't worry about noise on my account. A freight train coming right down the middle of my bed couldn't wake me when I'm asleep."

Chapter Four

Katy had filled a pretty crock bowl with gravy and set it and a basket of piping hot biscuits on the table beside a platter of scrambled eggs and bacon.

Fiona poured two mugs of coffee and carried them to the breakfast table. "Do you think Jud overslept?"

"He's been gone for more than an hour. Left a note on the cabinet to say he's eating over at Toby and Lizzy's this morning," Katy answered.

A jab of disappointment stuck Fiona in the chest. She'd liked the banter the night before, loved sharing leftovers with him and talking to someone who expected nothing from her. She didn't have to be anyone but herself: no airs, no changing from who she was to who she could or should be—in essence, no bullshit.

Katy shoveled half the eggs and bacon onto her plate and passed the rest to Fiona. "You ready to go to work this morning?"

"Sure. Do you mind if I borrow your car when I need it?"

"Of course you can use the car. The first store task I'm turning over to you is the bookkeeping."

"Yes, ma'am." Fiona grinned.

The sun was bright against a sparkling white blanket covering the north part of Throckmorton County that morning when Fiona and Katy left Audrey's Place and headed into town. Christmas carols played on the radio and everything was good until Fiona remembered that she'd sold her laptop. How in the devil was she supposed to do anything in bookkeeping without a computer?

"Well, shit!"

"What?" Katy asked.

"I don't have a computer. I know you've always kept books by hand but I'm used to spreadsheets and a computer program."

"That can be fixed. Go down to Lizzy's store and tell her to get on hers and order you one. It can be here in two or three days, depending on the weather."

"Mama, I have less than three dollars in my purse," she said honestly.

"It's a business expense for the store. Or if you want it for your own use as well as the business, I'll pay for it and you can pay me back. Divide the payment into six and take that out of your weekly paycheck."

"It can be for the store," Fiona said quickly.

Katy pulled into her normal parking spot at the back of the store. "Bless your heart. And I mean that in a good way because when it comes to taking care of the business stuff, I'm six months behind, so get ready to pull your hair out. That new computer will damn sure pay for itself, I'm sure. I just don't know how to do that stuff and I'm too busy with your grandmother to learn."

"I would have worked for room and board," Fiona said softly.

"You are not the prodigal son. You are my daughter and we always paid you girls when you worked for us, remember?"

By noon, Katy had explained the basic delivery schedule and the payment agreement with each vendor, and Fiona had filled six pages of her notebook. "Any questions?" Katy asked.

"Just a couple of logistics things. If we moved the prepackaged pastries up to this end cut right here"—Fiona pointed to the first one inside the door—"then it would be an impulse buy. Folks coming in for coffee would see them and pick them up quicker than if they have to walk to the back of the store to find them. We could switch them out with the cleaning supplies and toiletries. People coming in to get those things are in an emergency situation if they're buying them in a convenience store."

"Then that's your next job. Anything else you might want to suggest?" Katy grinned.

"Are we still getting a couple dozen doughnuts from the shop in Throckmorton as he drives through on his way north each day?"

"Most days but it's a long holiday weekend," Katy said. "We still keep them under the glass dome just like your grandmother did when she ran the store. Why?"

"I wanted one." Fiona smiled. "I guess I'll wait until Monday."

"While you work on that switch you have in mind, I'm going to put on a pot of coffee. Even if it's a holiday, the old guys could come in for a gab session after they get chores done. Cows have to be fed and taken care of every day of the year," Katy said.

"Where's a dust rag? I'll clean as I go."

Katy set about making coffee in the two big pots at the back of the store. "In the back room right along with the spray cleaner. And thanks, kiddo. It's been at least two weeks since I've had time to dust the shelves."

Fiona found what she needed and set about her job. She'd barely gotten a good start when Jud swaggered into the store and went straight for the coffee machine. The smell of hay, aftershave, and some kind of manly soap all trailed after him. She gripped the cleaning rag and reminded herself to keep working or she would have fallen right in behind him like a little puppy.

"Where's the doughnuts?" he asked.

"Holiday," Fiona said.

"Well, rats. I had my mind set on a couple of those maple iced ones." He carried the coffee to a yellow-topped chrome table at the back of the store and pulled out a chair.

"So did I," she said. "We've got packaged pastries. Want one of those?"

"No, it wouldn't be the same. What are you doing?"

"Moving some stuff and doing some cleaning."

"Which is desperately needed." Katy pushed back a floral curtain covering the doorway into the back room. "I called Lizzy from the phone back there. She says she'll bring down her laptop. It's already got a bookkeeping program on it and she hates to do anything with it, so she's going to make a deal with us. We can have the computer if you'll do her bookkeeping and her taxes this year. Can I tell her that it's a deal?"

"Sure, but I would do all that for free."

"Not without a computer. Hey, Jud. No doughnuts today

but I'll order half a dozen extra maple ones on Monday," Katy said.

"Better make that a dozen." Jud flashed a grin. "Fiona might eat that many before I can get morning chores done."

"Well, would you look what the cat has done dragged in?" Herman Hudson stopped right inside the door and opened his arms.

Fiona walked right into them. Herman was the same age as her grandmother and had always been a friend of the family. He hugged her tightly with arms as big as hams and they matched his round belly and big square face.

"You are a sight for sore eyes, girl. How long are you home for this time?" Herman let her go and started for the coffeemaker. "Where's the doughnuts?"

"Don't get any today. Holiday, remember?" Fiona said. "But right here is a whole bunch of prepackaged things."

Herman turned around and came back, picked out a variety of things, and carried them to the table. "Put them on a ticket, along with mine and Jud's coffee. You didn't answer my question."

"I don't know but I'm going to stick around and help Mama run the store. She's got a lot going on and needs some help," Fiona said.

"That's good news. Real good news," Herman said.

Was it? Would she finally put down roots or would she still feel like she was misplaced after a few weeks or even months?

* * *

After a buffet supper of more leftovers at Audrey's Place, the guys retired to the living room to talk cattle, ranches, hay, and four-wheelers. The four women and the baby sat around the dining room table and talked about putting up the Christmas tree the next weekend.

"Promise me you'll stay for Christmas," Allie said.

"I wouldn't miss the holidays for anything, not even Florida in the winter. Besides, it's Audrey's first Christmas," Fiona said from the rocking chair in the corner where she was humming to Audrey.

"If you'd told me a week ago that Fiona would be home to stay indefinitely, I would have thought you were crazy," Lizzy said.

"Times change," Katy said.

Those last two words played through Fiona's mind that evening when everyone had left. Times did change. Sometimes a person had to walk through fire to get to the nice cool lake water. Even though she wasn't sure she would stay in Dry Creek for the rest of her life, it was home and it was good to be there.

Her apartment in Houston had been so tiny that she'd felt cooped up most of the time, so she'd spent a lot of time out on the balcony. It was barely big enough for a white plastic lawn chair but at least she had fresh air, could hear the constant motion of traffic, and could watch the lights of the airplanes coming in and going out. It beat feeling like the walls of the apartment were closing in on her.

That evening, she had a bout of the same claustrophobic feeling in her bedroom. She swung the drapes back and looked out at the stars in the sky, patches of white still dotting the landscape. There was no traffic noise, not a single plane in the sky; the only thing she could hear was the faint howling of a hungry coyote somewhere over on the Lucky Penny.

She opened her closet door and removed a quilt from the top shelf and carried it down the stairs. Fresh air! Just a breath of it, no matter how cold, would help. Her therapist would tell her that it was too much, too fast and she needed to step back from the forest for a little while.

A cold breeze rattled the bare mesquite tree limbs and shivers shook her from shoulders to toes, even though she'd remembered to put on a winter coat from her closet. Her breath created little puffs of smoky fog in front of her as she headed for the swing in the shadows of the porch.

"You feelin' a little cramped tonight, too?" Jud asked.

How in the hell did he do that? She always knew when someone was approaching her or when they were looking at her even from across a room. "You scared me. What are you doing out here in the cold?"

"Same thing you are, I expect. Getting some fresh air even if it would freeze the spikes off the devil's little red tail. I'll share the swing if you'll share that quilt. It's colder out here than I thought it would be," Jud answered.

Fiona sat down on the other end of the swing and spread the quilt out over both of their legs, pulling the corner of hers up to her chin. "I've lived simply for more than a year. This is all overwhelming. Most days I worked, went home to read a book from the library, and didn't talk to anyone unless Lizzy or Allie called."

"Groundhog?" Jud said.

She nodded, remembering the old movie, *Groundhog Day*, where every single day was the exact same as the one before it. "Pretty much. I still saw the same customers almost every day, talked to the same coworkers about important world-changing things like whether we should restock the small cups or the large ones before we closed up every evening. But when I went home, I was alone."

"Family rallies around when you need them." Jud

tugged his share of the quilt up to his neck. "What did you expect when you came home?"

She shrugged.

"Well, you are here now and it looks like you're going to do all right, darlin'."

"Don't call me that," she protested.

"Then how about honey pie, sugar, or sweet cheeks?" he teased.

"None of the above. Do you call your sister darlin'?"

"Sometimes, when I'm not mad at her." He grinned. "And, Fiona, we might have joint kin folks, but we are not related at all."

"Thank God!" she spit out. "I'm sorry. That came out wrong."

He chuckled. "Sometimes it's easier to talk to someone who isn't related, who isn't even your friend, isn't it? Got something on your mind, Fi-o-na?" He dragged out her name, stretching each syllable.

"Nothing except getting outside," she said. "You?"

He set his jaw firmly. "I feel like a fifth wheel and I'm a little jealous. We pooled our money for this big adventure, but then Blake and Toby wound up married and happy as piglets in a cornfield before I even got here. It's not the same as it would have been for three bachelors sharing the same house and arguing over who has to fix fences or who has to cook supper that night."

"Find you a woman and get the same happiness they've got," she suggested.

"I just might do that," he declared.

"Well." She inhaled. "I didn't plan to come back here at all and I've had enough of the marriage scene, so I'm not looking for anyone to settle down with."

"Why?"

"I didn't want to live in Dry Creek, so I went to college, got a good job, and thought I had my fifty-year life plan all in order. Then it all fell apart, so I'll start all over, only this time without letting a smooth-talking guy upset things," she answered.

He laughed.

"What's so funny?" she asked tersely.

"Man plans but God or fate or whatever you want to call it has a sense of humor. You've proven that, haven't you?"

"I saw a therapist a few times until I realized that I was running out of money and wasn't going to get a decent job. She helped me admit that the divorce was partly my fault."

The hard north wind stung Fiona's bare cheeks. "Let's go inside and make some hot chocolate."

"I'm all for that but what makes you think the divorce was your fault?" he asked as he folded the quilt and handed it to her.

"I was pretending to be something I wasn't." She opened the door and hurried inside like a moth driven to the warmth of a flame. Shedding her coat and leaving it on the bottom step, she looked over her shoulder to see Jud hanging his on a hook on the coat rack.

"Did your ex, Kyle, ever come to Dry Creek with you before you were married?"

"A couple of times. He was bored to tears." She led the way into the kitchen, flipped on the light, and found the hot chocolate mix right where it had been when she was a little girl. She heated two cups of milk on the stove and removed the whipped cream from the refrigerator.

"Then he knew, Fiona. He knew what you were, where

you came from and how you'd been raised, so he knew your inner heart."

"But I didn't want to be that person. I wanted to be that hotshot woman in high heels and power suits with a leather briefcase."

Jud poured a packet of hot chocolate mix in each of the mugs. "When did you stop wanting to be that woman? Did you talk to Kyle about it?"

She carefully poured the milk into the mugs and stirred. "I did talk to him and told him that I wanted more time with him. I was ready to start a family and spend more nights at home than out at fancy restaurants or events with potential or existing clients."

He added a dollop of whipped cream to each and carried both mugs to the table. "And?"

"It was not good. He told me he married a career woman with the top of the ladder always in sight. He didn't want children, not until we were close to forty, and then he only wanted one son. Within six months he handed me divorce papers. I won't make the same mistake twice."

"Does that mean you don't trust men?"

Her brows drew together. "Lizzy and I had this conversation. I trust men. I'm not sure I trust my judgment yet or that I ever will. I'm scared that if I find some guy who makes me feel all oozy inside and I marry him, I might realize I still want to be that woman with the briefcase and high heels. It happened in the reverse. Who's to say that it wouldn't turn around and happen again?"

He sipped at the hot chocolate. "I got no answers for that one. But I can tell you this is some fine chocolate and it's warming my insides. Do you feel better for sucking down some of that bitter cold wind?"

She nodded emphatically. "I do. When I finish this, I might even be able to sleep. How about you?"

"Hot chocolate is always good after being outside. Mama made it for me and Josie when we were kids after we'd go out and play in the snow. She had a rule. We could go out there and play as long as we wanted but when we came in, we had to stay inside. According to her, running in and out, getting hot and then cold, over and over again would make us sick."

"Same rule here. Must be a mama thing," Fiona said.

Was that where she was in her life? She'd gone out to play in the cold and stayed out there seven years. Now she was back in the house drinking hot chocolate. Did that mean she'd have to stay in for the rest of her life?

"You're fighting demons, aren't you?" he whispered softly.

Lord have mercy! Jud's whisper was even sexier than his slow Texas drawl. She'd been thinking about her own life and hadn't given a thought to the insane sparks that passed between them when they were in each other's presence. Then suddenly the brain gears switched and now she wanted to kiss Jud Dawson.

Sure, he'd listened to her. And, yes, it had been over a year since she'd shared a bed with a man. And the way his eyes coveted what his two cousins had with their wives left no doubt that Jud wanted the same. And Fiona wasn't even going to think about the way his whole face lit up when he held Audrey. Oh, yes, sir! This cowboy wanted a wife, children, and a home in Dry Creek. History would definitely, guaran-damn-teed not repeat itself with the third Logan sister.

He pushed the chair back, rinsed his mug, and put it in

the dishwasher. "We all fight the demons in our head from time to time. Just stand your ground and don't let them win."

When he passed her chair, he tipped up her chin and brushed a soft kiss across her lips. "Good night, Fiona."

"You don't kiss your sister like that, do you?" she sputtered.

"You are not my sister and you've needed a kiss for a long time."

"How do you know?"

"I'm a Dawson, remember?"

He disappeared into the darkness.

She touched her lips to see if they were as hot as they felt and found them to be surprisingly cool. It was a kiss, not a damn proposal, and it would not happen again.

Chapter Five

The little white church in Dry Creek had two rows of pews with a center aisle. The side aisles were barely wide enough for a vacuum cleaner between pews and wall, so few people used them. The Logan pew on the left side of the church was full that day with Fiona sitting next to the wall and Jud Dawson at the far end, leaving the two married couples between him and Katy, who sat next to Fiona that morning.

"How long has it been since you've been to church?" Katy whispered as the preacher took his place behind the pulpit.

"I worked seven days a week, Mama," she answered.

"Then you haven't been in church in a year?"

Fiona grimaced. "That's right."

"Another reason you should be home."

The preacher cleared his throat. Straying eyes went forward and those who had been slumping sat up tall and straight. God was not going to find a reason to fault a single person in the church that morning.

"Good morning. I hope you all had a wonderful Thanksgiving in spite of that bad weather." His deep voice hardly needed the microphone to reach the back pews. "And now it's time to think of Christmas. Since Christmas is on Sunday this week, we will have our holiday program the Wednesday night before, and our usual morning services that Sunday will be postponed until evening. That way all you folks can have the morning with your family."

He looked down at his Bible and Fiona got ready for the sermon. She would do her best to pay attention since she hadn't set foot inside a church in a year.

"Before I begin, the ladies have said that after our Wednesday night Christmas service we will have a leftover potluck dinner in the fellowship hall. So be thinking along those lines and bring your leftovers to the potluck that evening for some time of fellowship. Please open your Bibles to Matthew 22, where Jesus said for us to love our neighbors as ourselves. Would you hurt yourself? Would you say mean words to yourself? Would you deny yourself food or shelter?"

Fiona drifted away from the preacher's booming voice. She felt someone staring at her from the pew behind her. She glanced over her shoulder to see Truman O'Dell and his wife, Dora June, both giving her the evil eye. Dora June, God bless all three of her chins, had decided to step in and give her sisters advice since Granny was in a care facility and had damn sure rubbed them the wrong way.

But what in the hell had Fiona done to bring the wrath of the O'Dells down upon her? She'd only been in town three days. Surely a year-old divorce wouldn't be enough to bring out the cross and nails to crucify her. Those two old codgers should be taking in the sermon and thinking of being nice to their neighbors.

"In this upcoming season of love, we should remember to treat our neighbor right, even if they treat us wrong. When our Lord and Savior was on the cross, he asked his Heavenly Father to forgive the people who done that horrible deed to him," the preacher went on.

Finally, the preacher asked Truman O'Dell to deliver the benediction. The roof came nigh to rising up a good three inches when everyone in the church sighed. Not because the sermon went five minutes over twelve o'clock but because Truman always thanked the almighty for everything from the snow that would bring extra nutrients to the soil, to his goats, to the church building, and the offering that morning. The roast beef in most folks' ovens would be dried up into jerky by the time they got home to Sunday dinner.

Fiona imagined the church roof lowering back into place when Truman raised his head and said, "Amen." The quietness ended and folks began to talk in low tones as they moved toward the door where they'd shake hands with the preacher. Then they'd brave the bitter north wind to their vehicles and drive like bats set loose from the bowels of hell to get home and save what was left of the dinner.

Somehow Fiona got separated from the rest of the family when Lucy Hudson grabbed her arm and gave her a hug. "Lord, honey, I hate it when Truman gives the final prayer, but I suppose Preacher Lyle was trying to get him to see that he's been a horse's ass the past year."

Fiona raised an eyebrow.

"You look like your granny Irene when you do that," Lucy giggled. "Don't tell me your sisters haven't told you about his vendetta against the Lucky Penny. He's strutted around like a peacock talkin' crap about how he'd buy that ranch yet from them when they got tired of hard work and moved away." Her eyes shot toward the ceiling. "Forgive me, Lord, but it's not judgin'; it's the Gospel truth. Anyway, he's been talkin' bad about the Dawsons ever since they got here."

"Why?" Fiona asked.

"No one wanted the Lucky Penny, what with its reputation for being so unlucky for anyone who buys it. But Truman wanted it real bad, only he's tighter with his money than a bull's butt in fly season and he was trying to hold out for a better price when the Dawsons showed up and bought it," Lucy whispered.

"That's no reason to be ugly to Blake and Toby and now Jud."

Lucy nodded emphatically, the gray bun on top of her head bobbing as if it would tumble off and go flying across the pews. "I know and everyone else in town knows but Truman and about three women. I won't call any names but one of the women is Truman's wife and the other two are her friends. Dora June don't give a damn"—another eye roll to the ceiling and the sign of the cross over her heart—"about the ranch but she's upset because Allie and Lizzy wouldn't listen to them about them Dawson boys. What with y'all's granny in that place with her problems, those three old biddies thought they could step right up and give Lizzy advice."

Fiona stifled a giggle.

Lucy patted her on the back. "As if anyone could give Lizzy advice, right? After that preacher wannabe broke her heart, she grew a bigger pair than most men in this place."

The giggle escaped. "Survival causes that."

"Yes, it does. Anyhow, I'm glad you are home and real happy that you are going to help your mama out in the store. I been worried about her for a while now with all she's got on her plate. I heard you are taking care of Lizzy's books. Would you be interested in taking on some more work in that line? Me and Herman is getting too damn old to keep up with all these newfangled tax laws," Lucy said.

"We could talk about it," Fiona replied.

Lucy hugged Fiona again. "I'll come on by and talk to you first of the week, then."

Allie worked her way through the crowd until he was right beside Fiona. She cupped her hand over Fiona's ear and whispered, "We're supposed to love Truman? God's asking a lot this morning, isn't He? Come with me to the nursery and we'll get Audrey. It's the first time I've left her, but last week she made such a fuss that Dora June and Truman were both giving me dirty looks all during services."

"Well, if I've got to love Truman and Dora June after the way they've acted, then I guess y'all had best pack my casket full of sunblock because I'm bound for hell," Fiona said softly.

Allie laughed so loud that several people turned around to stare at her. Fiona didn't care if it was right there in the sanctuary. The scripture said that even David from the Bible was a noisy fellow. He played the musical instruments and danced around rejoicing when he bested his enemies and the good book said that he was the apple of God's eye. So if Allie wanted to laugh in the church house, then by damn she could.

Allie poked her on the arm. "You've been standing next

to Lucy too long. That expression on your face looks like her when she's ready to tear into someone."

Fiona's mossy green eyes went from angry to twinkling in a split second. "I'm hungry and you know what that means."

"Bitchy," Allie said.

Nadine grabbed Fiona by the arm. "Hey, girl, I wanted to invite you to the café for Sunday dinner to welcome you back to Dry Creek."

Allie waved over her shoulder and disappeared into the crowd.

"I should eat with the family. Rain check?" Fiona asked.

"Anytime. Got to get going. I only leave the café for the hour that church services are going on. Mary Jo is working until I get back. She, Sharlene, and I take turns on Sunday so that only one of us three misses church," Nadine said.

Dora June touched Fiona on the shoulder. "It's good to hear that you are back in town. I hope you are smarter than your sisters."

Dora June was Truman's opposite. He had a squirrelly little face with small squinty eyes that constantly darted around and a hump in the middle of his nose. But Dora June, now, she was a different story. Not more than five feet tall, she was square built and had at least three chins hanging below a moon-shaped face.

"I always considered Allie and Lizzy to be geniuses," Fiona said.

The three chins quivered when Dora June shook her head. "In business, they are but, honey, when it comes to men, well, you are the smart one. Where is that husband of yours?"

"Living with his new wife, I would expect," Fiona said.

Dora June's hand was a blur as it went from Fiona's shoulder to the chubby woman's cheek. "I had no idea. I'm so sorry."

"Thank you, but I'm fine now."

"Well, you should steer clear of that Jud Dawson, honey. Show a little more sense than your sisters."

"Dora June, I think my sisters are the smartest women in the whole county, maybe the whole state of Texas when it comes to men because they are married to men who adore them."

Dora June quickly changed the subject. "Do you have your Christmas tree up yet? I got mine all done yesterday." She lowered her voice. "Truman hates it but then he's an old Scrooge when it comes to the holidays. Maybe he would have been different if we'd have had kids but then maybe his attitude is why God didn't see fit to give us any. I'll be seeing you at the store, I'm sure." She leaned in even closer. "Listen to me. The Lucky Penny isn't kind to the folks who own it. Your poor sisters will wind up having to leave their businesses and move away from Dry Creek. Your mama will only have you left to help her."

She was gone before Fiona could say a single word. When she finally made it to the door, shook hands with the preacher, and the cold north wind whipped her long red hair around to slap her in the face, her family had gone. All but Jud, who was two people behind her and the last person to shake the preacher's hand.

"Guess we're the last two people on earth," Jud said. "Good thing I brought my own truck or we'd both be walking a couple of miles." He looked down at her shoes. "Or maybe I'd be walkin' and carryin' you."

"Don't fool yourself. I can run as fast in these shoes as you can in those boots," she said.

"But aren't you glad we don't have to?" He escorted her out across the parking lot with his hand on the small of her back.

Truman drove past them so slow that Fiona could have reached inside and hugged Dora June if the window had been down. Not that she would have wanted to, not as sour as they both looked.

"The gossip will have us sleeping together by morning since you are taking me home and well, you know, your cousins and my sisters, their stories are only going to fuel the blaze of the whole thing," Fiona groaned.

"Might as well have the game if we're going to have the name," Jud drawled.

"Not in your wildest nightmares, cowboy." Fiona pulled free from him and let herself into the truck.

"Now they'll say I'm only sleeping with you. That I'm not even a gentleman who'll open the doors for you," Jud teased.

"Just drive us home. Small towns!" She folded her arms across her chest and looked straight ahead at the dark clouds rolling into Dry Creek.

"Ain't they wonderful?" Jud started the engine, pulled out of the parking lot, and turned south to go to Audrey's Place. "Didn't you miss it when you were in the big city?"

"I missed family and potlucks but not the gossip," she answered.

"But that's where the fun is." His beautiful smile, just slightly crooked on the left side, lit up the interior of the truck. "It makes folks so happy to spread secrets whether they are true or not. The preacher said we should love our neighbors, didn't he?"

"As in food, shelter, and necessities for life, not as in rumors. I don't like gossip, so if I love my neighbor as myself, then I don't have to like their gossip, either," she argued.

"Am I your neighbor since we are sharing food and all that other stuff?" he asked.

"No, that makes you my roommate," she said. "A neighbor doesn't live in the house with you."

"If we considered our bedrooms as our apartments and the landing as the hallway between our apartments, then we would be neighbors. Then you would be heavenly bound to love me, right?" he teased.

"Is that a line you use in bars to pick up women?"

"This ain't no bar and we didn't just have a dozen beers, Fiona."

"Why do you care if I love my neighbor, namely you? We can share a house without loving each other like it says in the Bible. Lots of married folks do." She unfolded her arms and held her hands in her lap.

His chuckle was every bit as deep as his drawl. "I like your sense of humor."

The chuckle developed into laughter. She tried to bite back the smile, but it didn't work and for the first time in months, Fiona laughed until her sides ached. About nothing. About everything. And when he parked the truck beside the others in front of Audrey's Place, she felt freer than she had in more than a year. Not even her therapist had set her soul free like laughing with Jud Dawson over something that wasn't even funny.

For that she owed him.

"For something that wasn't supposed to be funny, that was sure a hoot," he said.

She nodded, swung open the door, and caught a snowflake on her tongue. The warmth and the buzz of conversation welcomed her into the house. She and Jud hung their coats on the rack inside the door.

Jud brushed against her shoulder on his way to the living room and snappy little bursts of heat made their way through her bright green sweater and to her skin. She'd have to be stone cold dead for a cowboy like Jud Dawson not to affect her but she'd have to be a deluxe idiot to act on that attraction. She wasn't dead for sure but she wasn't going to be an idiot, either.

"Hey, Fiona, you can set the table while I help Mama with the gravy," Allie said.

Lizzy brought in an armload of plates with cutlery rattling on the top plate. "Mama is already serving up the food. If Truman had prayed much longer, we'd be eating salad and bread or going to Nadine's. The roast is well done but still edible." She lowered her voice. "So are you going to love your neighbor?"

Fiona scooped forks, knives, and spoons up in her hands and placed them around the table. "I do love my neighbors. You and Allie live right across the fence."

"I'm talking about the one across the landing from you," Lizzy teased.

Fiona shot Lizzy a dirty look. "Are you going to love your neighbor, as in Truman and Dora June?"

"Of course," Lizzy said quickly. "I love them, but I damn sure don't like them. I'm very grateful they aren't my neighbor in the physical sense. Deke can have that honor and I'm sure he's even glad that their house is on the far side of their property and not right over the fence from him."

"Dora June started meddling right after church," Fiona said.

Katy set a bowl of potatoes and carrots on the table. "I know she's a gossip and gets into everyone's business but she and her three friends do work hard at the church. They've turned an unused Sunday school room into a nice little clothes closet and food place for anyone who's down on their luck. Folks donate and the ladies keep everything organized. Last month a young couple with a toddler came through, down on their luck trying to make it up to Ryan, Oklahoma. Dora June made sure they had a tank of gas, food, and even gave them clothes for that baby."

"I heard about that," Allie said. "They had a warm coat day last week. Let any kid in the school who needed a coat pick one out. Henrietta washed the donated ones and repaired any tears or missing buttons. But, Mama, it was those four that caused you to quit the ladies' group."

"The Lord works in mysterious ways. If they hadn't been so judgmental of you girls and put you out of the group, I wouldn't have resigned as president. If I hadn't, then I would for sure be even more exhausted these days," Katy said.

"Silver lining?" Fiona asked.

"Something like that." Lizzy finished setting the plates. "But if they hadn't gotten all self-righteous with me and Allie, then one of us could have taken over your duties at the church while you were gone."

Katy patted her on the shoulder as she passed on the way back to the kitchen. "And you would have hated being tied down to it. I did at times and I didn't have a handsome husband waiting for me at the end of every workday. It is what it is and that's enough *buts*."

When dinner was on the table, everyone took their seats as if they'd been assigned. Toby seated Katy at the end and she motioned for Jud to sit at the other end. The only chair left for Fiona was the one to Jud's right. He pulled it out with a flourish and seated her before taking his place.

"Deke will say grace," Katy said.

Deke said the shortest prayers of anyone in Throckmorton County, and Fiona had no doubt that her mother called on him for that very reason. One minute after their heads were bowed, he said *amen* and the food started around the table. As luck would have it, every time a bowl, platter, or bread basket was passed, Jud's fingertips brushed against Fiona's and a whole bevy of sparks blasted every time it happened. It was definitely time for her to get back into the dating scene, which she would do as soon as she started over in a brand-new place. Until then, she could endure her hormones wanting a little something, something.

"Be sure to save your fork." Katy smiled when they were nearly finished with dinner.

"Dessert?" Fiona forgot all about Jud.

"Warm chocolate sheet cake with vanilla bean ice cream," Katy said.

"I love you!" Fiona squealed.

"Is that all it takes to make someone love you?" Deke asked. "I know a bunch of rough old cowboys in this area who'd gladly borrow Katy's recipe."

"Nobody can make it like Mama does," Fiona countered.

"Hey, now!" Allie and Lizzy said at the same time.

Fiona slowly shook her head. "You both can make it but it ain't like what Mama makes. She throws in mama love."

"I can do that," Allie said.

"And Audrey will think yours is the best in the world someday. Everyone finished with their plates? I'll clear them away while Mama cuts the cake."

Half an hour and two helpings of the rich chocolate cake later, several cell phones rang at the same time. Deke, Toby, and Blake fished theirs out of their pockets and were on their feet before they hung up. Katy, Allie, and Lizzy all found theirs in the pile of purses tossed on a chair in the living room.

"Come on, Jud. That was the volunteer fire department. There's a fire somewhere down past Deke's place. You can help," Blake said the second he'd finished listening to the call.

"Down past Deke's place on which end?" Fiona asked.

"It's Truman and Dora June's house," Katy called out from the living room. "Get your coats on, girls, and bundle Audrey up, Allie. You can stay in the truck with her but Dora June might need us."

Chapter Six

Smoke, darker than the clouds rolling in from the southwest, billowed upward until the wind caught it and spread it out over the whole county. The blaze had engulfed the whole house, and even though the firemen sprayed every drop of water they had on it, the house and all its contents were devoured.

Truman and Dora June stood beside their pickup truck, shock written on their faces as they watched fifty years of their married life go up in flames. Katy wasted no time in marching right up to Dora June and wrapping her arms around her.

"It's all gone." Dora June broke down in sobs against Katy's shoulder.

"Don't cry, Dora June," Truman said. "I hate it when you cry, but if you hadn't left them Christmas tree lights on..."

Dora June pushed away from Katy, put both hands on Truman's chest, and shoved him backward against the cold truck fender. "Don't you go blamin' me. It was probably that extension cord you wrapped duct tape around because you were too cheap to buy a new one."

"You don't need to talk to me like that..."

Dora June's forefinger shot up. "Truman O'Dell, you are a scrooge."

Katy stepped between them. "Why or how this happened is not as important as where you go from here, as in right now, so both of you settle down. Do y'all have a place to go tonight?"

Dora June shook her head. "Martha's granddaughter is getting a divorce and staying with her until she gets on her feet. Henrietta's got a grandson and his family over at her place until after Christmas. He's got a month's leave in between duty stations in the service. And Ruby has company coming next week. I guess we'll have to go to Throckmorton or Wichita Falls to a hotel."

Fiona moved to stand beside Katy. "Mama, you aren't going to...," she whispered.

"Love thy neighbor," Katy whispered back, and then turned to Dora June. "Don't be silly. Audrey's Place has lots of room. You can stay there until you make a decision about this place."

Fiona sucked air right along with her sisters. Had her mother really just offered to take Truman and Dora June home after the way they'd behaved the past year? Lord have mercy! It might be the Christmas season when love abounded and the preacher might have preached on loving your neighbor, but Truman and Dora June? Fiona's nose twitched and her eyes dried out before she remembered to blink.

"I'll live in my old store building on Main Street before I live in a whorehouse," Truman snapped.

"You might but I'm not," Dora June smarted back at

him. "Katy, I appreciate the offer but I can't climb steps with these old knees."

"You and Truman can have my bedroom. It's downstairs. It even has its own private bath," Katy said.

Dammit! Why didn't her mother simply smile and nod? Everyone could appreciate the lovely Christian gesture without having to endure the pain of the reality if they took her up on the offer.

"I will not sleep in a room where a whorehouse madam did and you are not going to either, Dora June." Truman crossed his arms over his chest.

"Then you go sleep in that drafty old rat-infested building that doesn't even have a shower. Last time we checked, the potty wouldn't flush and the sink wouldn't drain. You can take your meals at Nadine's. I'm going home with Katy since she's been so sweet." Dora June turned around and marched over to Katy's car.

"You are welcome to change your mind," Katy said.

Fiona clamped her jaws shut tightly to keep from saying anything. If Truman and Dora June moved into Audrey's Place, then Fiona would spend her evenings over at the Lucky Penny with her sisters. Hell, she might even move in with them or else take up residence in the travel trailer if Jud didn't.

Truman stomped over to Katy's car and opened the passenger door. "I'll go, but I don't like it one bit."

Dora June crawled out of the car. "Well, you ain't goin' to like this a bit better. We're going to the church to get some clothing to last for a few days until we can shop."

Truman groaned and rolled his eyes. "I hate charity."

"Pride is a dangerous thing," Fiona told him, repeating the words her mother had said to her.

"Listen to her." Dora June crawled into the truck. "Be glad we weren't at home takin' our usual Sunday afternoon nap or we be dead. And be thankful that we still have a truck to drive and that your livestock wasn't burned up. God's been good to you, Truman."

"If he'd been good to me, I'd be sleeping in my house right now and not watching it finish burning to the ground. Come on, woman. I'll take us to the church and then to that horrible house," Truman snorted.

"We will see you in an hour, and thank you, Katy," Dora June said.

"Mama, what in the hell have you done?" Lizzy whispered.

"I've loved my neighbor. And you will, too. It will teach us all some patience."

"It might get me thrown in jail."

In a few long strides, Jud joined them.

"For what?" he asked.

"Mama just invited Truman and Dora June to live with us," Fiona said.

"That's sweet of you, but I'm surprised Truman agreed," Jud said.

"It's amazing what an old coot will agree to do when it's freezing outside, his house is gone, and the toilet won't work in his shack of a building on Main Street." Fiona sighed. "And we were going to have a family evening one day this week and put up the Christmas decorations."

"We still can," Jud said. "Christmas is my favorite holiday and not even Truman is going to ruin it."

Blake joined them but he was not smiling. "Katy, are you sure about this? Allie and Lizzy are not happy."

"We can't do any good here," Katy said. "So we're going back to the house and y'all are going to help me clear out my bedroom and move my things to one of the rooms upstairs."

"Yes, ma'am, but—" Fiona said.

Katy held up a palm. "No more *buts*, remember?"

* * *

It was really happening. Katy gave orders and everyone, including Jud and Deke, obeyed. Clothing was carried up to another room. Drawers were emptied and the dresser cleaned off—everything gotten ready for guests. Lizzy and Allie had put clean sheets on the bed and fresh towels out in the bathroom.

"Now we've got about five minutes before Dora June and Truman get here." Katy led the way into the living room. "Lizzy, tell me what it says about heaping coals in the good book."

"It says something about being kind to your enemies and it will be like heaping coals of fire upon his head. Poor old Truman's brain is most likely burning like hell about now," Lizzy said seriously.

"He probably won't even come out of his room when we come over here for a visit," Blake said.

Katy nodded and smiled. "Dora June loves Christmas, so she'll love helping with the tree when we put it up. Besides, it will help her feel some normalcy after losing everything she had. I bet some of the ornaments on her tree were handed down from her mother and grandmother, just like ours were."

Allie nodded. "That which does not kill us makes us stronger, right?"

"Who are you trying to convince? Yourself or the rest

of us? And if that saying is true, I'll be able to bench press a damn steer by the time Christmas rolls around." Fiona rolled her eyes.

A soft rap on the kitchen door brought Katy to her feet. "Fiona, you'd best come with me to welcome them."

"That's only fair since she's had to put up with the least crap from them," Lizzy muttered.

"I expect I'm about to make up for that at least twelve-fold," Fiona said through clenched teeth.

"You sure you don't want to move back into the travel trailer?" Blake asked Jud.

Fiona transferred her mean look toward her brother-in-law. "No, he does not. I need all the backup I can get, so don't you even answer that question, Jud Dawson."

"Smart sister you got there, Lizzy," Toby said.

"I told you she got all the brains." Lizzy rolled up on her tiptoes and kissed Toby on the cheek.

Fiona stood to the side and let Katy open the door. Looking at those two old folks standing there with plastic grocery bags full of used clothing, she felt a stab of pity and guilt. Not so much that she didn't still wish they'd have been able to find housing at one of Dora June's friends, but she knew what it was like to hit rock bottom.

"Come right in and from now on, this is your home, so you don't have to knock," Katy said.

"Can I help you with those bags?" Fiona asked.

"We've got it. I've been here often enough with committee meetings to know where to go. Thank you again, Katy." Dora June headed across the kitchen, through the dining room, into the foyer, and to the bedroom at the end. "I'll be right back."

"How much rent do you want?" Truman stopped inside

the door, his thin face set like stone and his nose tilted up a couple of inches.

"We won't take a penny from you," Fiona said.

"I don't take charity. I'll pay you same as if it were a hotel."

"Truman, pride carries a lot of pain with it, so let go of it and hush about charity," Fiona told him. "I'll show you the way to your room."

Dora June met Truman in the doorway. "You go on and take your afternoon nap or take a shower to get all the smoke off you if you want to. I've got things to say to this family and then I'm going to help clean up those dinner dishes from the dining room table."

"You don't have to do that. You are guests," Fiona said.

"If I don't have to knock, then I'm not a guest." Dora June tilted her head up, stretching all of her chins. "Is everyone waiting in the living room?"

"Yes, ma'am," Fiona said.

Dora June removed her coat and tossed it on top of the bags, smoothed back her gray hair, and marched back through the foyer. She didn't stop until she was in the middle of the floor with the family all around her.

"Here's what I'm going to do," she said with authority. "Truman will be gone over to our place taking care of things like normal. He'll be here for breakfast, lunch, and supper because that's the way he is. Tomorrow we are going to the grocery store and I will buy food and do the cooking for whoever wants to come around for those meals."

"That's not—" Katy started.

One of Dora June's palms shot up. "Let me finish. If I had to live in a hotel, I'd be crazy in a week with nothing to do. You've given me a nice place to stay and I *will* take care of the cooking and the cleaning of the downstairs. I can't climb them steps with my knees or I'd do the whole house, but the rest is what I need to do to keep myself from thinkin' about what has happened today."

She sat down in a rocking chair. "Truman ain't none too happy anyway and he'll feel less like he's takin' charity if I help out around here. It won't be but a few weeks at the most while we decide whether to build or just buy a trailer and park it somewhere on our property, but while we are here, let me help, please."

"Thank you." Jud smiled. "That will give me more time to work on the Lucky Penny. I bet you cook like my granny back home in Muenster."

Dora June smiled for the first time. "I'll fatten you right up, Mr. Dawson."

Fiona followed Jud's lead. "It will take a load off me and Mama when we have to work all day at the store, so thank you, Dora June. But you don't have to buy all the groceries to feed us."

"Yes, I do and yes, I will. Now I'm going on back there to take a nap with Truman. He's an old bear and he hates Christmas, so if Jesus Christ himself told him the lights didn't cause that fire, Truman wouldn't believe him. But I know how to handle him, so don't worry." Dora June stood up and a few minutes later they heard the bedroom door shut softly.

"So you get a maid and a cook," Allie said.

"Silver lining, but it don't mean the cloud isn't jet black," Fiona answered back. "You want a maid? I can send them over to you."

"No thank you," Allie and Lizzy said together.

* * *

Jud removed a gallon of milk from the refrigerator and filled a glass to the brim. He set that on the table and went back to the cabinet to cut a slab of chocolate cake from the pan. He had just put the first forkful into his mouth when Fiona peeked around the door frame.

"Whew!" She wiped her brow dramatically. "I thought it might be Truman in here for a late night snack and I sure don't want to deal with him tonight."

"Just me, but if you think he might prowl around, we could take it to the hall upstairs and sit on the floor," Jud said.

"Sounds like an excellent idea. I'll meet you up there in five minutes. I came after the same thing you've got going," she said.

Nine doors flanked the two sides and end of the wide hall. Six led into bedrooms and one into a linen closet. One opened up to a set of stairs leading to the attic. The ninth door had a cute little plaque on the outside that let everyone know it was the *necessary* room.

Tucked into one nook was a pair of dark crimson wingback chairs that flanked a small table with a lamp. An old oak credenza stood straight across the hall from it. The bathroom at the end of the hall sported an ancient clawfoot tub, quite possibly put into the house when it was built.

Jud had cracked the bathroom door enough to let a sliver of light out and was hidden at the end of the credenza when Fiona showed up. She tiptoed even though she was barefoot and walking on carpet. One hand held a glass of milk, the other a chunk of cake twice as big as what Jud had. She sat down to his left and balanced the cake on her lap. A picture of Rudolph all tangled up in Christmas lights was printed on her knit sleep shirt. The faded red bottoms were baggy enough that Jud had no doubt they could have fit Dora June, but she looked so damn cute he could hardly keep his hands off her.

"So you couldn't sleep, either? Worried about the new houseguests?" His voice was barely above a whisper.

"I'm not sure I'm comfortable turning so much of the housework over to Dora June. I know she can do it and she wants to, but dammit! I like to cook and this is the first time in ages that I can make anything I want. I've been looking forward to making Christmas cookies and decorating them," Fiona admitted.

"Just tell her that you are making cookies or candy or cakes. Do you make those Martha Washington candy things? I'll shoot them both and drag their bodies off to the back of the property if they get in your way of making those. Next to Aunt Bill's fudge, they are my all-time favorite and I don't get either very often."

Fiona nodded. "Yes, I make both but I didn't have anyone to eat them with this past year. And I was too busy to make candy or cookies when I was married."

The thin ray of light from the bathroom lit up a smear of chocolate icing on the corner of her mouth. He shifted his position until he was in front of her, sitting with his legs crossed and his knees touching hers.

"What?" she said as he leaned forward.

"Chocolate. Be still." He wiped it away with his thumb and then licked it off.

Little lightning bolts shooting around in the landing were so real that he expected to hear thunder rolling, but nothing happened. Women had never affected Jud Dawson like that, but there was something about those luscious full lips that begged to be kissed and it was far different than any bar bunny he'd ever picked up.

She scraped the icing stuck to her plate with her finger and licked it off.

He followed her lead and cleaned his plate with his finger. "Want me to take the plates down to the kitchen? No need in both of us going."

She shook her head. "We'll leave them on the credenza and take them in the morning. Good night, Jud."

He stood up, took the dirty dishes from her, set them on the credenza, and then offered her his hand. When she took it, he pulled her to her feet and kept right on until she was plastered against his chest. He hadn't planned on kissing her until he saw her moisten her lips with the tip of her tongue. He shut his eyes and simply followed sparks right to those sweet lips he'd wanted to kiss all evening.

* * *

The bristle of Jud's beard tickled Fiona's face as his lips moved over hers. She'd never been an impulsive person, so why in the devil was she kissing Jud so passionately? Using both hands, Jud brushed her hair back, kissed her on the forehead, then the tip of her nose and moved back to her lips.

His tongue eased its way into her mouth, igniting fires that she thought she might never feel again. Her insides went all oozy, begging for more than a touch, more than a series of hot perfect kisses.

She covered his hands with hers and gently pulled them away from her face. "Enough," she whispered hoarsely.

"Depends on who's calling the shots." His sexy drawl had deepened to a rasp.

"Let's not start something we can't finish," she whispered, and then gasped when she heard the turn of a doorknob across the landing.

She backed up against the wall just as the door opened and Katy stepped out in a long flannel nightgown that went from neck to toes.

"There's more cake in the kitchen if y'all can't sleep." Katy yawned.

"We just had some and were about to turn in," Jud said, as if nothing had happened.

"Well, then hand me those dirty dishes. I woke up hungry and I'm going down to the kitchen for a glass of milk. Good night to you both," Katy said.

"I feel like a sophomore," Jud chuckled when Katy disappeared down the steps.

"Me too, but we can't do this again." Fiona's breath came out in a long gasp.

He ran a finger down her jawbone. "Why? I kind of enjoyed it."

She turned around and opened her bedroom door. "I'm leaving town, maybe not next week or even before summer. But still, I'm not going to be here long-term. Can't get any simpler or easier to understand than that."

"But you'll be around for a little while. I'm not asking for a lifetime commitment here, Fiona. We are two adults and we could have some fun. Besides, it might help you forget that rotten ex of yours," he said.

She had a smart remark on the tip of her tongue that got lost in his soft brown eyes. She wanted to kiss him again. Hell, she wanted to do more than act like sophomores in high school. She wanted to be half of a consenting adult couple and pull him through the open door into her bedroom.

No, no! the voice in her head screamed. *Get a hold of your emotions or you'll make the second biggest mistake of your life. This is not a part of your new plan.*

"What are you thinking about so seriously, Fiona? A few kisses don't mean a stroll down the aisle. I enjoyed kissing you," Jud said.

"I was thinking of my new plan, and it doesn't involve getting into a relationship of any kind," she said honestly.

"You are beautiful when you are serious. But then you're pretty damn cute when you are kicking the shit out of a blown truck tire." He grinned.

It had been a very long time since anyone had told her that she was pretty or had teased her about her temper. "I guess it goes with the red hair and green eyes. I'm told that the original owner of this place, Miz Audrey, had red hair and a wicked temper."

"Hey…" He braced his back against the wall. "Since you don't like it here and you could live anywhere in the whole world, where would it be?"

"Any big city where no one knows me or my past," she answered quickly. "I've been thinking about Austin or maybe San Antonio. What about you?"

"Right here. I've waited for the Lucky Penny my whole life."

"Why?" She frowned. "It's a run-down old ranch except for the part that Lizzy bought from Deke. Even that isn't anything to brag about."

"Because all three of us have always wanted to build something from nothing. To be able to tell our kids when we are old that no one gave us this land or this ranch, that we had to dig it out of the earth and work our asses off to have it. There's something satisfying about that," Jud said.

"Didn't Toby already do that with some place he had up around Muenster?" She looped her hands around her legs and braced her chin on her knees.

"He did but it wasn't nearly the challenge this is. We were all born a hundred years too late, I guess. We should have been ranchers back in free-range days or when the state was being settled."

"You wouldn't have had bulldozers and tractors in those days," she said.

"We would have had Audrey's in all its glory. I wonder what those ladies who lived in our bedrooms looked like." He grinned.

She slapped at his shoulder. "I hated the stigma of this place when I was a teenager. Boys thought Lizzy and I would be easy because of the reputation it has."

"Not Allie?"

"No, she started dating Riley when they were kids and she never went out with anyone else. It broke her heart when she found out he'd been unfaithful their whole married life."

"And you? How bad was your heart broken?"

"At the time, I was more angry than hurt. Especially about my job. We'd been fighting so much that divorce had crossed my mind several times."

"Y'all still up?" Katy asked as she topped the staircase and headed to her room.

"Just going to bed now. Good night, Miz Katy," Jud said.

"'Nite, Mama." Fiona took a couple of long strides and gave her mother a hug.

She'd started back across the hall when Jud put a finger over his lips and pointed. Sure enough, there was the squeak of the refrigerator door as it opened and then the definite sound of the light switch. After that they heard Dora June asking Truman if he'd eaten half the chocolate cake and him fussing about not having a single bite.

"Sleepy?" he whispered.

She shook her head.

"It isn't even ten o'clock yet. Let's take this conversation into my room. I promise to leave my bad boy ways out here and you can have the rocking chair," he said.

She followed him into his room and noticed he hadn't been lying about neatness. Everything in the room was in place. Not even a magazine thrown on the dresser or a pair of boots kicked off beside the bed.

She sat down on the edge of the bed, feet on the floor, hands folded in her lap. He took the rocking chair and nonchalantly propped his bare feet up on the footboard of the bed. Her imagination jumped the tracks and went completely wild. What would it be like to have those feet tangled up with hers in this very bed? Would they be cold in the night or would his whole body be as hot as it looked in those Dallas Cowboy pajama pants and that navy blue thermal knit shirt?

"My sister, Josie, and I argue about everything, but I miss talking to her since I came here," he said.

"I thought you'd been living out in the panhandle and working for an oil company. Did you major in geology in college?" Fiona pulled her feet up on the bed, glad that she was wearing socks. There was something personal and even sexy about bare feet.

"Josie and I both did. Geology with a business agriculture minor for both of us. The oil company gave us a trailer to live in as part of our benefit package. She's still got a couple of months left on her contract and then she'll decide whether she wants to sign on for another year or not."

Fiona propped two pillows behind her and got comfortable. "I've missed adult conversation, too. Talking to my sisters on the phone was nice, but it's better to see who you are visiting with."

Especially when he was a damn fine-looking cowboy.

"So tell me more about Fiona the businesswoman," Jud said.

"She was a hardworking woman who went in early, stayed late, and got the job done. She had a few promotions and raises and then it all went in the crapper and she found out how the other half lives."

"Starbucks?" He laced his hands behind his head and leaned back in the overstuffed rocker and recliner combination. "Would you please toss me one of those throws on the end of the bed?"

She picked it up and threw it over the footboard as he pulled the lever on the side of the chair. Suddenly his feet disappeared. He covered them with the burgundy throw and looked at her from a reclining position.

"Not Starbucks. Just a little coffee shop that went belly-up when Starbucks put in a shop at the end of our block," she answered, disappointed that he was covered completely.

"I worked flipping burgers one summer at a Sonic," he said. "And one summer in college, I spent the whole three months doing gigs as a rodeo clown. Josie wants to invest in rodeo stock—bulls mostly. She would like to ride but she's about as coordinated as a hippo on ice skates."

"She sounds like she could be my friend," Fiona said.

"Probably. You are both strong-willed, determined, and outspoken," he chuckled.

They talked until midnight when Fiona made a joke about turning into a pumpkin and stood up, stretching from one side to the other with her hands over her head.

"And now it's time for Cinderella to rush away across the hall in her golden coach, right?"

She giggled. "This Cinderella doesn't even have a rusty old pickup anymore."

He popped the recliner down and walked her to the door. "I'll take you anywhere you want to go."

"Ahhh," she sighed theatrically. "My Prince Charming will race to my rescue in a big black club-cab truck."

"You bet your sweet little Southern ass he will." Jud tipped up her chin with his fist. "He will even let you ride in the front seat."

She fought the desire to roll up on her toes for a good night kiss. "Thank you for that and for the conversation."

He kissed her on the forehead. His soft lips right above her eyes at that time of night when everything was so intimate anyway was almost more than her nerves could stand.

She had to get out of his room or else drag him back to the bed, tear that shirt up over that muscled abdomen, and slip her hand beneath the elastic band of those Dallas Cowboy pajama pants.

With that vision in her head, she backed out of his room and hurried to her own bedroom. She threw herself on the bed and stared at the dark ceiling. It was going to be a long, long winter.

Chapter Seven

Fiona awoke to the aroma of bacon and coffee blended with something sweet reaching her nose as she threw the covers back. Noises across the hall told her that her mother and Jud were getting around, too, so that meant Dora June was serious about taking over the kitchen. The sun wouldn't be peeking over the horizon for another hour, but things had always started early in Dry Creek. The store was open by seven so the old guys could come for their morning coffee and discussion of politics.

"Politics, aka town gossip," she said to herself. She was used to getting up early because she'd had the early shift at the coffee shop. Folks who had to be at work by eight wanted time to drink the first cup in the shop and then take one with them to sip on throughout the morning.

Fiona dressed in a pair of skinny jeans and a soft dark green sweater and fished an old comfortable pair of cowboy boots from the back of the closet. Seven years she'd been gone and had only been home for a short while and yet old habits had come back as if she'd never left. Shaking the bugs out of her boots. Sitting on the step to put them on. Tucking the legs of her jeans down into them.

Katy laid a hand on her shoulder. "Good morning. Ready to go to work again?"

Fiona stood up and hugged her mother. "Good morning to you, too. Hey, I forgot to tell you that Lucy Hudson wants me to take over her books, too. She might come by and talk to me this morning."

"Ladies?" Jud stepped out of his room. "Books? What books?"

"Fiona went to school to be an accountant. She's always been good with figures," Katy said.

The pride in her mother's voice made Fiona's heart swell. She'd always known that her mother loved her but that morning she felt it down deep rather than just heard the spoken words.

"We might need to talk about the Lucky Penny business, then," Jud said.

Fiona blinked and tried looking away, but it didn't work. Wearing snug jeans, a dark blue thermal knit shirt with the top two buttons undone and the sleeves pushed up to his elbows, and scuffed cowboy boots—well, that was definitely sex-on-a-stick right there. Then add in bedroom eyes that hadn't had enough sleep and blond hair that curled when it was too long, and it was enough to make a saint sit up and take notice.

"Mornin', Jud," she said. "I'd be glad to take on the accounting for the Lucky Penny."

He nodded slightly toward her and then turned his attention to Katy. "Smells like Dora June was serious."

"I love home cooking." Fiona started down the stairs.

"My girls have always had healthy appetites," Katy giggled.

Dora June was bustling around in the kitchen. She wore a red sweatshirt with a picture of Santa Claus on the front and green sweatpants that were rolled at the hem. "I know I must look crazy but I love the way this feels. All soft and Christmas like." She pushed the sleeves up to her elbows. "Sit right down and have a nice cinnamon apple muffin while I fix y'all some eggs. I didn't want to cook them until you were here because cold eggs are horrible."

"Dora June, you don't have to wait on us." Fiona buttered a warm muffin and rolled her eyes. "You should be baking for a fancy coffee shop. These would sell for five dollars each where I used to work."

Dora June beamed. "Aah, honey, wait until you taste my orange cranberry. I like to make them in the holiday season. Speaking of that, I make cookies every Saturday during the season so I can have them for my Sunday school class. Y'all will have to eat the broken ones."

"Well, now, that is surely a chore I will look forward to." Jud smiled. "Where's Truman this morning?"

"He eats at five every morning and goes out to do chores by six. I expect he's over at the house trying to prove it was the Christmas tree that caused the fire. I cried and worried until after midnight, but finally a voice in my head had a talk with me and I'm fine with things this morning. I'm sixty-eight years old and..." She prattled on as she cracked eggs into a bowl and whipped them into a yellow froth. "I've been praying for two years that God would show Truman that it's time for us to retire and do something else. I didn't want the answer to be what it was, but who am I to question God?"

Fiona buttered another muffin and got the message as loud and clear as if it had been delivered through the voices in her head. The old truck barely making it to Dry Creek, the way things were working out, they were all answers to the prayers that she'd had in her head those weeks when she ran out of food and had no money. She'd been led to Dry Creek for a reason.

"Now Truman"—Dora June poured the eggs into a cast-iron skillet with melted butter in the bottom—"he's got to make his own peace and God has a little harder time convincin' him than he does me. He'll be back in the middle of the morning and we're going to Wichita Falls to buy clothing."

"Don't worry about supper," Fiona started.

"Oh, we'll be back by then. I've got a chicken in the slow cooker and plan on making dumplin's tonight."

After he'd finished breakfast, Jud carried his dishes to the cabinet, rinsed them, and put them in the dishwasher. Fiona followed so close behind him that she caught a whiff of his aftershave with every breath.

"Y'all been raised right," Dora June said seriously. "Now get on out of here and go to work and I'll busy myself with my jobs."

Fiona wanted to remind Dora June that she wasn't the boss, that she might have taken on the job of chief cook and maid, but that didn't give her any parental rights or even grandparent rights, but she kept her tongue.

"You got that right, Miz Dora. I'm procrastinatin' going out there in the cold wind to feed cows but I suppose it's got to be done," Jud said. "Thank you for the mighty fine breakfast. You mind if I tuck a couple of those muffins in my pockets for a midmorning snack?"

Dora June beamed. "Let me get you a couple of them plastic bags to put them in. Don't want crumbs in your pockets drawin' ants. You want to take along one or two, Fiona? There's plenty."

"I'd rather have two biscuits stuffed with leftover eggs and bacon. That would make a great lunch," Fiona answered.

"I'll get the bags and, honey, around here it's *dinner* and *supper*."

Fiona nodded and pasted on a smile.

* * *

Katy parked beside a line of five pickup trucks with their engines still running and old ranchers huddled down over the steering wheel like a buzzard over roadkill.

"Mercy, the old guys are here early today," Fiona said.

"They're always waitin' for me to open up on Monday so they can talk about the whole weekend. Men gossip every bit as much as women," Katy laughed.

Doors slammed as the guys crawled out of their trucks and followed Katy and Fiona into the store. They'd barely gotten inside when the pastry man arrived bringing in the usual order of pastries. Katy flipped on the lights and adjusted the thermostat while the fellows headed for the table in the back corner. Before Fiona could get the coffee made, Herman Hudson yelled at her to bring a dozen doughnuts to the table.

"I know Miz Lucy made you a good breakfast," Fiona said.

"That was two hours ago, darlin'. Man my size has to eat more often than three times a day. Besides, these old codgers here are going to help me out with the doughnuts," Herman chuckled.

Herman lived in bibbed overalls and always had a smile for anyone he met. He and his wife, Lucy, had been friends with Fiona's grandmother, Irene, since long before Fiona was born. He'd always felt more like a surrogate grandfather than a customer and he'd fallen right back into that place that cold November morning.

"Old! Who you callin' old?" one of the other men said. "And where in the hell is Truman this mornin'? I wanted to talk to him about that fire."

"Lickin' his wounds, I imagine," Herman said. "Katy took him and Dora June in over at Audrey's Place. He didn't want to go, but Dora June... well, let's just say she stood up to him and he don't mess with her when she takes a stand. She'll put up with a lot of shit but when she sets her mind, he'd better go on and do what she says."

"I'll be damned," another old guy said.

"He'll get over his snit, I expect, and we'll see him right here tomorrow mornin'," Herman said.

"Hey, I heard that them boys has got half the land cleared at the Lucky Penny. I swear they're going to make that ranch something to sit up and notice for sure. They ain't afraid of hard work or long hours neither one."

While her mother took a couple of doughnuts up the street to Lizzy's feed store, Fiona refilled the coffee cups and went back to dusting shelves. Besides, she could hear what those old codgers were saying a lot better from that vantage point than she could back behind the counter.

* * *

A blast of warm air greeted Jud when he pushed his way into the feed store that morning. Lizzy looked up from the counter and licked the chocolate frosting from the second doughnut from her fingers. It was the eyebrows and the shape of the faces that proved the Logan ladies were sisters. And maybe the attitude and that hip-swaying walk that made men take a second look and drool.

"Gettin' colder. Feels like snow out there," he said.

Lizzy laid a catalog to one side. "Weatherman says we're in for another cold blast. I can't believe we're getting hit two years in a row. How's things with Truman in the house?"

"Haven't seen him. He was gone at breakfast. According to Dora June, he leaves earlier than we do. I feel sorry for them. It can't be easy losing everything like that, but Dora has accepted it."

Lizzy poured a mug full of coffee and handed it to him. "She surprised me last night. I thought he always ran the show but it sounds to me like whenever she digs in her heels, he'd better obey."

Jud sipped the coffee. "They've been married a long time. I guess she picks her battles. This is so good after being out in the cold all morning."

Lizzy motioned the last chocolate doughnut. "Help yourself if you want."

"No, I just ate two big muffins that Miz Dora gave me this morning."

"What are you in town for?" Lizzy hopped up on the counter and crossed one leg over the other.

"About ten bags of cattle feed," he answered.

"I heard that Lucy Hudson is going to talk to Fiona about doing bookkeeping for their ranch. We should get her to take care of the Lucky Penny."

"I've been thinking the same thing all morning. We all hate to do the paperwork and there's lots of it with a ranch."

"I worry about her, Jud. She thinks she won't be happy here."

"Do I hear a *but* in there?" Jud asked.

Lizzy nodded. "But I'm not sure what it is. We've always wanted her to come back, but it has to be her decision or she will never be content."

"Why did she leave?" Jud asked.

"All I know is that she wasn't happy here."

"Here's my credit card. I'll go load up the feed and run back through here to sign the bill. And, Lizzy, you and your older sister are wise to love her enough to give her wings to fly and not try to hold her down."

"Thanks." Lizzy smiled.

Jud didn't actually need a thing from the convenience store that morning, but he wanted to see Fiona.

Tell a man he can't have something or that he can't do something and that will give him incentive to go after either with a full head of steam. The voice in his head sounded remarkably like his grandfather's.

A few flakes of snow fell from the sky as he stepped out of his truck at the convenience store. It was shaping up to be a second hard winter in Dry Creek. Last year Blake had to run things by himself. At least this year there were three of them to share the work load, plus two women who were absolutely the best rancher's wives in the whole state of Texas.

"I'm in the back room at the table trying to make heads and tails of Mama's books. Holler when you get ready to check out," Fiona yelled.

He stopped long enough to pour a cup of coffee and carried it to the door where a floral curtain had been pulled to one side. "Looks like you aren't going to get any moss on you today."

She looked up and frowned.

"A rolling stone gathers no moss," he explained.

That netted him half a smile.

She laid her books aside. "Well, there won't be a bit of moss on me if that's the truth. I'll be here until eternity dawns getting Mama's books in order. If she'd ever been audited, they'd have never found their way through the maze."

"I heard Lucy Hudson is bringing her things to you, too."

Fiona rolled the kinks from her neck. "That's probably fifty years' worth of work."

Jud removed his coat and hat and tossed them on the table in the corner, set the coffee on the end of the desk, and rounded the end. He stopped behind her chair and massaged her shoulders and neck muscles, his fingers digging in the knots that had been there far longer than the four days he'd known Fiona.

"Why are you a rancher?" she asked.

"Because I love the job," he answered.

"Women would pay big bucks for you to do this for them. If you did it naked from the waist up, you could charge double," she teased.

"And if I did it totally naked?"

"Oh, honey, the sky would be the limit."

"Want me to close that curtain and take off my clothes?"

Fiona shook her head. "I'm just sayin', not askin'."

"You need a break. Come up front and have a cup of coffee with me," he said.

"After that massage, I'd follow you to the moon and back." She stood up, got her foot tangled in a cord, and stumbled right into his arms.

"Whoa, there, darlin'. I know I worked the kinks out of your neck, but I didn't touch your legs," he teased.

One second she was straightening up; the next he was looking down into her green eyes and then his lips closed on hers. The kiss set off bells and whistles so loud that he couldn't hear a damn thing but ringing in his ears. Her lips were soft and the way her hands pressed against his chest sent bursts of heat right through his shirt to his skin. Dammit! Dammit! He'd never been so attracted to a woman in his whole life. It wasn't fair that fate had put her in his pathway and then said he couldn't have her.

"Hey, Katy, where are you?" Sharlene yelled. "I need a cup of coffee. Okay if I pour it?"

Fiona took a step back and frantically licked her lips. Jud picked up his hat and coat from the table.

"I didn't even hear the bell," she whispered.

"I thought it was just more of those going off in my head after that hot kiss." He quickly settled the hat on his head and put the coat on, more to cover up the bulge in his jeans than for warmth.

"I'm in the back, Sharlene! Be there in a minute. Mama ran over to Nadine's," Fiona called out as she started from the back room into the store.

"Fiona, is that you? What are you doing here?"

"Yes, it's me," Fiona said. "I'm helping Mama through the winter. You must have lost your touch, girl. I remember when you had all the gossip firsthand."

Sharlene, one of the biggest gossips in town, flipped her shoulder-length blond hair over her shoulder and ran her hand up Jud's arm. "Hey, handsome. Fiona, I haven't lost my touch at all. I was in Abilene for the holiday with my boyfriend and I just got back today. I'll be catchin' up on all the news soon as I get to Nadine's for lunch, but I wanted to run by and get a cup of coffee and visit with Katy first."

Jud waved and started for the front door.

"I've got a boyfriend or I would simply have to sample the goods you bring to the table," Sharlene teased.

"Your boyfriend is one lucky feller." Jud flashed a brilliant smile and took two steps away from her.

"Oh, honey, as sexy as you are, just say the word and I won't have a boyfriend in thirty minutes."

"I might change my mind in that length of time."

Sharlene laughed. "Poor baby! I don't cheat when I'm in a relationship and my boyfriend is out of cell phone reception for thirty more minutes, so it can't happen today. But don't give up hope."

"Never," Jud drawled. "See you at home this evening, Fiona. I've got to get the feed out to the ranch." He tipped his hat but his eyes were on Fiona. "Ladies..."

* * *

Sharlene watched Jud until he was in the truck and then turned back to Fiona. "I heard about Dora June and Truman's place burning."

"They're staying with us at Audrey's," Fiona said. She couldn't fault Sharlene for flirting or for watching that cute little tight-hipped swagger because she was doing the exact same thing.

"You're kidding me." Sharlene gasped. "After all the trouble they've caused?"

"Speak of the devil and he shall appear," Fiona whispered with a nod toward the door, where Dora June and Truman were pushing their way inside the store.

Both wore coats that were too big. As usual, Truman

looked like he'd been sucking on lemons and Dora June had a big smile on her face.

"Hello, ladies," she said. "Sharlene, did you hear about the fire?"

Sharlene crossed the floor in a couple of long strides and wrapped Dora June up in a bear hug. "I'm so sorry to hear what happened to your place. If I had room, I'd sure ask you to come and stay with me, but my rental house only has one extra bedroom and Mary Jo is using it until she can get on her feet and find something."

"We're very comfortable where we are, but thank you so much, honey." Dora June patted Sharlene on the shoulder. "It's so nice to have good folks in a community when tragedy strikes. I came to ask you if you have a key to the house, Fiona. Your mama gave me one so we can come and go, but I got worried that maybe you didn't have one, so I thought it best to stop and ask before we leave town."

"Yes, I do have a key and if you aren't home when I get there, I'll get the dumplings started," Fiona said.

"We'll be there," Truman said tersely. "Come on, Dora June. It's an hour up there and an hour back." He tucked her arm into his and led her outside the store.

"Poor old things," Fiona said. "You get a gold star for that performance, girl. I swear if I didn't know you so well, I would have believed that you really did want to give them a place to live."

Sharlene smiled brightly and bowed. "He's probably hating the taste of that crow pie he's having to chew on right now. He's an old bear but then I would be, too, if everything I had just went up in smoke," Sharlene said. "Thank God I don't have a spare room because I can't imagine living with him. You are a brave woman, Fiona Logan."

"I know they've been difficult but I feel sorry for them. No children and now their house has burned," Fiona said.

"Me too, but I sure don't want to live with them," Sharlene said. "Now what's this I hear about you being divorced?"

"For a year now," Fiona said.

Sharlene and Allie had gone to high school together, so Fiona knew the woman but she and her sisters hadn't ever been close friends with her. Still, Sharlene had no scruples or pride when it came to diving right into the personal lives of anyone she had a speaking acquaintance with.

"And Jud?"

"What about Jud?"

Sharlene tilted her head to one side and lowered her eyelids slightly. "Is he a roommate in that big old house or something more?"

"Good Lord, Sharlene! I've only been home four days. Right now, Jud Dawson is someone who lives in the house with me and Mama because he's kin to my two brothers-in-law," Fiona said.

"Good! The way he was flirting, I might change my mind about him." Sharlene winked and started for the door. "I still can't believe that you came back to Dry Creek. We all wished we had your backbone when you left and didn't even glance in the rearview mirror."

"I'm not sure I'm staying forever."

"I couldn't do it. This is home and I'll be here until they drag me out by the heels. See you later." The bell above the door sounded loud and clear when Sharlene left.

"I'm still not staying forever," Fiona said. But there was a little part hiding down deep in her soul that didn't believe a word of it.

* * *

Dark comes early in the last days of November in Texas, especially when the sky is a solid sheet of gray. Katy had left from the store to go with a couple of her friends down to Abilene for a steak supper. Her car looked pretty small when Fiona parked it next to Jud's big club-cab truck.

The cold wind cut through Fiona's denim coat on the way from the yard to the house. If there wasn't snow or sleet in those clouds, she'd be willing to eat a dirt sandwich for supper. The wonderful aroma of chicken filled her nose when she stepped through the back door into the utility room.

"So how was your day?" Jud sat at the kitchen table.

Her eyes were drawn to his big hands wrapped around that glass of sweet tea. "Busy," she answered.

"I got here about thirty minutes ago. I took the chicken out of the slow cooker and just finished boning it. I don't know how to make dumplin's, but I got that much done."

She removed her coat and hung it on one of the long row of nails inside the back door, kicked off her boots, and padded across the kitchen floor. "We'll pour the broth into a pan and while it's heating up to boiling, I'll get the dumplings ready and stir up enough dough to make a quickie peach cobbler for dessert."

"I love cobbler. What can I do to help?"

"Sit right there and stay out of my way," she said.

"Yes, ma'am. I think I can handle that with no problem."

She added a can of cream of chicken soup to the broth. By the time the broth reached a boil, the dough was ready to start dropping in half a teaspoon at a time, and the little cobbler was in the oven.

"Do we eat it in bowls like soup or do we fix other things to go with it?" he asked.

"Mama always served it like soup with thick slabs of buttered bread, cheese cubes, and sweet tea."

"Mine did, too, except that we didn't have the cheese." Jud carried his empty glass to the cabinet and refilled it.

She had her back to him, and when his hands snaked around her waist, she jumped to one side and whipped around, a spoonful of dough in her hand. He backed up quickly, hands raised like she was holding a gun, and chuckled.

"Don't hit me with that. I'd have to either change shirts or eat bare-chested and it's too cold for that," he said.

"Jud, we can't... you know... start something we can't finish..." She stumbled over the words.

"I was moving you to one side so that I could get into the cabinet. I wasn't fixin' to throw you over my shoulder and carry you off to the bedroom." He lowered his hands.

"Just tell me to move," she said bluntly.

"Move, Fiona. I need to get another glass out of the cabinet to fill with ice and tea for you."

She stepped to one side.

"Don't be so touchy," he said.

"Don't be so handsy," she smarted right back.

"I like kissing you."

At that, she had no words.

When the dumplings were almost done, she pulled the bubbling, crusty pie from the oven and set it on a hot pad. "That will be good with a scoop of ice cream on top. It's always better warm, but I can eat it cold, too." She went back to dropping dumplings into the broth. "I like kissing you, too, and that's the problem," she blurted.

"A problem, why?" He leaned on the counter, his big biceps straining the sleeves of his plain shirt open to show a thermal knit under it that stretched across his broad chest.

Before she could answer, a blast of cold air brought Dora June through the door. A few snowflakes were stuck to a brand-new navy blue coat and stocking hat pulled down over her gray hair. "We're home. And bless your darlin' heart, you started supper." She sniffed the air. "Is that cinnamon I smell?"

"I sprinkled a little bit on one of those quick peach cobblers and the dumplings will be ready in about ten minutes. Y'all need help with packages?" Fiona asked.

Dora June removed her coat and carried it to the coat rack in the foyer. "I ain't had a new winter coat in twenty years. Truman can bring in the sacks. It'll do him good the way he's been fussin' about how much money we had to spend. You'd think we were paupers. Maybe totin' things inside during a snowstorm will cool down his temper."

"Soon as he gets done, we can eat," Fiona said.

"I'll get my coat on and go help him." Jud was out the back door in a flash.

Truman could be in a pout if that's what he wanted, but Fiona fully intended to ignore him. It had been at least two, maybe three years since she'd had dumplings or peach cobbler and she wasn't letting Truman O'Dell ruin it for her.

He glared at her when he and Jud toted in the first set of bags back to the bedroom. By the second trip, he just looked like a tired old man who wanted to eat supper, lean back in his favorite chair, and drift in and out of sleep while he pretended to watch television. Fiona felt so sorry for him that she could have wept.

When they sat down at the table, Dora June looked at

Fiona and cocked her head to one side. Did she have dough on her chin or in her hair? Her hand went up to check.

"Fiona, you are the lady of the house. It's your place to call on someone to say grace," Dora June finally said.

"Truman, would you please?" Fiona blushed.

It was by far the shortest prayer she'd ever heard him say. When she raised her head, everyone stared at her again.

"What?"

"You want to dip the dumplings or should I?" Jud asked.

"Go ahead." She'd spent a year eating at the cabinet or over the kitchen sink. The years she was married she had used her kitchen very few times. She'd forgotten all about the duties the lady of the house had in Dry Creek.

"Good dumplin's," Truman said after the first bite.

Fiona came close to dropping her spoon.

"Yes, they are and that pie looks real good, too. This is a treat to come home to food already fixed," Dora June said.

"Thank you," Fiona mumbled.

That was the extent of the conversation. Other than asking for something to be passed, they ate in silence, which was just fine and dandy with Fiona. She'd rather have quiet than an argument that would keep her from enjoying her supper. After they'd finished dessert, Jud refilled his sweet tea glass and carried it to his room. Truman muttered something about Dora June bringing a cup of coffee to their room when she had the kitchen cleaned and he disappeared.

"I haven't changed my mind about you and that cowboy," Dora June said bluntly.

Fiona cut her eyes around at Dora June. "Oh?"

"They might be hardworking cowboys like Lucy and

Herman say all the time, but that ranch is what it is and no one has ever been able to change it. When their savings run out, they'll leave and take your sisters with them. I'm not wrong. I've seen it happen too many times through the years. And just because your mama was kind enough to let us stay here don't mean that I'll change my mind."

"Frankly, I don't care if the whole family leaves Dry Creek because I'm not planning on sticking around a minute longer than necessary, either. Maybe we'll all just leave together and the feed store and Mama's store will close up. Whole town will probably fall into decay and die if that happens."

Dora June narrowed her eyes into slits. "Your mama wouldn't do that, but Jud will break your heart. Trust me, Fiona, this one is trouble."

Fiona frowned. "I'm not sure that's a bit of your business."

"Your granny Irene was my best friend. I miss her."

"What's that got to do with you trying to tell me what to do?" Fiona snapped.

It started as a chuckle and grew into a laugh that had every one of Dora June's three chins wiggling. She finally wiped her eyes with the tail of an old faded apron that had evidently come from the church clothes closet.

"You do have her temper. Nobody ever told Irene how to run her life. I always wished I could have gotten some of that for myself."

"Never too late," Fiona said. "Want to make some cookies tonight?"

"No, I do not! I'm going to wash a load of underwear so me and Truman can have clean things after our shower. I never wear under-britches right out of the packages and it was a real leap of faith for me to put on the ones I got at the church last night, but when you ain't got anything else, you learn to be grateful for what you can get."

"I'm going to make cookies and I'll finish cleaning up the kitchen. You can get your laundry started," Fiona said.

"Are you telling me what to do now?" Dora June raised a gray eyebrow.

"Yes, ma'am, I am."

The older lady pursed her lips and settled her chins together in one big blob under her chin as she tilted her head down and looked up at Fiona over the top of her wire-rimmed glasses. "Just like Irene. Bossy as the devil. And look where it got her. Her mind is gone and she don't even know her family."

"Living with Truman, I'd think you would be praying that you'd get Granny's dementia so you wouldn't know him," Fiona told her.

"Hmmmph!" Dora June snorted but her eyes twinkled in merriment. "Living with you ain't goin' to be easy."

Chapter Eight

Fiona ate one cookie out of each bunch that came from the oven, so by the time the six dozen were finished, there were only five and a half left. Of that, she placed six on a plate and the rest in an airtight container and left them on the counter in case Dora June or Truman wanted a late evening snack.

She filled a quart jar with milk, twisted the lid on it, and took it along with the cookies up the stairs. If there was no light shining from under Jud's door, she'd take the treats to her room. If there was, she'd set them on the floor, knock gently, and go on to her room.

His door was wide open. Jud was lying back in the recliner with a laptop resting on his knees and the wires from earbuds hanging down past his shoulders. He grinned and motioned her inside.

With a few flicks of the wrists, whatever was on the laptop disappeared and the earbuds were gone. "Hey, is that what I hope it is? I left the door open so none of the smell would be wasted."

"Chocolate chip cookies and milk." She set them on the nightstand beside his chair.

"Stay a while and talk to me. I was watching a show because I'm bored. If it hadn't started snowing and wasn't so damned cold, I'd be out on the porch or taking a drive."

She sat down on the edge of the bed. "What were you watching?"

"Some episodes of *Justified*. I really like the first season. I hated it when the series ended, so I bought all six seasons." He bit into a cookie and smiled. "Just like Mama makes and warm right from the oven."

"That's when they're best," she said. "So on a normal Monday night in your life before the Lucky Penny, what would you be doing?"

"Probably sitting in the living room watching television. Maybe drifting off to sleep because I'd partied too hard over the weekend. You?"

"Didn't have the money or the friends to party with over the weekend. So I would probably be propped up on my bed reading. The television in the furnished apartment I rented didn't have cable and only got one channel that usually played cartoons. The library was a block down from the coffee shop where I worked. On Saturday morning before my shift started, I'd go by and check out half a dozen books."

He picked up the second cookie. "What do you read?"

"I like romance, but not paranormal. And mystery, but not the cozy stuff. Recently I've gotten into some cowboy romance by Katie Lane and Laura Drake."

"Oh, so you like cowboys?" His eyes took on that dreamy I-would-love-to-take-you-to-bed look.

"I like to read about fictional cowboys. Real ones are a whole different story." She paused and then went on. "Jud, do you think people or even places change in the course of time?"

He twisted the lid off the milk and took a few gulps. "Now, that's an interesting change of subject. I was about to say that I'm fond of Jeffery Deaver and James Patterson and I did like Nicholas Sparks's *The Longest Ride*. It's about a cowboy. Now back to your question about change over the course of time. Water can turn to ice if it's kept in the freezer long enough or it can change into steam if it's boiled. According to the circumstances, things can change," he said.

"You think you can turn the Lucky Penny's reputation?"

"Absolutely. We've already started. In three generations, what they say about it will be urban legend. By the time I have grandkids, folks will be flocking to this area *because* of the Lucky Penny. It will raise the best beef cattle in the state and possibly be pumping enough oil to put Dry Creek back on the map. Main Street will be several blocks long and every store building will be full and the population will be ten times what it is now," he said seriously.

"All the way up to five thousand?" A smile toyed at the edges of her mouth.

"Maybe more." He nodded.

"Optimistic, aren't you?"

"Beats the hell out of pessimism. What else you got on your mind tonight?"

She shrugged. "You think people can change. I was sure hoping that Truman could change. I hate the tension when he is at the table. Just knowing he's in the house right here at Christmas puts a damper on the whole holiday.

He's worse than Scrooge. What was Mama thinking? They could have lived in the church. It's got a kitchen, and when they redid the nursery they put a shower and a sofa bed in there in case visiting preachers needed a place to stay."

"Maybe it's time to turn ice into steam," Jud answered. "And, yes, people can change. It's got to do with whether they want to down deep in their hearts but nothing, not one single thing, is permanent on this earth. Not green grass or attitudes."

"Thank you," she said. "But Truman is frozen pretty solid. How do we even get him out of the ice tray?"

"What'd you do with the rest of the cookies?" Jud pushed the footrest down and stood and twisted his back, working out the kinks of the day.

He could stand in front of her and do nothing but move like that for an hour and she'd be content to watch the show. It was far sexier than any dance move she'd ever seen and the way his biceps flexed—well, that reminded her of the way his arms felt around her when they were kissing, and her imagination created images that made her blush.

"I put them in a container but I left some on the counter," she answered.

"That's a step in the right direction. Nothing starts to un-freeze a feller like good cookies. Let's make it our Christmas mission to unthaw that old codger."

She pushed up off the bed. "I'm not sure there's enough Christmas magic to turn that old scrooge into anything but a bigger old scrooge."

He held out his hand toward her. "We need a plan. Come on, I'll walk you to your door. Never know what might be lurking out there in the shadows of the hall."

She put her hand in his and he laced their fingers together. His calloused fingertips caused bursts of warmth throughout her whole body. Big hands like that would protect a woman as well as make love to her. She wished it were a quarter of a mile to her room instead of less than ten feet so she could examine all the feelings that his touch evoked.

"Thank you for the cookies and milk," he whispered.

"You are so welcome. Thank you for the conversation." She opened her door and let go of his hand.

"No good night kiss?" he asked.

"Jud, I—"

She didn't get another word out because his lips were on hers, moving expertly and erasing every sane thought from her head.

"Good night, Fiona," he breathed into her ear when the kiss ended.

"No, Jud! Not good night. We've got to talk about whatever this thing is that has sprung up between us." She crossed her arms over her chest.

He put a finger over her lips and she had to concentrate to keep from losing every shred of common sense in her body.

"One thing at a time, darlin'. Right now we've got to turn Scrooge into Santa Claus."

Then he crossed the landing and shut his bedroom door behind him. For the second night in a row, she threw herself backward onto her bed and stared at the ceiling.

* * *

Truman didn't look too happy for Jud to be joining him and Dora June for breakfast but he didn't say anything other than to tell Dora June that he'd take three over easy eggs with his bacon and biscuits that morning.

"And you?" Dora June asked Jud.

"Same as Truman is having." Jud poured himself a cup of coffee, topped off Truman's, and then sat down at the table.

"What made you get up so early?" Dora June cracked three eggs into a big cast-iron skillet.

"Have a problem I need some help with and was hoping Truman might be willing to hear me out."

"I got work to do. Ain't got time for none of you Dawsons' problems. Got enough of my own," Truman said coldly.

"Then I'll help you with chores this morning so you'll have the time. It's just a matter of a little hike. If you're too old to do much walkin', I guess I could just tell you what the problem is."

"Boy"—Truman set his jaws in a clench— "I could out-walk you any day of the week. I'm used to hard work."

"We'll see about that." Jud smiled. "I'll help you get your work done and then we'll see if you get winded on the hike back to the place I want you to take a look at."

"Hmmph," Truman snorted.

Jud pushed back his chair, hurried across the kitchen floor, and took the two plates from Dora June. He set one in front of Truman and the other across the table. "I'll ride with you and then we can come back here when we're done. The place I need you to see can't be reached by truck. You'll need to bundle up so you don't get sick."

"I'm used to the weather, so don't tell me how to dress. Maybe I don't want you to ride with me. Can't you get it through your thick head that I don't like you or your kin? And what's to say that after you work for me that I turn around and don't go with you?" Truman dug into the breakfast Dora June set before him.

"You might be a jackass, Truman, but you are an honest man, so if I work for you, then you will do what I ask," Jud said.

Dora June brought a plate of muffins to the table and sat down beside Truman.

He buttered a muffin and laid it on the side of his plate, then shot a dirty look across the table at Jud. "Jackass, am I?"

"I didn't stutter," Jud said.

"Well, if you're going to ride with me, you'd better get to eatin' because I'm not waitin' for you," Truman said.

Jud had never shoveled food in so fast or gotten his boots and coat on in such a hurry. When Truman came out of the house, Jud was leaning on the fender of the old guy's truck. The look on Truman's face was absolutely priceless.

"It ain't locked," Truman said. "I only open the doors for Dora June."

Jud nodded seriously and crawled inside. Truman got in, ignored the seat belt, and started the engine.

"I reckon we're in for a hell of a winter. Only hope I've got enough hay in the barn to carry me through," Truman said. "You boys are going to be hurtin' big-time."

"I don't think so. We put up enough for the herd in the worst conditions and then added another forty big bales to that number, plus we always use some cattle feed to keep the weight on them in the cold weather," Jud countered.

Truman turned right at the end of the lane. The Lucky Penny lay to the right, and down the road a bit was Deke's new place over on the left. Just past that, Truman turned into his lane, drove past the charred remains of what used to be his home, and drove on out to the barn.

"What kind of stock are you runnin'?" Jud asked.

"Twenty goats and a hundred head of cattle."

"Why goats?" Jud asked.

"Dora June thinks the babies are cute in the spring and I sell off the stock in August. It gives her a little extra money to put in her jar."

Jud opened the door and got out of the truck. "What does she do with the money?"

"Never asked. It's hers and it's her business."

"Okay, goats first and then cattle?" Jud asked.

Truman nodded. "Load up two bags of them pellets and we'll drive over to the goat pen."

Jud hoisted a bag up on each shoulder and tossed them over into the back of Truman's truck. "Now what?" he asked.

Truman almost smiled. "I'll drive and you can dump it in their feeder. Be careful around that old billy goat. Dora June is the only person he likes. He's put me over the fence more'n once."

Jud fought the urge to pump his fist in the air. A smile from Truman was a hell of a lot of progress for one morning's work.

"Okay. You want me and my cousins to bring the dozer over here when this weather clears up and take care of that fire mess?"

"Hell no!" Truman raised his voice. "Insurance ain't decided what they're going to do yet. Don't know why they're actin' like it was arson. It was that damned old Christmas tree Dora June puts up every single year."

"Did you hear that the whole family is coming over for supper tonight and we're putting up decorations?" Jud asked.

"I ain't goin' to be involved in that shit. I'll stay in my room," he said.

"Why?"

"I hate Christmas," Truman said.

"That's sad."

"I don't need your pity. I can hate it if I want to," Truman declared.

"I guess that's your choice. I love Christmas. It's my favorite holiday."

Truman grunted.

It wasn't far to the goat pen and the herd seemed oblivious to snowflakes drifting down from the cold gray skies. The younger ones romped around playing king of the mountain on a couple of hay bales. The older ones pawed at the snow so they could get at the brown grass beneath it. The two bags filled the feed trough and the billy goat was far too interested in eating to mess with Jud.

That job finished, he hopped into the truck, removed his gloves, and rubbed his hands together. "It's getting colder by the minute. The flakes aren't wet anymore but dry and they're coming down faster."

"We're in for another bad winter. Dora June's knee hurts when the weather is changin' and she's right every time," Truman said. "Let's check on them cows now. I put several bales out yesterday mornin' but it's been cold. Probably need to load up another one and take it out to them."

"So you use the small square bales?" Jud asked. "Most ranchers have gone to the big round ones."

"I ain't spendin' my money for all that equipment to make the big bales when this size has worked my whole life. Ain't you strong enough to throw a few bales off the back of a truck?" Truman said without even cracking a smile.

"To get you to answer my questions, I'll restack the whole barn for you," Jud shot back at him.

Truman's eyes twinkled even if he didn't smile. "I won't ask you to do that but you can load the truck and ride in the back so you can throw the bales off when I stop."

The old fart was enjoying the company whether he'd admit it or not. Jud settled back into the seat, glad that Truman didn't have hogs to feed or horse stalls to muck out in the cold weather. Hoping that the snow didn't fall any faster—or worse yet, make a reverse and decide to turn into sleet—Jud hoped that he didn't kill Truman with the hike through the mesquite when they got back home.

Truman backed his truck into the barn, stopped right inside the big wide doors, crawled out, and grabbed his hip with a wince. He limped a little as he made his way around the truck to lower the tailgate, but he'd worked the kink out fairly well by the time he picked up a bale. He did fairly well until he reached the truck, where it took two tries before he got the sixty-pound bale onto the tailgate.

"I reckon we'll need about ten bales today," he huffed.

No wonder Dora June worried about him and wanted to get out of the ranching business. Jud had a bale of hay in his hands and was about to suggest that he do the heavy lifting but the voice inside his head told him that would offend Truman. *He'll take three steps back instead of two forward,* Jud thought as he brought a bale to the back of the truck.

"Hey, Truman, it would go faster if I carried the hay

over here and tossed it into the truck bed and you stacked it up so I could get at it easier out there in the field."

Truman nodded and pulled himself up into the truck bed. Never in his life had Jud wanted to help someone so much, but he held back and let the old guy do it on his own. Then Jud went to work, carrying the rest of the hay.

"First bale ain't so heavy but this tenth one wears on a man," Jud said.

"You younguns ain't got what it takes to ranch. You got all that fancy machinery and all you got to do is sit in an air-conditioned cab all day," Truman panted as he stacked the last bale.

"We still make small bales over on the Lucky Penny. I'm kind of lookin' forward to hauling hay next summer," Jud argued.

"Well, when you're so sore you can't move that first night, you call Dora June and she'll send over some of her liniment, but you'll have to send one of your kin after it because I ain't bringin' it to you," Truman declared.

"She make a good kind, does she?" Jud rubbed at his arm even though it wasn't a bit sore.

"Everything Dora June makes is good. We going to stand around her jawin' or are we goin' to feed the cattle? And since you are workin' for me this mornin', we do things my way," Truman said.

"And that is?"

"I like to go down to Katy's store for a cup of hot coffee and a little visitin' with the men folks after chores."

"You aren't afraid to be seen with a Dawson?"

Truman narrowed his eyes at Jud. "I ain't afraid of nothing but losin' Dora June."

"Then why do you fuss at her so much?" Jud asked.

"It's our way," Truman said bluntly.

"Folks might think you are changing your mind about the Dawsons if we go to Katy's store."

All he got in response was another grunt.

* * *

Jud wished he could have taken a picture of Fiona's face when he walked into the store with Truman and headed back to the table where half a dozen old geezers were discussing the weather over their morning coffee.

She raised an eyebrow.

Jud smiled and said, "Two cups of coffee and bring us a dozen of those doughnuts. I'll treat the guys this morning."

"You got a new runnin' buddy?" Herman Hudson asked.

"Hell no! I ain't about to start runnin' with a Dawson. He needs my help, so he had to work to get it."

"If I could get him to work for me, I'd pay him whatever he asked," Herman said.

Fiona set a tray with two cups of coffee and a dozen doughnuts on the table. "Any of y'all need a refill?"

"Not me. I got to get out to the Lucky Penny and do some wood cuttin'. I swear, all that mesquite they've been clearing has been a gold mine to me and mine these past two winters." Herman picked up a doughnut and shoved it in his mouth, holding it there while he put on his coat. When he finished, he bit off a third of the doughnut and asked Fiona to put his coffee on his bill.

"I'll take care of it all," Jud said. "It's my first day to sit here with you fellers, so I'll buy it all today."

"Thank you," Herman said seriously. "You'd do well to get to know these guys, Truman. They're the hardest workin' crew I've ever seen."

"When hell freezes over, I might think about it."

Jud caught Fiona's eye and winked. He could hardly wait until everything settled down that night so he could tell her about the morning.

"So is there anything I can do for you so I could get you to work for me some morning?" Herman asked.

Jud took a sip of his coffee. "Nothing I can think of, but I'll keep it in mind."

"I'm ready now to show you that I'm not too old to take a hike. Where is it we're goin'?" Truman said abruptly.

"Back behind Audrey's Place," Jud said. Truman was jealous of Herman and that was something Jud could file away for later use for sure.

"On the Lucky Penny? I said I wouldn't step foot on that place," Truman declared.

"You goin' back on your word to help me after I did my part?" Jud asked seriously.

"I give my word and I'll do it, but I think you tricked me and I don't like that."

"You don't have to like it, Truman. I didn't like getting out there in that goat pen or lifting all that heavy hay, but I did it anyway, so we'll be even when we take care of this. Right now I'm going to pay our bill and I'll meet you in the truck."

Fiona figured up the amount and made change for the twenty-dollar bill Jud laid on the counter. "What is going on?" she whispered.

"I'm melting ice." He grinned.

"By fighting with him?"

"Can't be too easy on him or he'll figure out what I'm doing. Bring cookies to my room and we'll talk later," Jud said.

"Deal," she whispered, and placed the change in his hand.

Truman drove back to the house, parked the truck, and glared at Jud. "It's your party from here. Where do we go?"

"See that clearing over there behind the yard fence?"

"Why's it there?"

"Because Toby wanted to make a path for some reason. I expect he found that old well and wanted to check things out," Jud answered.

"That where we're going?"

Jud nodded.

"Then let's get on with it. Can't imagine why you'd want to talk about that place. It's as unlucky as the rest of your ranch." Truman bailed out of the truck, turned up his shirt collar, and pulled his black felt hat down tight on his head. His ears stuck out the sides like Elmer Fudd's. Judd half expected him to start stuttering as he took off at a pace that kept Jud moving right along.

The old coot was trying to prove that he was still twenty years old. If he dropped dead from a heart attack, Dora June would shoot Jud.

"Hey, slow down. It's not that far that you have to run," Jud yelled.

Truman stopped until Jud caught up. "Younguns! Y'all can't keep up with us old folks in anything. I know exactly where we're going," he panted. "There's an old well back here and it ain't good for nothing. Never was. Just another thing that went wrong on the Lucky Penny. What do you want me to tell you about it? That it produces water. Well, it don't."

Jud led the way back to the clearing where the well sat over in the far corner. He removed the board and looked down into the blackness. "Why doesn't it have water in it? Why drill a well if you haven't done your homework and know there's a water table down there that's got good water?"

"Because the folks that live on this ranch ain't got sense. It was back before I was born when they sunk this well. My daddy told me the story about it. The folks had notions of building a house here for some of their kin. A grandma or a mother-in-law. I don't remember that part. I remember wondering why in the devil they'd want a house this close to that old brothel, though."

"Why did they stop drilling or digging or whatever they were doing?" Jud asked.

Truman cut his eyes around at Jud. "Why are you so interested in this old well?"

"It's part of the Lucky Penny history and I want to know all I can about the ranch."

"My dad said they hit rock. Limestone about forty feet down and plumb give up. They should've filled it in but I guess the next owners used it to hoodwink their buyers into thinking there was water over on this part. Ain't never been water in that thing, so if you're planning on irrigatin' with it or pumpin' water out for your cattle, you're shit out of luck."

"Some days you get good news; some days you get bad news. Thanks, Truman, for telling me about it," Jud said. "I'm going on over to relieve Blake from the bulldozer now. You want to come help us mow down mesquite? I'll let you drive my equipment. I'm not stubborn and mean like you."

"Hell no! I ain't helpin' y'all do a blessed thing and I'm moving out of that old brothel soon as the damned insurance settles and Dora June and I decide whether to build or buy a house," he said.

Chapter Nine

Fiona hummed Christmas carols all day long as she waited on customers at the store and worked on the accounting in the back room. It had been years since she'd been home on the evening they decorated the tree, and her spirits were high, even when she had to enter miles and miles of numbers into the computer.

At noon, Katy went up to Nadine's and brought back a couple of big juicy burgers and they had lunch together at the yellow table. "You are in one fine mood today," Katy said.

"I can't wait to decorate the tree, and Dora June said she was making cookies." Fiona bit into the burger and groaned. "I love good burgers. This is amazing. Nadine should have put in a café years ago."

"She's doing a good business. Speaking of businesses—do you remember my friends Trudy and Janie?"

"Those are the women you went to supper with the other night, right?"

"Yes," Katy said. "They're both retired and they're going to Florida for three months. They asked me to go with them. They've rented a condo right on the beach where a bunch of retired folks go for the winter. Trudy has done this for years but it's Janie's first time to go with her."

"And?" Fiona held her breath.

Katy laughed. "Don't panic. I told them no. I can't be away from Audrey for three months or your grandmother, either."

"But you could be away for a week or maybe even two. Are they flying?"

"No, they're driving in Trudy's van," Katy answered.

"You want to go, don't you?"

"I haven't been away like that in . . ." Katy paused.

"Did you even have a honeymoon when you and Daddy married?" Fiona could never remember a time that her mother had been out of Dry Creek for more than a day.

"We went to Dallas for the weekend but he had to be back on the job Monday morning and I was helping Mama run this store so . . ." Katy shrugged.

Fiona shoved some paperwork to the side and reached across the table to lay a hand on her mother's. "Go with them. Stay a week or two and then fly home. You can be back in plenty of time for Christmas, and I'll see to it that Audrey gets lots of love and I'll check on Granny every Sunday afternoon that you are gone."

"But . . ."

Fiona gently squeezed Katy's hand. "You told us girls no buts, so I'm sayin' the same thing to you. I can hold down this place for a couple of weeks. Getting away will do you a world of good. When are they leaving?"

"Tomorrow," Katy sighed.

"Perfect. The tree will be up. Granny can spend the evening with us, so you'll get to have that time with her and then you can leave in the morning. That's only two Sundays and I'll visit her both of them, I promise, and take care of anything that comes up with her. You're only a phone call away and if something drastic happens, you can be home in a few hours. Planes go from there to Dallas every day."

"You should have been a lawyer rather than an accountant. You present a strong case." Katy smiled.

"Then you'll do it?"

"I'll think about it."

"Fair enough," Fiona said.

* * *

Fiona was not one bit disappointed when she and Katy came home that evening. The lights coming from the windows of Audrey's Place cast a yellow glow on the falling snow, creating a picture fit for a Christmas card. The warm house smelled like pine and sugar cookies mixed in with something chocolate and was that chicken? A blaze crackled in the fireplace and Christmas carols were playing. Fiona removed her coat, hat, and gloves and took it all in like a thirsty person who'd just crossed the desert with no water.

"Well, let's get started decorating the tree?" Irene started to unbutton her coat.

"I'll help you." Fiona hurried to her grandmother's side.

"Bein' forgetful is a bitch, but it don't make me helpless." Irene pushed Fiona's hand away. "I'm hungry. I hope there's Christmas cookies with icing on them in the kitchen."

"I bet there is." Fiona stood back and let Irene hang up her own coat.

The whole family was there to help put up the decorations and supper was laid out buffet style on the dining room table. Chicken salad sandwiches, chips, three kinds of dip, and all kinds of cookies and finger foods. Dora June was bustling around like she did at a church supper, playing with Audrey one minute and fussing about no one eating enough the next.

"What in the devil are you doing here, Dora June?" Irene asked as she removed her coat and hat. She handed them to Fiona and went straight for the table, where she picked up a cookie. "Did you make these?"

"I'm staying here for a while," Dora June answered. "My house burned down and Katy is letting us stay with her. And, yes, I did make the cookies."

"You ain't lost your touch." Irene picked up a second one. "Allie, you need to take that baby into the living room. She won't remember today when she's old as I am but we will remember the look on her little face when the tree is lit up."

"Yes, ma'am." Allie crossed the room and hugged Irene. "How was your ride down here tonight? Were the roads clear?"

"They were. According to the weather report, the snow stops just north of us and is going to the east," Katy answered.

"Hey, y'all, I hear there's a tree decoratin' goin' on tonight." Deke swept into the house through the kitchen door, hung up his coat and hat, and grabbed two sandwiches on his way to the living room. "Granny! I didn't know you were going to be here."

"I'm always here when it's time to decorate," Irene said.

"It's a Christmas miracle," Dora June whispered to Fiona. "She's good tonight."

"I know." Fiona nodded.

For someone who had put up such a fuss about Allie and Lizzy marrying those two Dawson brothers, Dora June sure was acting like a loving grandmother that night. Maybe since she'd figured out she couldn't lick them, she'd join them as the old saying went. Truman was nowhere to be seen, but then Fiona didn't expect him to come out of his cave and be civil.

"We've been waiting for y'all to get home," Lizzy said. "The guys brought down all the Christmas decorations, and we're ready to start putting up the tree. The outside will have to wait until the weekend. We can't get the lights up out there in this blinding snow."

Fiona picked up a sandwich and ate it on the way to the living room. "Holy smoke, Allie! There's enough stuff in here to decorate half the state of Texas."

"Ain't it wonderful." Dora June almost swooned. "This is the most exciting day I've had in as long as I can remember. Give me that baby and let me sit in the rocker and just watch. Come and sit beside me, Irene, and we'll talk about old times."

Irene stacked three more cookies in her hand and followed Dora June to the living room, sat down on the end of the sofa, and asked Dora June to tell her about the fire.

Allie put Audrey in Dora June's lap. "When it comes to putting on the ornaments, you have to help."

Fiona sat down on the other end of the sofa and watched the guys put together the eight-foot artificial tree. Thank goodness they built houses with high ceilings in the early part of the previous century.

"I can't believe Allie and Lizzy are nice to me. I've been so nervous about this all day that I almost spent the evening in the bedroom with Truman, but I want to watch the Christmas decorations going up and I do love holding a baby. This is my favorite season of the whole year," Dora June whispered behind her hand to Fiona.

"Us Logans don't carry grudges...not for very long," Fiona said softly. "Besides, it's Christmas and miracles happen at this time of year."

"Thank you, Lord." Dora June looked toward the ceiling.

"I love Christmas," Irene said.

"You think if I invited Truman to join us it might help?" Fiona asked.

Dora June shook her head. "If he comes out of the room, it has to be his decision. He didn't help with decorations, but he did sit in his recliner and eat cookies the day that I put the tree up. He's not much of a shopper, but he does pick out a card every year and he puts a hundred-dollar bill in it for me to spend on whatever I want. He might have been different if we'd had kids, but the mumps fixed Truman right before we married."

"I'm sorry. You would have made a good mama and grandma," Fiona said.

"I wanted a family but we've done all right except for the Christmas thing. Maybe it was because he had the mumps at Christmas and that soured him on the holiday. But I love it and I've had my tree and my decorations every year. I'm glad y'all are putting up one here since mine burned," Dora June said sadly.

"Fiona, Jud needs help getting the lights on the tree," Katy said. "I do believe y'all will have to wait until the weekend to get the outside stuff up and running. That wind is getting fierce out there."

Fiona whipped around to lock gazes with her mother. "You've decided to go?"

"I have. I called Trudy while you were tidying up your paperwork and told her to pick me up in the morning," Katy answered. "And thank you."

"Go where?" Allie asked.

Fiona draped an arm around her mother's shoulders. "She is going on a two-week vacation to Florida with her friends."

"I can..."

"We will..."

Jud and Dora June both spoke at once and then stopped.

"Nothing needs to change. The only difference in the routine is that I won't be here," Katy said. "Now let's get started on this tree. Fiona, you help Jud. Lizzy, you and Allie unpack the other boxes of decorations."

"Are you sure?" Dora June asked.

"Absolutely. You'll need to keep an eye on these two kids I'm leaving in your care." Katy grinned. "And you two kids will have to keep a watch out for Dora June and Truman. Don't let them work too hard."

"Well, I think it's a great idea for you to get away for a little while—long as you don't decide to stay down there," Allie said.

"Me too. I'd sure want you here for Christmas," Lizzy chimed in.

"The timing is perfect." Fiona started clipping lights to the tree. "Mama can have the fun of the trip and be home a few days before the holiday. Don't go so fast, Jud. This part takes time and patience."

"Oh, honey," Jud whispered for Fiona's ears only, "I can go fast or I can have patience, depending on whatever you want."

"Hush." She blushed.

"Dora June can hold Audrey while we do all this," Allie said.

"No, that's my job since I won't see her for a couple of weeks." Katy took the baby from Dora June and sat down on the sofa with her. "We are going to watch this whole process together. Dora June, darlin', will you unpack the ornaments and line them up on the coffee table so that they'll be ready when the time comes?"

Dora June clapped her hands. "I love looking at the pretty ornaments and it's a special year when me and Irene can put them on the tree together."

When she turned around to pick up the box that had been marked *ORNAMENTS*, Fiona noticed that she wiped a tear from her eyes.

Fiona felt a sting of sadness for Dora June. She'd never had a big family around her as she decorated her tree. Even with Truman sitting in the background enjoying her cookies, it had to be lonely. Then another shot filled her heart as she watched Irene struggling to hold on to everything she held dear. Two old ladies: one with family that she didn't even know some of the time, the other who wished she had family.

Lizzy bumped Fiona on the shoulder. "Time to get busy if we're going to get this done tonight."

"What are you and Allie going to do while I'm doing the hard work?" Fiona asked.

"We're unpacking the boxes with the stuff in them like Mama said."

"Mama lets me help with the ornaments," Irene said.

"You can help tonight," Katy told her. "You and Dora June can do that job together."

"I think I'm supposed to be mad at Dora June but I can't remember why," Irene whispered.

"Y'all aren't mad at each other anymore." Katy patted her on the shoulder. "The miniature nativity scene goes on the mantel and the collection of snowmen goes on the top of the bookcase and the secretary and wherever you can find a place," Katy said. "This is the last year we'll put them on the end tables. Next year Audrey will be walking and she might hurt herself if she knocked one off and broke it."

"And the snow globes?" Lizzy asked.

"Exactly in all the traditional places this year. We may have to rethink things next year since Audrey will be walking by then," Irene answered.

"Have the lights been tested?" Fiona asked before she clipped another one to the branches. "This tree is artificial but I swear I smell pine."

"I lit a pine-scented candle," Dora June said. "And thank you, Katy for letting us continue to stay here while you are gone."

Fiona's hand brushed against Jud's bare arm and the electricity was nothing short of pure static. How no one else saw it was a complete mystery.

"To answer your question about the lights, Fiona, the guys and I did that before you got home," Jud answered.

Tradition: that's what her mother said years ago when she asked why they still used the ancient lights on their tree when everyone else had gone to the flashing twinkle lights.

He stopped and she took another step, her whole body plastering against his, sending little spurts of heat from her toes to the ends of every red hair.

"Where does a person even buy the bulbs for these antiques anymore?" she murmured breathlessly as she took a step back.

"Anywhere," Jud answered. "They sell every color imaginable for night-lights now. Same size as these are. My grandparents still use this kind. I saw a place online last week that's selling strands of these again and I plan to buy some when I have my own home and Christmas tree."

He bumped against her hip and more sparks flashed around like dozens of stars falling from the sky. Everyone talking at once covered Fiona's quick intake of breath, thank God. She clipped the bulb to the tree and took a step, putting a foot of space between her and Jud but that didn't do much for the heat between them.

"I'd offer you a penny for your thoughts but I bet you wouldn't sell them that cheap," Jud whispered.

Sweet Lord! She wouldn't sell what she'd just been thinking for any amount of money.

"You got that right." Crimson filled her cheeks.

"Are you blushing? Now I really want to know what you were thinking." His warm breath caressed that soft spot on her neck, sending shivers up her back.

"You aren't getting them spread out enough. We've only got two more strands and they have to do the whole tree," Lizzy bossed from the sidelines.

"You worry about your job and leave me alone. The nativity is off center. The shed and manger go smack dab in the middle, or you won't have enough room for all the rest of the animals," Fiona told her.

"The joys of sisterhood." Allie winked.

Toby unpacked figurines of sheep, a donkey, a few

cows, and a couple goats. "Hey, where is Truman? I found goats."

"Not even nativity goats would get him out here," Dora June said above the noise. "The music has stopped. Someone needs to start another CD. I always play music when I'm decorating."

"It ain't Christmas without music," Irene said.

"Yes, ma'am." Blake crossed the floor to the corner where the CD player was located and chose an album with a mixture of country music artists.

Fiona wiggled her hips to the song, "Rockin' Around the Christmas Tree." When she stopped and went back to work, Jud nudged her with his shoulder.

"Great moves there. Want to go out Friday night and do some dancin'?" he asked.

"Are you asking me for a date?" she whispered.

"I guess I am. We could go to Wichita Falls or maybe to a place called Frankie's." He drawled so low that only she could hear him.

"Frankie's? How do you even know about that place?" Her big green eyes widened and she cocked her head to one side.

"Deke offered to take me. He took Lizzy, you know."

"No!" Fiona gasped. "Does Mama know?"

"Have no idea. You'll have to ask her," Jud said.

"What are y'all whispering about?" Dora June asked.

"I was asking her to teach me to do that dance. I can two-step or swing dance, but I can't do the shuffle and she's really good at it," Jud answered.

"It looks like a pagan mating dance to me," Dora June huffed. "Y'all get on with the lights so I can help put the ornaments on. Audrey gets to put the star on the top when we get done. I promised her she could do it if she wouldn't go to sleep. That way she'll stay awake and then sleep good tonight for her mama."

"But"—Allie glanced over toward the rocking chair—"she's not even two months old, Dora June. How is she going to put the star on the tree?"

"We'll really put it on the tree." Dora June smiled.

"Blake will hold her up there beside it like she did it," Irene said. "Y'all can take a picture of her up there beside it. The rule in our house says the youngest kid gets to put the star on the tree. Who knows? It could be the only year she'll get to put the star on the tree. She might have a little brother or a cousin next year at this time."

"Bite your tongue," Allie gasped.

"One never knows what another year will bring. I sure wouldn't mind giving Audrey a little cousin next year," Lizzy said.

Dora June's eyes shifted to Fiona.

She popped up both palms, fingers splayed out in defense. "Don't look at me. I'm not in the market for a baby, not even to put the star on the tree."

"Best be careful. God has a way of throwing monkey wrenches into the best plans," Dora June giggled.

"So no babies before next year but we could go dancing. Last time I checked that didn't produce a baby," Jud flirted.

"Can you guarantee that?" she asked.

"For sure," he said.

"What are you two talking about?" Lizzy asked.

"We are going dancing on Friday night," Fiona said. "But it's not a date. It's just two people going out for a good time." She tucked the final light in exactly the right place. "Now it's time for Dora June and the rest of y'all to put the ornaments on. Jud and I have done our job."

"Oh, really? Was I fast or patient?" Jud's eyebrows went up.

"You finished well," she said.

"I always do," he whispered.

She started to say something else but noticed that Irene's eyes had begun to dart around the room.

Katy went right to her side and held her hand. "Are you okay, Mama?"

"Where am I? I don't know this place. Did we get new nurses?" Irene frowned.

"We hired help to decorate the lobby. Are you ready to go to your room?" Katy asked.

Irene nodded. "I am very tired." She glanced out the window. "Maybe tomorrow we can build a snowman if it snows enough."

Deke had been helping Lizzy set snow globes on the higher places but he turned and headed toward the kitchen. "Let's take Miz Irene home in my truck. I'll feel better if I go with y'all and if the roads get slick, then my truck is heavier."

"Thank you," Katy said.

"No problem. See all y'all tomorrow, folks."

Fiona started across the room to hug her grandmother but Katy shook her head. Allie looped her arm through Fiona's and Lizzy laid a hand on her shoulder.

"She thinks we are hired help and those folks would not hug her," Allie said softly.

"We've learned how to handle it," Lizzy said.

"This is so hard." Fiona swiped at a tear clinging to her long lashes.

"Yes, but we'll be thankful that we had her for a couple of hours. That's a miracle," Allie said.

"Just one minute, Katy," Blake said.

Even though all the ornaments weren't on the tree, he fixed the star to the top and held Audrey up for everyone to take pictures. "I don't want you to miss seeing the real thing." He grinned.

Jud plugged the end of the cord into the outlet and the multicolored lights lit up beautifully.

"Thanks." Katy smiled as she helped Irene into her coat and hat. "Look at Audrey's eyes. I'm so glad you did that for me, Blake. That's a precious memory I will cherish forever."

Fiona inhaled deeply. Lizzy was right. They'd had Granny for a little while and that was a miracle. Audrey's little eyes had lit up so bright when the lights came on that Fiona couldn't even find words to describe the joy in her heart. She made a vow right then that she'd always come home the weekend after Thanksgiving and enjoy this tradition. It didn't matter where she lived; she would never miss making memories like this again.

"Carols!" Dora June clapped her hands. "We haven't had a caroling in years. We've got enough folks in this room right here to have one. We can ride on the back of a flat-bed trailer and sing all the old carols. We'll have to figure out an evening."

"Can you sing?" Jud asked Fiona.

"No, she can't," Allie said. "But we don't care because she can dance."

Lizzy nodded emphatically. "Yes, she can. If it hadn't been for her, I'd have been a scared rabbit at my proms. She taught me all the newest dance moves and I was the queen of the prom."

"Well, if you can dance that well, I'm really looking forward to Friday night," Jud said.

"Friday night? What's going on Friday night?" Allie asked.

"We are going to visit Granny and then go to a country bar up near Wichita Falls for some dancing," Fiona answered.

"Oooooh." Dora June's eyebrows shot up.

"Just as friends," Fiona quickly clarified.

The eyebrows settled back into place.

"If you aren't nice, I will sing, Jud, so remember that," she said.

"Is this your song?" He nodded toward the stereo.

Fiona cocked her head to one side and listened to "The Angel and the Little Blue Bell" by Brenda Lee. She had not heard the song since she was a little girl. The lyrics were about a little blue bell that couldn't ring and said that an angel appeared and told the little blue bell that she'd come to dry his tears. She changed him to gold, gave him the perfect tone, and on Christmas Day he could ring.

"No, it's not, because I don't expect an angel to appear on Christmas Eve and give me a voice of gold," she answered.

"What if it's symbolic of what the angel could bring you?" he asked.

"The angels deserted me a long time ago." She took a step away from him and went to the turntable. The angels had really turned their backs the day she was born. They had put wings on her shoulders instead of giving her something to hang on to so that she could find a place to light and call home.

Jud followed her. "How did they desert you?"

"All I ever wanted was a place to belong like Lizzy and Allie, but the angels turned their backs on me. I didn't fit into the little town of Dry Creek or in the big city of Houston. Maybe I'm one of those souls who will wander for her whole life and never find a place to call her own."

"Maybe you need a good reason to put down roots," Jud said.

"Family should be a good reason, right?"

"Maybe you need more," he answered.

She found a CD with several of the older country artists featured on it. Loretta Lynn started out with a fast song and Fiona's shoulders wiggled to the music.

"You've really got music in your soul whether you can sing or not," Jud said.

"Yes, she does," Lizzy said. "And we've missed that around here."

"I missed all this," Fiona said honestly.

Jud grabbed her hand and twirled her several times before bringing her back to his chest. "Don't look now, but Truman is peeking around the edge of the door. He's itchin' to come in here and join us but he's too damn stubborn."

"Like I told him before, pride is a dangerous thing." Fiona fell into step to a country waltz as Loretta sang about the chill on the air because Daddy wouldn't be there.

"I've got a cousin in Kuwait right now and he's got two little kids. It puts a tear in my eye when I listen to this song. This was about Vietnam but I'm sure it's the same feeling," Jud said.

"I'm sorry," Fiona said.

George Strait started singing "Christmas Cookies" and the mood of the whole room jacked up a notch. Allie put the baby in her carrier and grabbed Blake's hand for a dance. Toby wrapped his arm around Lizzy and they joined the other two in a fast swing dance. The lyrics said that every time she put a batch in the oven there was fifteen minutes for kissing and hugging.

Jud leaned back and laughed. "I got gypped."

"What are you talking about?"

"Fiona made cookies yesterday, but I didn't get in on the fifteen minutes of fun while they cooked," he said honestly.

Dora June shook a bright red and silver ornament in their direction. "As long as I'm in this house, there had better not be any of that fifteen-minute stuff. Miz Katy would fire me from my chaperone job and throw me out in the snow if that happened."

Jud bowed at the waist to kiss Fiona's fingertips when the song ended. "Thank you for the dance, ma'am."

"You are very welcome," Fiona said.

Blake slid a more modern CD into the player. "I think it's time for some Alabama."

"Hear, hear!" Toby agreed.

Dora June swayed to "Christmas in Dixie" as her eyes shifted around the room. Her whole face shined with excitement when she stared at the nativity scene. A big smile covered her face at the snowmen looking out from every corner of the room. And when she looked at the snow globes, she nodded so hard that all chins were set into motion.

"This is wonderful," she said. "There's something about having all you kids around me that I can't even explain."

Fiona could relate well after the lonely holiday she'd spent the year before.

"We need presents under the tree. Fiona, will you take me shopping on Sunday after church?" Dora June asked.

"We could go see Irene while we're up there. I should be whipped for not going to see her more often. That's saying if the weather will let us."

"Of course we can," Fiona said. "Matter of fact, maybe we'll make it a girls' day out. What do you say, Lizzy and Allie?"

Her sisters both shot bewildered looks across the room and she understood them. They'd put up with Dora June's crazy meddling. Fiona had been ready to shoot her right between chin number two and three more than once, but if they were going to turn Dora June and Truman into allies rather than enemies...well, it had to start somewhere.

She caught Truman's frown as he peeked around the door frame again and that solidified her determination. "We'll take Audrey with us."

"Oh, that would be wonderful." Dora June grinned.

Lizzy nodded. "I haven't shopped for this sexy husband of mine and that would be a great time to do so."

Allie's nod was slower. "I haven't even started my shopping, so I guess I do need to go."

"Rule number one, Dora June. No bossing us or telling us how to run our lives," Fiona said.

"Rule number one, Fiona." Dora June pointed a chubby finger at her. "You need bossing and I'm like your granny. I speak my mind."

"It should be an interesting day for y'all," Jud muttered.

It was past ten when everyone finally left, but the whole downstairs was decorated for the holidays. A lovely poinsettia and candle centerpiece graced the dining room table. Red candles with greenery around them were arranged on the foyer table and the kitchen curtains had been taken down and replaced with pretty red and green plaid ones.

Fiona took one long, last look at each room before she turned out the lights in the kitchen. She carefully picked up two bottles of cold beer and carried them upstairs, along with a platter of leftovers from the supper buffet.

A thin line of yellow light cut across the neutral-colored carpet of the hall but it grew to a wide band when Jud threw the door wide open. "I thought I heard you. Weatherman says we're in for sleet off and on all day tomorrow and Thursday, but the sun will come out on Friday and melt most of it, so we should be good to go dancing. Want me to tell Deke we'll go to Frankie's with him?"

"No! I'm not going to Frankie's. I can't believe that Lizzy went. That's just a glorified brothel. I'll go up to the Rusty Spur with you, though, as long as you let me pay my own way," she said. "Hungry?"

"Not right now, but I'll take one of those beers," he said. "How'd you get those anyway?"

"Deke sneaked them in when Dora June's back was turned. But we have to drink them tonight because she'll find them tomorrow."

"Bless old Deke's heart." Jud twisted the top off and drank a fourth of the contents. "Icy cold, too. Come on in. I've been dying to tell you about what happened with Truman."

Setting the platter on the end table, she settled in on the bed with pillows behind her back. She removed the lid from her beer, then hurriedly sipped the froth when it threatened to overflow the bottle. "Don't want to waste a single drop of this precious stuff. You do know that Throckmorton County is dry and we have to cross the county line to get anything to drink."

"That's the first thing Blake moaned about last winter."

Jud settled into the recliner. "Do you realize that we're like two old married folks? You have your spot and I have mine."

"We're more like a couple of high school sophomores, sneaking beer and kisses behind the principal's back," she laughed.

"And the principal is Miz Dora June O'Dell, right?"

She raised her bottle and leaned forward. He did the same and touched his to it.

"You could have knocked me over with a feather when you and Truman walked in the store together, so talk." She bit into a chicken salad sandwich. "These are so good. I have to ask Dora June what spices she uses. But back to the Truman story."

"Well, I got to thinkin' last night about how to knock some of that jackass attitude out of him, so I got up early and went down to breakfast." Jud told the whole story between sips of beer and bites of three cookies.

"Wow!" she said.

"I'm having breakfast with him again every day for the whole time they're here. He's either going to shape up or else leave because he hates me so bad," Jud said.

"Why were you interested in that old well? We always thought it had water in it and maybe the folks who lived there had their house burn down and that was the reason the house was gone. Did you do your homework?" she asked.

"About what?" He reached for a sandwich at the same time she did.

The reaction when his hand touched hers didn't surprise her anymore, but that didn't mean she had to do anything about it. She could ignore it until it got bored and went away.

"This whole area was filled with military forts because this is where they housed the Indians about the time Texas became a state. So there could have been houses all over the place, and that old well could have been the main source for water during that time," she explained.

"Well, according to Truman, that well never had water because they hit limestone, which he thought was a hoot. He figured he was delivering bad news to me, but it was really good news. I'm going to talk to Blake and Toby first, since this is a joint venture but..." He paused.

"You think you are sitting on oil?"

He nodded. "Or natural gas, but my nose says it's oil."

She leaned forward and held out her nearly empty bottle to clink with his again. "That's fantastic. Good luck with it. Are you going to use your old work connections to drill it for you?"

He shook his head. "No, I'm going to subcontract a rental agreement for the equipment and sink it myself. It will take every dime of what I've got saved and my inheritance from my grandparents, but if I hit oil, it will all come back to the Lucky Penny."

"And if you don't?"

"Then I'll be broke, but at least I won't have cost the ranch anything," he said. "It will take a few months to get it going, and Josie might even want to partner with me. She's thinking about it."

"That's a big risk."

Another nod. "Life is full of risks. We make a decision based on what we have to work with that day, not the day before because that bronc has already been ridden or the day after because that wild horse isn't ready to ride, but today."

Fiona drained the last drop from her beer bottle. "I had no idea you were a philosopher."

His slightly lopsided grin warmed her heart. Why had she not noticed that his smile wasn't perfect?

"Me? I'm just a rough old cowboy with a pretty good nose for oil. That's why I couldn't get here before now. I had another year on my contract with a company based out in the panhandle. I'm not bragging, but if I said to drill in a certain place, they sunk a well."

"You ever wrong?" she asked.

"One time, but I stopped the job before it started."

"What happened?" she asked.

"Josie thought it was a mistake and the more I listened to her, the more I realized she might be right. I went back over my notes, went back to the site, and I had doubts. So they didn't drill. Usually Josie and I agreed, but that time she was right and I was wrong."

Fiona picked up an extra pillow and hugged it against her stomach. "Did it hurt to admit that to your sister?"

"Hell, yes, it did. And she rubbed it in for weeks," he chuckled.

*   *   *

There was something about Fiona's fire that drew Jud to her like a gypsy to a bonfire. He looked forward to the evenings when they talked. He missed having breakfast with her. His heart skipped half a beat when he walked into the store and there she was either behind the counter or at that table in the back room with the laptop in front of her.

It could simply be because they were thrown together, living in the same house, kin to the same people, working in a town with a population of less than five hundred people, so there weren't many folks to talk to. But that argument wouldn't hold water if he was honest. He was flat out attracted to her.

She threw her legs off the bed. "I'll take care of the beer bottles if you'll take what's left of those dirty dishes in the morning."

"What are you going to do with them?" he asked.

"Hide them in my coat pockets and then toss them in the Dumpster out behind the store. It's an old trick us girls perfected years ago." She smiled.

"You drank beer under your mama's nose?"

"When we could get it," she said. "But never more than one or two at the most. Us Logan girls cannot hold our liquor worth a damn. Both Lizzy and Allie had their first drunk experience after your brothers came to the Lucky Penny. I won't be following in their footsteps."

"Did Blake make them do his hangover cure?" Jud asked.

"Oh, yes, and from what I hear it's a miracle, but I hate, absolutely hate, bananas."

"Noted. No bananas for you." Jud stood, handed her his beer bottle, and slung an arm around her shoulders. "Let me walk you to your room."

"I'm pretty sure I can make it on my own," she laughed, and rolled her eyes. "But I appreciate the gesture."

"Aw, where's the fun in that?"

Jud wanted to kiss her again. No, he wanted to kiss her lots of times and then slowly lead her back to his room, tumble her onto his bed, and make slow, sweet love to her all night. Instead, he kissed her knuckles one at a time and then cupped her face in his big hands and lowered his mouth to hers for a long, lingering kiss.

"Good night," he whispered, and turned around to go back to his room.

"Jud," she called out.

He glanced over his shoulder and wiggled his eyebrows. "Change your mind?"

"Dora June would catch us for sure," she giggled. "These old beds have squeaky springs."

"I wouldn't worry about her hearing the springs nearly as much as hearing your screams," he teased as he shut the door to his room.

* * *

The next morning, Jud hit the floor with determination to make progress on thawing Truman a little more. Fiona had been right about the squeaky springs, because he heard her tossing and turning as he tiptoed past her bedroom door early that morning. A picture flashed through his mind of the two of them making beautiful music with those springs, but he quickly made himself think of other things.

Truman and Dora June were both at the table when he reached the kitchen and immediately Dora June pushed back her chair.

"Three eggs? I got biscuits and sausage gravy and the waffle iron is hot," she said.

"Sit still, Miz Dora June. You don't have to wait on me."

"It's all on the stove," she said. "I appreciate you gettin' it for yourself, Jud. My old knees are feelin' this cold weather."

"Can I warm up either of y'all's coffee while I'm getting mine?"

"I'd love a warm-up, thanks," she said. "And Truman's cup is nearly empty, so he'll take more, too."

Jud filled all their cups and then set the coffeepot back

on the warmer. "I thought I'd go with you this morning, Truman. It's a nasty day out there. Are your cell phone batteries charged?"

Truman puffed out his chest. "I don't carry one of them damn things. They are the ruin of society and I didn't ask for your help."

"You could fall and freeze to death in this weather if you're out there alone." Jud carried a plate of food to the table. "You don't have to use it unless you need it. Miz Dora, we need to buy him a pay-as-you-go phone for Christmas."

"If you do, I'll throw it out in the yard," Truman declared.

"Well, you're not big enough to throw me out in the yard," Dora June said. "So either Jud goes with you until this weather clears up or I'm going with you every morning. Your choice but you need to make it now because I'll have to get into my warm clothes."

"Hmmmph." Truman snorted. "I ain't takin' you out in this weather. You'd catch cold and maybe pneumonia. I guess Jud can go with me."

"Thank you for offering, Jud. I do worry," Dora said softly.

"So would I if it were my grandpa out there without a phone or any way to get in touch with us if he got hurt," Jud said.

"I'm not your grandpa," Truman said tersely.

Jud let him have the last word but he caught the sly wink from Dora June.

Chapter Ten

It was time for Fiona to go to work, but she lingered over her coffee that morning. "Mama, I need one more hug before I leave. You will call when y'all settle into the hotel for the night, right?"

"I will." Katy wrapped her arms around her youngest daughter. "I'll make sure to have time to hear all about your first day on the job."

"I love you. Please be careful." Fiona's voice almost cracked.

"No tears," Katy whispered. "This is an adventure for both of us. I get a vacation and you get to run the store all by yourself."

Fiona took a deep breath and hugged her mother even tighter before she let go and stepped back. "Wish me luck. I've never been the boss."

"You'll be a wonderful boss. Call one of Herman's granddaughters to help you if things start to get overwhelming. But I have faith in you." Fiona kissed her on the forehead. "That's your kiss on the forehead. You gave them to us when we were little girls and we thought they were magic."

"They were and I'm sure this one is, too," Katy said. "Now go before you make me cry. I can be on the next flight home if you need me or if anything happens with your grandmother."

"Go and don't worry," Fiona urged her.

"Get on out of here. I bet the old guys are fuming because the store isn't open so they can catch up on the gossip and eat doughnuts," Katy said. "I'm looking forward to warm weather, a little sunshine, and the beach."

"Without a single guilt trip, right?" Fiona opened the door and waved.

She'd been home almost a whole week. This was her third day at the store but her first one without her mother there. She made sure the coffee was brewing, but the pastry guy had left a message on the store's answering machine saying the roads were too slick, so he wouldn't see her until Monday. The guys weren't going to like that one bit. They'd have to eat the prepackaged things off the shelf if they wanted their snacks today.

Sleet fell sporadically. The tiny pellets beat against the windowpane for five or ten minutes, put down enough ice to lay a coat on the snow that had already fallen; then it stopped. But it was just teasing. In ten minutes it would start all over again and the roads would be even greasier.

Fiona shut her eyes and imagined sitting on the beach with a book in her hands, watching the sun setting over the Gulf of Mexico. In her imagination, she could hear the children laughing and making sand castles, see their parents walking hand in hand across the beach, all with the sounds of Christmas music in the background.

How often had she wished for a chill in the air to make it seem like Christmas? How many parties had she attended when they'd turned down the air-conditioning so the ladies wouldn't sweat in their cute little velvet cocktail dresses? Now she had real Christmas weather and she was dreaming of the beach.

She could not have her cake and eat it, too, but that morning she was determined to worry about nothing other than her old guys who wouldn't have their morning doughnuts.

The phone her mother gave her as an early Christmas present rang. She fished it out of her pocket and smiled when she saw Katy's picture appear. "Yes, Mama," she answered.

"I just wanted to tell you that Trudy has snow tires on the van and that we're heading due south all the way down to Interstate 10. Fifty miles south of us the roads are completely dry. But the main reason I called is that you need to put the snow tires on the car. They are in the storage shed out back. I haven't used them since last year, so get Jud to check the air in them."

"I'll do that. Now go on and have a great time," Fiona said.

"I'll call when we check into a hotel so you can give me an update on the store. Bye, now!"

"Bye, Mama."

"Hey, Fiona!" Sharlene shook snow from her blond hair and fluffed it back away from her face. "Is the coffee ready? The electricity is out at our house this morning. Can you believe this weather? We've still got another day left in November and it's snowing and sleeting. It's downright crazy."

"Y'all need a place to stay?" Fiona asked.

Sharlene hung her coat on the back of a chair. "No, we'll be fine. We've got a gas hot water tank and gas heat, so we aren't going to freeze, but the cookstove is electric and so is the coffeepot."

Fiona picked up the biggest cup and filled it. "Here you go."

Sharlene grabbed two honey buns on the way to the back table. She set the coffee and the pastry on the table. "I'm starving and really glad I don't have any kids arriving at the day care this morning until nine. You got any of your Christmas shopping done?"

Fiona couldn't do a lot of shopping on less than three dollars, but she didn't tell Sharlene that. On Friday she would have a paycheck and she planned to buy a few gifts each week until Christmas arrived.

"Not yet but Lizzy, Allie, and I are going with Dora June after church on Sunday to do a little bit." Fiona left the counter, pulled out a chair, and sat across from Sharlene.

The cellophane paper around the honey bun crinkled as Sharlene pushed it across the table. "Want a honey bun?"

Fiona sent it sliding back across the table. "No, thanks. Dora June made a big breakfast this morning."

"I envy you for having Dora June's cooking, but I still wouldn't want to live with either of those old farts. Do you miss the city?"

"Sometimes, but being home for a few months isn't a bad thing, especially during the holidays. How about you?"

One of Sharlene's shoulders inched up toward her ear.

"Remember, I had both. I commuted from here to work. So I got all the fun of the small-town gossip and close-knit community and then when I was in the city I got Starbucks and lunch specials at all the restaurants."

"Does Mary Jo miss it?" Fiona asked.

"She loves having her own beauty shop and not having to commute an hour to work every day. Sounds like the coffee bunch is here," Sharlene said as truck doors slammed outside. She slipped on her coat, then picked up the extra pastry in one hand and the coffee in the other. "Figure up my bill and I'll give them the table and scoot across the street. I need to get ready for my first batch of kiddos. Who would have ever thought I'd enjoy a day care so much, but I do."

"Having a day care and having kids of your own are two different things," Fiona said.

"I know, but I just love them all. Someday I'm going to run that family that has nineteen kids some competition. Oh, look. It might be snowing but I'd know that swagger anywhere. That's Jud Dawson going into Mary Jo's place." Sharlene pointed to the salon across the street. "I'd love to get my hands all tangled up in that blond hair of his."

Fiona had no right to be jealous, but she was.

"You forgot to ring up the coffee," Sharlene said.

Fiona fought against the crimson filling her cheeks, but it didn't do a bit of good. "Coffee's on me today. You'll need it since the kids can't go out in the backyard and play."

"You got that right, darlin'," Sharlene said. "But don't think that blush escaped me." She leaned across the counter. "And don't worry. If you *didn't* have the hots for him, I'd worry about you. What you do or don't do about it, that is your business, but if you ever decide to act on that attraction y'all have for each other, I will expect a full report."

Three men, including Truman and Herman, pushed through the door and stomped the snow from their feet on the coarse welcome mat. "Mornin', Sharlene. How's that babysittin' business goin'?" Herman asked.

"It's keepin' the bills paid and food on my table and it sure beats commuting in this weather," she answered. "Y'all boys have a good day now."

The door shut behind her at the same time Fiona picked up the coffeepot and three mugs to carry to the table. By the time the old guys had hung their coats on the backs of their chairs, she had filled their cups. "You boys are late today. I expected you to be waiting for me."

"Took us longer to get the chores done in this weather. Where's the doughnuts?" Herman asked.

"Y'all are out of luck today. You'll have to eat the prepackaged stuff on the shelf if you want a midmorning snack or go up to Nadine's. I hear she's making apple pies this morning."

"Just bring us a dozen of those things up there on the rack. If we go to Nadine's, the wives will get upset because we didn't invite them. This is just a convenience store. That's a real restaurant," Herman said.

Fiona picked up a red plastic basket, put a paper in it as if she were serving doughnuts, and filled it with honey buns, chocolate cupcakes, and powdered doughnuts. When she set it in the table, they were cussing the insurance companies. According to them, Truman's company should have already settled with him and a new house should be built right where the old one stood.

Fiona really had no right to watch the clock and con-
veniently be at the front of the store when Jud hunched
his shoulders against the cold as he left Mary Jo's Beauty
Shop. Hoping he might swagger on across the street, she
held her breath, but he got into his truck and drove away.

"Hey, if y'all need anything else, yell right loud. I'm going into the back room to do some book work," she yelled.

Herman waved to let her know that he'd heard her and
went back to listening to the next rant about insurance. She
whipped around and went to her desk, opened up Nadine's
files on the computer, and started inputting data.

Fifteen minutes later, Truman hollered that they were
leaving. "Put what we had today on my bill."

"Will do. Y'all be careful out there in that mess," she
shouted back.

"Hey, Fiona, your sister's comin'," Herman yelled as he
left the store.

Fiona set her work aside and in seconds, Lizzy carried
two cups of hot chocolate to the back room. Fiona had always envied her for knowing exactly what her path was
in life and never looking back once she made a decision.
She'd known in junior high that she would inherit the feed
store, and she never looked to one side or the other. She
strapped on the harness and took care of business.

"I just saw Jud leave Mary Jo's. Guess he got a haircut
this morning." Lizzy handed off one cup of hot chocolate
and sat down in the chair facing the desk. "How are things
really going in the house? Last night was all *Walton* wonderful, but still waters run deep. Are you going to be all
right with Mama gone and having to be in that house with
Dora June, Truman, and Jud?"

Fiona chuckled. "Remember when Granny used to

watch reruns of that television show and tell us no one in the world was that perfect?"

Lizzy warmed her hands around the mug. "But she'd watch them over and over again, wouldn't she? I miss her."

"Me too. I still expect to hear her cussin' down the foyer before she even appears in the kitchen or living room."

"It got bad there at the end. She ran away and it was awful the way she dressed. Either in sequins and mismatched shoes or else she'd run away in her nightgown and a robe with rubber boots on her feet. But I wasn't asking about Granny. How are things with you?"

"It will be fine. It's not forever and I enjoy Jud being there. It's nice to have someone to talk to in the evenings but..."

Lizzy set the mug on the desk. "But what?"

Fiona shrugged.

"But he's putting down roots and you still want to fly, so you aren't going to start anything, but he's a damn fine-lookin' cowboy and you haven't had time for a romp in the bed since your divorce." Lizzy stopped to catch her breath and then went on. "How close am I?"

"I've only been home a week."

Lizzy blew across the top of the steaming hot chocolate. "What's that got to do with my question?"

Fiona sighed. "Yes, you're right on all counts. We're going to the Rusty Spur Friday night, but it's not a date. Besides, what can we do with Dora June and Truman in the house? You know how the bed springs squeak."

"Oh, honey." Lizzy's grin said that she could tell tales that would make a sailor blush. "If that's the only thing holding you back, it can be arranged that they will be out of the house any evening of the week."

"That is a lovely sweater. I believe it belonged in my closet at one time," Fiona said.

"Nice way to change the subject. I can totally see you blushing, you know," Lizzy told her.

"Quit playing matchmaker with the hopes that if I fall for Jud Dawson I'll stay in Dry Creek."

Lizzy's head bobbed up and down several times. "I only do it because I love you and this is where you belong. You just don't know it yet. I should probably get back to the store, though everyone is holed up in this kind of weather and no one needs anything. I hope I don't die of boredom. Toby, Blake, and Jud are even painting the inside of my house because they can't do anything on the ranch until this clears up."

Fiona went back to her bookkeeping work when Lizzy left but she couldn't keep her mind on her work. Finally, she saved what she had done, drew up another cup of hot chocolate from the machine, and picked up a six-pack of miniature powdered sugar doughnuts on the way to the table. She propped up her scuffed cowboy boots on an empty chair and tried hard not to think of Jud, his kisses, that cute little crooked smile when he was amused, the sexy strut, or his drawl.

But it didn't work...

* * *

Deke was the tallest of the four men, so he got the job of rolling the white paint on the ceiling. Toby and Blake were already working on the walls when Jud arrived, and as luck would have it, the last one to the party got the worst job. He had to paint the woodwork. He opened the gallon can of semigloss trim paint, dipped the brush, sat down on the floor, and started painting baseboards.

"So, Deke, I heard you were out with a hot redhead over the weekend," Jud said.

Deke laughed. "So hot that butter would melt right off her naked body."

"Hot enough to melt an Eskimo's igloo?" Toby asked.

"Are we going to get into so hot stories?" Blake chuckled.

"You used to tell them better than anyone," Deke answered.

"You'll be reformed someday. When your baby daughter wraps her fist around your little finger and smiles at you for the first time, all those hot women stories will disappear," Blake said.

"Now that would take magic or miracles. I'm not ever settling down to one woman. There's too many out there all lined up for a little Deke love for that kind of nonsense." Deke grinned. "How about you, Jud?"

"Don't get me to tellin' lies." Jud dipped his paintbrush into the bucket and kept working.

"So you're ready to settle down?" Deke's hazel eyes popped wide open. "And here I thought I'd have one bar buddy for a long time."

"I didn't say a word about settling down," Jud said. "But changing the subject. I'm glad we're all here because I've got something I want to talk to y'all about." Jud went on to tell them about the old well and what Truman had told him.

"If there was oil on the Lucky Penny, don't you think someone would have discovered it?" Deke said.

"This ranch has been grown up in mesquite for years. No one even thought to look past the unlucky reputation that it has had all this time." Jud had a steady hand and was almost to the corner.

"In other words, no one looked beneath the surface and everyone thought that well had water in it. I was looking forward to using it this spring after we cleared the land around it," Toby said. "I got to admit, I'm a little disappointed. But if it yields a gusher, it would sure turn our five-year plan around."

"Well, I'd like to keep it under our hats until spring. I can have all the paperwork done for what we need in the meantime, and if it's got the potential I think it does, the Lucky Penny will finally live up to its name instead of its reputation."

"Good luck," Deke said. "Now, what's this I hear about you helping Truman? Did y'all see him peeking around the corner last night while we were decorating? What do you figure that was all about?"

"He's a lonely old coot," Jud answered. "Y'all remember Mr. Henry?"

"Who?" Deke started back to work.

Blake laid his roller down and gulped down a third of his beer. "Mr. Henry was the scrooge in Muenster for years."

"Like in the movies?" Deke asked.

"Exactly. He didn't give out candy on Halloween. He would call the police if a kid walked on his grass on the way home from school. Truman reminds me of him. He's even about the size Mr. Henry was and he's got that mean look in his eye," Toby said. "I was terrified of him when I was a little kid."

Deke stopped long enough to wipe a blob of white paint from his cheek. "What happened to him?"

"He died a couple of years ago," Blake answered.

"But a grandson that he didn't even know he had came

to live with him about ten years before that," Jud said. "The kid was probably twelve that year because he was a few years younger than me. Anyway, that boy turned Mr. Henry's life around. I intend to turn Truman's around. Mr. Scrooge is going to be Santa Claus on Christmas morning."

"I'll bet you fifty dollars that won't happen," Deke laughed.

"I'd rather bet a case of beer. If he's wearing a red suit on Christmas morning, you owe me a case of beer. If not, I'll buy you one," Jud said.

"That's a deal. Is our word good enough or do we need to shake on it?"

"Deke Sullivan's word is good enough for me any day of the week."

* * *

Jud had lots of things he wanted to share with Fiona, starting with a couple of beers he'd talked Deke out of after they'd finished the painting. She was sitting in one of the chairs in the hall outside her door, and when she looked up, his heart kicked in an extra beat.

"I'm returning last night's treat." He held the beers up. "Did Lizzy and Allie call you? If not, I'm supposed to tell you that we're expected at Lizzy's tomorrow night to help with Christmas decorations and supper. When we get done there, we're supposed to go to Allie's and help put up her stuff."

"They called already." Fiona headed to her spot on the bed. "Nice haircut."

"Thanks. Mary Jo does a good job." He grinned as he handed her a beer.

Jud sat down on the edge of the bed instead of in his chair. "I need a huge favor, Fiona."

"Which is?" she asked.

"I've talked to my cousins and Deke knows, too, about this oil business, but I don't want anyone else to know, including your sisters, until it's a done deal."

"Blake and Toby are good with not telling them?"

Jud nodded.

"Then I'll keep mum about it, too. No problem. I'm sure if the gossip gets loose that there's oil on the Lucky Penny, everyone will be clamoring, wanting to know if it's on their property."

Jud flipped around until he was sitting beside her, his back braced against the headboard. "And every oil company in the state would flock up here to get a piece of the pie. Everyone will think I'm crazy for drilling because of the Lucky Penny's reputation, but if I hit oil, I plan to reinvest my original money into equipment and start my own company with Josie as a partner. It will be a sideline business because ranchin' is my first love and we won't ever go big with it. But it would be a good moneymaker and could even bring some business to Dry Creek. We could give these folks a bigger cut of the profits than the big companies and still make a lot of money for us."

"What makes you think your sister will want to live in Dry Creek?" Fiona sipped at her beer.

"She came to Blake and Allie's wedding and loved the place. Said it had lots of potential. Who knows, if you stick around, you might have a city built around you in a few years."

"After living here the first eighteen years of my life, that's really hard to imagine, Jud."

"Nothing is impossible. It might all take time but sometimes even miracles still happen. Hey, I wanted to come by the store after my haircut, but the guys were painting and wanted me to help," he said. "How was your day?"

"I finished getting Mama's books in order. Now it's just a matter of a little weekly maintenance. Oh, and Mama called and told me to put the snow tires on the car because of this weather."

"I could do that for you," Jud said.

"I know how to change tires. Daddy made sure that all of us girls could do that and change oil."

"Then we could do it together."

"With any luck, we won't even need them since the latest report says the bad stuff will end at midnight and the sun is supposed to shine tomorrow. It'll be slushy by noon but not as slick. I'm just glad it's going to be cleared off by Friday night. I'm ready for a night away from Dry Creek," Fiona said.

"Me too. That reminds me. Deke wants to go with us. And Sharlene's boyfriend is out of the state for a few days, so she and Mary Jo are going along, too."

Well, damn it to hell on a rusty poker, Fiona thought. *I'd rather call it a date as be stuck between those two after they've been drinking all night.*

Chapter Eleven

When the clock struck five on Thursday evening, Fiona wasted no time locking up the store and heading to Lizzy's house. She was still in a snit that she'd have to ride all the way to Wichita Falls the next night in the backseat with Sharlene and Mary Jo and then most likely all the way home with them in a drunken state.

But that wasn't the whole ball of wax of her bad mood. If Jud's sister came to town, then he wouldn't need Fiona to talk to in the evenings, to bounce ideas off of or share secret beers with. He'd have Josie, and Fiona would be right back in her room—all alone. Fiona loved the evenings when she and Jud visited. It was something that she looked forward to all day.

Judging from the number of trucks out in the front yard, everyone was already at Lizzy's when Fiona arrived. She checked her reflection in the rearview mirror, shook her hair out of the ponytail she'd worn all day, and reapplied her lipstick.

"Hey." Lizzy met her halfway across the room with a hug. "You're just in time for dinner."

Fiona peeked over her sister's shoulder. "Your place looks amazing! It looks...like a brand-new house." She took a step back so she could see the whole living room and kitchen. "I love the soft off-white with the pure white woodwork. You did good picking that out, Lizzy."

"I hear we're going to make a party out of tomorrow night. It's been years since I've danced with you." Deke nudged Fiona on the shoulder.

"Be prepared to be worn out by the night's end."

"I expect whoever I take home will finish the job," he laughed.

"Let's eat and then we'll put up my first Christmas tree in my new home with my new husband," Lizzy beamed. "Tonight Toby is going to hold the lights and the garland and I'm going to place them on the tree."

"Just like Mama and Daddy did when we were kids," Fiona said softly.

"That's right. Deke, say a quick grace for us and we'll have supper," Lizzy said.

Since the small kitchen table would only seat four people, Lizzy declared that the guys could eat in the kitchen. The ladies would take their food to the living room and sit on the floor around the coffee table.

Allie chose the outside because she wanted to be close to Audrey's infant seat. Lizzy claimed the far end, leaving the other for Fiona. The low buzz of conversation and laughter in the kitchen came through the walls, but Fiona couldn't make out individual words. She could easily distinguish each man's unique drawl and knew who was talking at what time and wondered if Jud would miss talking to her in the evenings when his sister came to town.

"So how do you feel about going out with Sharlene and Mary Jo?" Allie's nose looked as if she'd smelled something bad.

"Not my choice," Fiona mumbled.

"What was he thinking?" Lizzy whispered. "But you said you didn't want to make it a date, so it's your own fault."

"I don't want to talk about it. Where are you putting your Christmas tree?"

"Well, I'm going to put my two cents in and then we'll talk Christmas," Allie said. "Don't let this one horrible evening dictate your decision about the future."

"Enough about the future. Let's enjoy the right now. Now, about that tree? And this is really good soup, Lizzy, but then you always were a good cook."

"Just not a good housekeeper." Lizzy smiled.

"What are you giving Toby for Christmas?" Fiona diverted the subject away from the next night.

"I found one of those coupon books online and ordered it. It's for all kinds of sex things and it does not expire until Christmas day of next year. Other than that I have no idea," Lizzy answered. "Confession time, though. Allie, I kept back a box of decorations from the attic when we brought them down. We always had way too much stuff for one tree since Mama bought more every year when it went on sale."

Allie patted her sister on the shoulder. "So did I! I stole the one marked the year I was born. I think it probably has a lot of Granny's stuff in it. You aren't mad at us, are you, Fiona? We'll share what's on the tree at Audrey's Place with you if you move away, or if you stay, it can all be yours."

"No, I'm not upset at all." A picture of a huge tree in her house in Houston flashed through her mind. It sat in a twelve-foot expanse of glass overlooking an acre of green grass. All done up in blue with a huge bow on the top rather than a star or an angel, it had been designed by someone on the firm's payroll. When she and Kyle had their Christmas party, the tree, with the blue and white striped packages underneath, was a huge success.

Last year, she'd bought a twelve-inch fake tree at a discount store for three bucks, fluffed out the limbs and strung microwave popcorn for a garland. She'd bought a few ornaments at the thrift store and made a construction paper and glitter star for the top. The presents that her mother and sisters mailed dwarfed the little tree but she'd been proud of it.

"You ready for me to bring in the tree?" Toby yelled from the kitchen.

"Yup!" Lizzy hollered back.

"Did you get a real tree? You rat! I bought a fake one in Wichita Falls last week when we drove up to see Granny," Allie said.

"I've always, always wanted a real one, but Granny was allergic to them and cats. Now I've got Stormy out in the barn with another batch of kittens. She comes into the house when she wants to and she and Toby's dog, Blue, have become best friends. Toby and I went out in the pasture and cut down a tree before y'all got here. It's leaned up against the back fence."

* * *

The clock said midnight when Jud finally eased up the stairs, bypassing the squeaky step and going straight to his bedroom. He'd planned to come home right behind Fiona at ten-thirty but he and Deke got into a conversation about oil drilling and then he wound up over at Deke's place having a couple of shots of whiskey with him while they continued to talk.

Now it was too late to knock on Fiona's door. He slipped into his room, kicked off his boots and clothes, and fell into bed naked, shivering against the chill of the sheets. He felt cheated out of his nightly visit with Fiona and wished he'd begged off with the excuse of being sleepy rather than going to Deke's place.

Fiona was in his dreams that night. She drove her mother's little Chevy Malibu and they came upon a bridge, the likes of which he'd never seen before. It was an arch so tall that the top of it was buried in the white puffy summer clouds. There was enough steel bracing under it to verify that it was secure but it was only one lane wide and there were almost no side rails.

. Fiona stopped the car at the end of the thing and shook her head. "I can't do this. I'm terrified of heights. Always have been."

"I'm right here beside you. I've got faith in you, Fiona. Keep your eye on the road. Don't look to one side or the other. Just drive and in fifteen minutes, it will be over and we'll be on the other side."

She took a deep breath and held on to the steering wheel in a death grip. One simple swerve and they'd both plummet into a glassy blue river below them, but she made it across and pulled her car up to a place that required a passport for them to go on. She whipped hers out but Jud didn't have one. He woke up while trying to explain to the guards that he was with the woman and didn't need a passport.

He checked the clock to find that he'd overslept by half an hour. Truman would be finished with his breakfast and gone. The old codger didn't wait around for help and things had to be done his way.

Usually Jud had a morning shower to wake him up, but that morning he threw on a pair of jeans and a long-sleeved knit Henley shirt and carried his boots down to the kitchen. Truman, Fiona, and Dora June were all having coffee at the table. Hot cinnamon rolls were on the cabinet along with a pot of hot cereal, a pile of bacon, and a stack of toast.

Jud stopped inside the door and blinked half a dozen times. Truman at the table after six o'clock. Was the world coming to an end?

"If you wouldn't stay out until daylight, probably chasin' after hussies, you wouldn't oversleep," Truman barked.

"Truman O'Dell!" Fiona exclaimed.

Truman crossed his arms over his chest. "You best eat some of that oatmeal Dora June made. It'll stick to your ribs while we get the livestock taken care of this morning."

"Yes, sir." Jud dipped up a bowl full of oatmeal with raisins, pecans, and brown sugar in it. He set it aside and slipped two cinnamon rolls, two pieces of toast, and half a dozen pieces of bacon on a plate.

Dora June bustled around behind him, filling a cup with coffee for him and topping off everyone else's cup. "I've got a favor to ask, Fiona. You can say no, especially after the way we were with your mother last year when we excommunicated her from the ladies' group at the church. I always have the ladies of the church, not just the auxiliary group, but any ladies who want to come, to my house for a little Christmas get-together. We don't have presents, just food and a singing."

"And you'd like to have it here?" Fiona asked.

"Bunch of folderol if you ask me," Truman muttered.

"The house is beautiful and so big and I wouldn't have to take everything to the church to have it in the fellowship hall, but I can if you'd rather I didn't have it here with what all went on."

"When?" Jud asked.

"Tonight. That's why you can say no and I wouldn't feel bad. Henrietta says we can have it at the church, but we always do it on the first day of December. We got so involved with the fire and all that we plumb forgot until last night."

"Mama said to treat this like it was your home, Dora June, so of course you can have your party here. I'm going dancing with Jud, Deke, Sharlene, and Mary Jo, so you don't have to worry about us getting in the way."

"Thank you." Dora June smiled. "We were wrong in the way we handled things with your sisters, Fiona. At the time we thought we were helping them see the error in their ways."

"Water under the bridge. We aren't even going to think of it anymore, Dora June," Fiona said.

"Are you afraid of heights?" Jud blurted out, and immediately wondered if he'd said that out loud.

"Me or Truman?" Fiona asked.

"I ain't afraid of nothing," Truman said staunchly.

Fiona shivered. "Well, I'm terrified of heights. I don't even like mountains. Give me flat land. A few rolling hills like we have here is okay, but nothing any taller than this. And I don't like mice or spiders either, since we're talking of fears."

"Tall bridges?" Jud pressed on.

"Why? Are you thinking of taking some route to Wichita that involves a tall bridge? If so, don't. Just flat out don't or I'll get out of the truck and hitchhike back home. I hate big bridges with a passion. We had to cross one on a business trip over in Tennessee once and I almost fainted."

"Nope, just wondered." The fear she'd had in his dream was real. Now all he had to do was figure out what in the hell that bridge meant and why she needed a passport to get into whatever country they'd landed in on the other side.

Fiona's hair floated on her shoulders that morning with an errant curl falling on her cheek. He wished he had the right to reach across the table and push it behind her ear and then briefly touch his lips to hers, promising to do more later on when they were alone. She looked up and caught him staring and he gazed into her mossy green eyes for several seconds before he went back to eating his second cinnamon roll.

He had no doubt that she had the strength to cross that bridge even if it scared her half to death. She'd faced a divorce, losing her job, working for pennies, and living alone for a year. She could cross any bridge in front of her with no problem. But would she trust him enough to go with her?

"You are both awfully quiet this morning," Dora June said.

"It was a late night getting both Lizzy and Allie's trees all set up and done," Fiona said.

"Then Deke and I got into a long-winded conversation and it was midnight before I got home." Jud picked up the coffeepot and refilled his cup. "Anyone else?"

Fiona held out her cup and his fingertips grazed hers as

he poured. Her expression left no doubt she'd felt them, too. Well, hot damn! At least he wasn't rowing this boat alone.

"Deke thought we should leave at seven tonight. Is that okay with you?" Jud set the pot down.

"I suggest you hurry up and swallow the rest of that coffee and we get busy with what we got to do right now rather than worrying about tonight," Truman said shortly.

"Sounds good to me." Fiona's voice had deepened. "Are we going to pick up Deke and the girls or what?"

Jud shook his head. "Everyone is meeting here so we don't have to drive folks home."

Fiona rolled her eyes toward the ceiling. "If they're too drunk to drive, those girls are sleeping in Sharlene's van."

"Well, I should say so," Dora June agreed.

"Hussies, the both of them," Truman muttered.

"Now, Truman, it's Christmas and besides the preacher said we have to love our neighbors. Where would we be if Katy hadn't shown us some love and if these two kids weren't being nice to us?" Dora June fussed at him.

"I don't like Christmas and never will."

Jud winked at Fiona and she gave him a thumbs-up.

Chapter Twelve

Cover charge, ten dollars. Beers for ladies on Friday night, three bucks. Since this was not a date, Fiona was insistent on paying her own way, though thirteen dollars was more money than she had spent on entertainment in more than a year.

"I'm buying the first round of beers to get us loosened up for dancin'." Deke motioned for the bartender to bring them five beers.

"Thank you," Fiona said.

Sharlene claimed the first one set on the bar. "Nothing better than a good cold beer drawn up in an icy mug."

Mary Jo reached for the second one. "Unless it's a single cowboy who'd like some company."

Fiona cut her eyes around to Mary Jo, but neither she nor Sharlene were giving Jud a come-hither-and-sleep-with-me look. Deke downed part of his beer and zeroed in on a tall blonde across the room. By the time the band started the next song, he was hugged up so close to her that they looked like one person with two heads.

A short red-haired cowboy with freckles across his nose and a winning smile sidled up to Mary Jo and she wasted no time wrapping her arms around his neck and swaying to the slow country song the band played.

"See that lonesome cowboy in the corner? The one with the red and black plaid shirt? He looks like he needs to unburden his soul and I'm just the woman to listen to him." Sharlene turned up her mug and drained it.

"You have a boyfriend," Fiona reminded her.

"Won't hurt to listen to troubles and have a few dances with him. I'm making you the guardian of my soul, Fiona. If I get drunk, carry me out, throw me in the truck, and take me home but don't let me go home with that boy or anyone else."

"I don't want that job," Fiona said.

Sharlene patted her on the cheek. "You don't have to like it. You just have to do it or else you'll suffer the consequences."

"Which are?"

"I won't have a boyfriend tomorrow and then I'll go after yours," Sharlene said just loud enough for Fiona's ears.

"I don't have one for you to go after," Fiona said tersely.

"Bullshit!" Sharlene motioned for the bartender to bring her four shots of tequila and she expertly wove in and around the dancers until she reached her destination. The cowboy grabbed a shot in each hand and threw them back one after the other before he pulled out a chair for Sharlene.

Jud held out a hand. "Guess that leaves you and me. How 'bout a dance?"

"That's what I came here to do." She put her hand in his, much like she did most nights when he walked her across the landing. But tonight the excitement in the place, the loud music, the warmth in her belly from the beer all combined to make the vibes between them even hotter and wilder.

He led her to the edge of the floor, pulled her arms up around his neck, and then dropped his hands to the lower part of her back. The female singer in the band sang "Breathe" and every lyric in the song felt as if it were written especially for Fiona and Jud for that night.

When the song ended, a male singer took the microphone, and Jud buried his face in her hair and sang the lyrics to "Amazed," along with the lead singer. Lord have mercy! Was every song going to be a love song? Was that all the band knew how to play and sing?

"I am amazed by you," Jud whispered.

"Why?"

"Hell if I know, but like the man says, everything that you do amazes me more than the last thing you did," he answered.

"Is that your best pickup line?"

"No, but wait." He pulled her even closer and swayed to the next song. "This one is talking about a wild child with a whole lot of gypsy." Then as the tempo picked up, he swung her out and brought her back to him in a twirl as the words said that she drove him wild. "That would be my pickup line if I was trying to talk you into going home with me. I'd ask you if you were a wild child with that gorgeous red hair and green eyes."

Fiona laughed. "Where do you get this stuff?"

"Had lots of practice and tutoring from my older two cousins. They are the pros at women. Me, I just listened and learned, but they were the ones who were never going to settle down. I've always wanted to fall in love with the right woman."

Fiona wasn't sure how to answer that comment. Thankfully the female singer in the band stepped up to the microphone.

"Hey, you ladies, this one is for you. You cowboys plant your boots, stand still, and let the ladies strut their stuff." The first guitar strands introduced "Any Man of Mine," and the singer did a fine job of sounding like Shania Twain.

Fiona got lost in tormenting Jud with her dance. He folded his arms over his broad chest and he flirted with her with his eyes the whole time she twirled around him, gyrating to the beat, touching his cheek and running her hands across his wide shoulders. She was so involved in the dance that she didn't notice when the rest of the dancers dropped out of the crowded circle one by one.

* * *

Shake a little more red in her hair and she could be Shania's kid sister. The angles in her face were basically the same, but her smile was unique to Fiona Logan and she had far more curves than Shania did.

Jud couldn't have taken his eyes off her if he'd wanted while she expertly moved to every word the singer belted out. Every time she touched him, he wanted to throw her over his shoulder and drag her back home. He didn't want any of the cowboys in the place getting any ideas about her dancing like that for any of them. When she moistened those sexy red lips and ran her forefinger down his jawbone, he was so involved with her that he didn't notice they were the only ones on the dance floor until the song ended and the applause started.

"Now, folks, let's all get back out on the dance floor

and you ladies stand still and let your cowboys show you their swagger." The steel guitar came to life and the singer started Josh Turner's "Your Man."

Fiona started for the bar but Jud grabbed her hand and twirled her around to stand before him. "My turn. Listen to the words, darlin'."

Jud's granny always said what was good for the goose was good for the gander, so he moved slowly, teasing her with his eyes and his dance moves but not touching so much as her pinky finger. Her shallow breathing told him all he wanted to know.

When the song ended, they were alone on the floor again and the band broke into another Josh Turner song, "Why Don't We Just Dance." The singer told them this one was for both parties and it was a fast swing dance. Jud had never danced with anyone like Fiona. She totally lost her soul and body to the beat of the music, as if no one was around but her partner.

The scent of her coconut shampoo mixed with a floral perfume perfectly to take his imagination to a beach where they were dancing under the stars. The sand was warm on their bare feet and his heart kept a steady beat with the sound of the ocean waves lapping at the seashore. He opened his eyes to realize they were in a bar full of people and not all alone on a deserted island with no one else around. His hand grazed the curve of her waist as he adjusted his hold on her and his breath caught in his chest. He'd held women in his arms, so why was this one different?

A question that would take some pondering but right then all he wanted was to never let go of Fiona, to dance off into eternity with her still in his arms. He remembered his conversation with the guys when they were painting. Not one of his previous women were anything near as hot as Fiona and none of them had ever made him turn a blind eye to everyone else in the bar.

Jud caught Sharlene's eye as she was going back to the bar for more tequila shots and she winked. Deke bumped him on the shoulder during one dance. Jud dreaded giving up the best dance partner he'd ever had, but Deke just gave him a thumbs-up and two-stepped away with his tall blond lady.

The song ended and Fiona blinked, grabbed Jud's hand, and started toward the bar. "I'm thirsty."

He pointed toward the bottle someone was holding and then held up two fingers to the bartender. His long arm shot over the top of a dark-haired Latina beauty to get the beers. The sultry way she stared him up and down, starting a few inches lower than his belt buckle and then up to his face, would have had him inching closer to her a few weeks ago. Tonight he noticed, but he wasn't interested.

When he turned around, Fiona was gone and the dance floor was filled with line dancers. He finally caught sight of her making her way through the crowd to Sharlene's table. Taking the longer but faster route around the edge of the room, he made it to the table at the same time she did.

She took the beer when he offered it and sat down beside Sharlene, leaving him the one empty chair in the whole place. Sharlene touched Fiona on the arm, leaned over, and cupped her hand around Fiona's ear to say something, threw back the last tequila shot, and patted the kid on the cheek when she stood up. Evidently, the therapy session was over and Sharlene was ready to dance.

"She's a good lady," the kid slurred.

"What's your problem, cowboy?" Jud asked.

"Woman problems. What else would drive a man to drinkin'?"

Jud held up his beer and the kid nodded; then suddenly the dullness left his eyes and he pushed back his chair. A woman wearing a long denim skirt and a bright green Christmas sweatshirt stopped right in front of him. With her ponytail swinging and her mouth set in a firm line, she popped her hands on her hips and glared at the grinning kid.

He laid a hand on her shoulder. "Darcy, darlin'."

She flipped it off like it was an irritating fly. "This is your last chance, Tommy. Next time, the wedding is off."

"I'm so sorry," he slurred. "I won't ever do it again."

"If you do, it's over. Go home, sober up, and I'll see you in church Sunday morning."

"Will you walk me out to my truck?" he asked.

She took his arm and they disappeared into a fog of smoke and line dancers.

One of the perks of a loud bar is that a person has to get close to another to be heard when they speak. Jud moved his chair around so he was right beside Fiona and touched his beer bottle with hers.

"To never needing one last chance," he said.

"Wonder how many chances he's already had?"

"I'd say by the look in that girl's eyes that it's been too many. What's the odds they'll make it to the altar?"

"Pretty good. The girl evidently wants a wedding. It's the odds that they'll stay married that are slim," she answered.

"Speaking from experience?"

"I didn't give a damn about a wedding. Got married at

the same courthouse where we got our divorce. So, no, I'm not speaking from experience."

Deke slid into the chair the kid had left and set a fresh mug of beer on the table. "Band is fixing to take a ten-minute break, so figured I'd better get something to drink before the bar is so crowded that I couldn't get to it. Y'all looked real good out there." The last song ended with a fancy bit of play from the drummer and then the noise factor dropped by fifty percent.

"Thank you." Fiona flashed a smile across the table. "I haven't been dancing in such a long time."

"How long's it been since you were in a bar? Those fancy clubs in Houston don't count, either. I mean an old country bar like this one."

"Seven years," she said honestly. "I had to use a fake ID last time, but you should remember that. You were with me."

"Whole bunch of us had a good time that night, didn't we?" Deke laughed.

The blonde tapped him on the shoulder and crooked her forefinger. "It's hot in here. Let's take our break out in the cool air. Maybe in your truck? I bet you've got a really big truck." She all but drooled on his shirt.

"I came with some other folks, so I don't have a truck here," Deke said.

"Then we'll see if my car is big enough to hold a sexy cowboy like you," the woman said.

Deke pushed his mug across the table. "Here, Fiona—don't let this go to waste." Then he was gone into the same fog that the kid and his girlfriend had vanished in.

"It's cold out there? They'll either freeze or die of car-bon monoxide poisoning if they leave the car running long enough for..." She hesitated as a blush worked its way up from her neck to dot her cheeks with crimson.

"I don't think either of them is going to mind the chill in the air or stay long enough to die of any kind of poisoning," Jud chuckled. "You ever go outside to cool off after dancin'?"

"Honey, I was only in a bar twice. Once on graduation night and then again the weekend I left for college. My life plan was set in stone and I didn't have time to screw around with boot-scootin' cowboys in those days."

"And now?" he asked.

"And now I'm enjoying this night and not thinking about any of that. I've figured out that even the best laid plans can be wrecked." She picked up Deke's beer and tasted it, then went back to the bottle. "But nowhere in any of my plans, past, present or future, do I expect anyone to crawl up on the water tower and paint 'Dry Creek, Texas, home of Fiona Logan' on it in John Deere green or ever Christmas red."

"Hey, can we sit with y'all?" Mary Jo and her red-haired fellow, each holding a margarita, appeared behind Deke's chair.

"Sure thing. Got room for two more folks here," Jud said.

"Tables are hard to get," Mary Jo said. "Y'all, meet Scooter. Scooter, these are my friends Jud and Fiona."

Scooter tipped his hat and held a chair for Mary Jo. "Pleasure to meet you."

"Likewise." Jud nodded.

"Who left their beer?" Mary Jo asked.

"Help yourself to it. Deke's cooling off outside," Jud answered.

Mary Jo's laughter was loud enough that several people turned to look in their direction. She slapped a hand over her mouth until she could get control, then picked up the pint glass and downed half the contents. "Poor old Deke. I know that woman he's dancing with. He'd best be careful or he'll be listening to the pitter-patter of little feet. She's got wedding dresses on the brain right now."

"Seems like everyone does," Fiona said.

"You got something to tell us?" Mary Jo pushed her brown hair behind her ears and licked the salt from the rim of the margarita glass.

"Not me! The band is getting set up again. I came to dance," Fiona said, taking a long swig of her beer and then standing up.

"We'll hold the table." Mary Jo moved close enough to wrap her arms around Scooter's neck and share the taste of salt with him through a long kiss.

* * *

The two singers each picked up a microphone, but the woman did the talking. "And now for the next hour we're going to kick off the holiday season with country music Christmas songs, starting off with Blake Shelton's version of 'Jingle Bell Rock.'"

Fiona's moves were right on, but her heart and soul weren't in it like before. Now she was more aware of Jud. Never, not even one time, had Fiona not been able to get lost in the music. It didn't matter if her partner was smooth on his feet or if he stumbled through the steps, she loved the way the music made her feel. But tonight the sound of the guitars and drums took a backseat to the way Jud held her against his buff body. Melting into him, listening to his heart beat against her breasts, feeling the heat of his hands on the small of her back was more important than the rhythm of the steel guitar and the drums. When that fast song ended and "White Christmas" started, Jud pulled her into his arms and started a slow waltz.

"Have I told you that you are beautiful tonight?" he asked. "That green shirt is the exact color of your eyes."

"Thank you," she mumbled.

"What are you thinking about? Your face is a mixture of emotions right now," he asked. "Are you tired of dancing?"

"Not at all. I'd forgotten how much I missed this," she answered.

"We could do this every weekend," he said. "Talking about dancing put a happy look on your face.

"Hey, don't tempt me." She smiled. "Do you read all women so well or am I that transparent?"

"It must be the vibes between us. You can't deny that they are there," he said.

"Let's talk about something else or just dance." She tucked her head into his shoulder.

"Long as you are in my arms and we're dancing, we can talk about anything. Do you want a white Christmas?"

"Do you?" she asked.

"I don't care if it snows on Christmas or if it's eighty degrees and the sun is shining. I just want family all around us." He stepped back, did some fancy footwork, and twirled her around a couple of times. "This is good holiday music."

"I like Blake Shelton. Met him once, and he's as country as his songs," she said.

"For real?" Jud asked.

"The rich and shameless get backstage passes at concerts," she said. "But before you ask, I'm not interested in being that high on the corporate ladder again. I would like to be a couple of steps up from the convenience store, though."

"What do you want to do?" he asked.

"I'm still working on that, but right now I want to dance some more."

Folks formed a line to dance to "All I Want for Christmas Is You." Sharlene fell in beside Fiona but she'd had so many shots with the melancholy boy that she had trouble keeping up with the moves.

"Lord, I'd better go sit out a few and just drink Coke until this gets through my system. Hey, where's my sad boy?"

"His woman came in and took him home," Fiona said.

"Well, good for her."

"Deke?"

"Cooling off outside."

Sharlene's eyes widened and she giggled. "He'd better be careful if he left with the woman that's been glued to his zipper all night. See y'all when we shut down the place."

"The wagon train leaves at twelve sharp," Jud said. "I've got to work tomorrow."

"Party pooper." Sharlene staggered off.

When midnight rolled around, Fiona still wanted one more dance with Jud, to feel his arms around her for a few more hours and to spend a little while longer looking into his fascinating brown eyes.

When they stepped out into the cold night air, there was no big lovers' moon hanging in the sky. Not even one little bright star could find a hole in the gray skies to push its brightness through. Other than the streetlamps on the four corners of the parking lot and a few headlights as folks headed home, it was a dreary night.

Fiona welcomed the fresh, icy air when she sucked it into her lungs. Jud laced his fingers in hers and hunched his shoulders against the bitter wind blowing from the north.

"I don't see any of them," she said.

"We'll call Deke from the truck."

Snowflakes had begun to fall from the sky when they were inside his truck. "White Christmas may be a reality if this keeps up all month," he said.

Her phone vibrated in her hip pocket. Deke had sent a text. Scooter would take Sharlene and Mary Jo home after breakfast. Deke had found his own way back to Dry Creek. They'd all see them in church on Sunday if not before.

"Guess we're on our own."

"They've all got plans, right?" he asked.

"Looks that way," she answered.

"Hungry?" He backed out of the parking lot and made a right-hand turn onto the highway.

"More tired than hungry, but we could get a burger to go at that McDonald's at the next exit," she said.

"So you know this area well enough to know that?"

"No, I saw a sign that said the golden arches were at the next exit when we were driving up here. This place has grown so much in seven years that I hardly know it at all."

"We'll get used to it together, then. We did our partying down around Dallas or else west of Gainesville if we didn't want to drive all the way into the big city, but this is all new territory to me." The lights were still on and the sign said the drive-through window was open twenty-four/seven, so he eased the truck up to the order place.

"Name your poison," he said.

She unfastened her seat belt and leaned toward him so she could see the menu. Remnants of shaving lotion, smoke clinging to his shirt, beer on his breath, tousled blond hair all worked together to send her hormones into a whining state.

"Burger with mustard and no onions, fries, and coffee," she said, but her mind damn sure wasn't on food right then.

The lady repeated it back. "Anything else?"

"Double that and add a chocolate shake to the order."

"Large?"

"That's fine," Jud answered, and handed her a bill.

Fiona opened her mouth to argue but he laid a finger over her lips. "I've had a wonderful time tonight. Just let me buy you a burger without a fight."

She straightened up. "Thank you. I can't remember the last time I had so much fun."

Fiona's phone buzzed in her pocket. When she checked it, there was a text message from Allie.

"Audrey needs diapers. We need to go to the store on our way home," she said.

The lady reached out and tapped on the truck window to get their attention. Jud hit the button and rolled down the window. She handed him the order and he drove forward to let the car behind him move up.

"So drive and eat or park and eat?" he asked.

"You might enjoy it more if we parked," she said.

He nosed the truck into a parking spot but left the engine running. She settled the coffee into the two cup holders at the end of the console and removed everything from the bag. She flattened the paper bag onto the console and made it into a mini picnic table. The two containers of fries became one big order when she poured them all out in a pile.

"Looks like you've done this before," he said.

"On payday, I treated myself to a burger. I went to the

park not far from where I worked, parked the truck, and put the console down just like this. Then I pretended Lizzy or Allie was in the passenger seat and I talked to them," she whispered.

Jud folded the paper back from his burger and bit into it. "You were really lonely, weren't you?"

"At times." She shot ketchup from two small packages onto one of the empty French fry sacks. "These are addictive, you know. They have a special salt they shake on them and it makes you keep coming back for more."

Like you, she wanted to say, but she crammed fries into her mouth to keep from talking.

"I like Allie's fried potatoes better. She makes them like my mama does, in a cast-iron skillet with onions. It's snowing harder. I thought the Lucky Penny was far enough south that we'd only see snow a couple of times a decade," he said.

"It's crazy weather all right. Maybe you Dawsons brought it with you from northern Texas. We might have had a white Christmas one time when I was growing up and we never had a white Thanksgiving. I remember an ice storm once when I was about ten." She removed the lid from her coffee and took a sip. "It snowed, but it never stuck around for more than a day and seldom ever covered the ground."

"So it's our fault?" Jud chuckled.

"Must be. You're the only thing that's changed."

"I believe two things changed. You came home, too," he argued.

"I came from the south. We don't get bad weather in Houston," she protested.

"Want to talk to me about those floods?"

"That's not snow and sleet."

"But it's bad weather all the same. Slide off the road with ice and snow. Get washed off with rising water. Either way, you're still off the road."

"Well, Mr. Smartass, you'd better finish your burger because the way this stuff is falling, we might find ourselves sitting in a ditch like Toby and Lizzy did last spring." She put the lid back on her coffee and wondered what it would be like to cuddle up next to Jud all night with nothing but a single blanket to keep them warm.

They were only two miles from the store and it stayed open twenty-four/seven. The parking lot was full, even though it was well past midnight, but they did snag a spot about halfway out from the front door.

"What's going on? Is this a Black Friday sale a week or two late?" she asked as she made her way gingerly toward the doors on the slick concrete.

"Not that I know of. I guess lots of people don't have anything better to do at nearly one o'clock in the morning other than go shopping," Jud answered.

"Oh. My. God." She gasped. "Look at that. My eyes may never be the same. I thought those pictures on the Internet were doctored."

The man rolling his cart out had a beard, tattoos up both arms, and a bald head. Yet, *bald* wasn't the right word. The whole top of his head was hairless but the rim around the edge had been let go until it was long enough to make a ponytail in the back. He wore camouflage leggings with a hot pink western shirt with pearl snaps and cowboy boots. But the crazy thing was the makeup job on his face. It looked like it had been applied by a six-year-old who'd spent the day with her grandparents getting sugared up on

candy and soda pop. And right there in the cart was another person—a woman with hot pink hair, wearing a red
prom dress that was two sizes too big and a plastic tiara.
She waved at everyone they passed like she was riding on
the top of a brand-new Caddy in a homecoming parade.

"Well, it is after midnight," Jud chuckled.

"But it's not Halloween," she said softly.

"Don't burst their bubble," he teased.

They were met by warm air when they walked through
the automatic doors. Fiona brushed the snow from her
shoulders and snagged a shopping cart. Jud walked along
beside her all the way to the back of the store where the diapers were shelved in the baby section.

"What size?" he asked.

"She didn't say," Fiona answered.

Jud picked up a package and read the print on the outside. "This one says up to twelve pounds. Does Audrey
weigh that much?"

"I have no idea. She was seven pounds and some ounces
at birth."

"She wears that number two," Deke said right behind
them. "I had to get some a few days ago when I was up here."

"What are you doing here?"

"Buying beer." He pointed at his cart. "Date didn't work
out too good. She wanted to go to her place, but when we
got there, I found them bride magazines strewed all over
the coffee table. That's my cue to run faster than the wind."

"Were you...did you use...oh, hell, tell me you used
protection when you were out in the car with her." Fiona
spit out the words but couldn't keep the blush from dotting
her cheeks.

"Geez, Fiona! Of course I did!" He grinned. "Y'all

might want to pick up some beer while you are here and maybe a cooler to keep in your room. Dora June wouldn't find it and y'all could have one when you want. Not that I mind sneaking a couple over to you, but it would sure make things easier. Besides, both of those old folks will be in bed when you get home, so it will be easy to sneak it inside."

"Smart idea." Jud tossed two packages of diapers into the cart.

"I'll see y'all tomorrow sometime," Deke said. "Be careful on the way home. Roads are getting slicker by the minute."

He disappeared into the food section and Jud took over the cart. "That idea of his was smart. I'm going to buy a cooler and a case of beer."

"I'm going to buy a bottle of strawberry Boone's Farm and see if it tastes as good as it did in high school," she said.

"I'll share my beer if you share your Boone's."

"It's a deal."

"Well, look who's out late?" Lucy said as they turned the cart around. "Y'all out making a diaper run for Allie?"

"Yes, ma'am, we are but we were already here. We went dancing," Fiona answered.

Lucy winked at Fiona. "I remember going dancing with Herman many years ago. In those days we sure didn't let anyone know what we'd been up to. But things change. We didn't have throwaway diapers then, either."

"Probably couldn't have afforded them if they were on the market," Fiona said.

"You got that right, honey. Did y'all see that woman in the cart? They're in the store somewhere. I wonder what they've been smokin'?" Lucy asked.

"I don't know but I don't want any of it," Fiona laughed.

"Oh, I don't know. It might be something wonderful to try." Lucy winked again. "I got to drag Herman out of the hardware stuff and take him home. We was up here at the hospital for our great-granddaughter. She was born tonight. Mama and baby are doing fine. They named her Dakota. Ain't that the craziest name for a little baby girl that you ever heard. See y'all later." She waved and hurried off toward another part of the store.

"Aren't you glad we didn't have the beer in the cart?" Jud whispered, his warm breath sending deliciously warm shivers down Fiona's back.

"Yes, I am. She would have told on us for sure."

"Then we would have had to share with Dora June," Jud said seriously.

Fiona slapped at his arm, getting another quiver down her spine when her hand brushed against his bare neck. "You are evil."

"And you are running with me," he teased.

* * *

Brightly colored Christmas lights lit the way back to Dry Creek. Farmhouses that she'd never noticed before and those tucked back down lanes had lights shining out through the huge snowflakes. Decorations had been strung up in the small towns of Holliday, Dundee, and Mabelle. Fiona didn't realize she was humming "Jingle Bells" until Jud started singing the lyrics.

"All these lights put me in the holiday mood," she admitted.

"Me too."

"Take the next left onto that farm road. It's a shortcut and we'll get home faster. Oh my! Look at that. Those folks strung lights across the top of their barbed wire fence.

I'm glad Mama didn't see it or she'd be shipping more twinkling lights home from Florida or telling me to buy enough to put around all twenty acres of Audrey's Place."

"Have y'all ever considered selling Audrey's Place?" Jud slowed down and followed her instructions.

"Why would you ask such a thing?"

"Just wondering. It's got the Lucky Penny on three sides of it and the townsfolk…well, some of them don't have a kind word to say about the ranch."

"Audrey's won't ever be for sale, not in my lifetime. Make a right at the next corner." For the first time in her life, Fiona felt a stab of guilt about leaving Dry Creek. In the beginning, there were two sisters still in the house. She had no problem with either or both of them inheriting the land and the house because she damn sure did not want it. Now they each had their own place and her mother wanted to retire. That left no one to hold Audrey's down until the next generation came along to claim it…except Fiona.

And I don't want it, she thought as Jud parked his truck beside Deke's in the front yard. *I don't want anyone else to have it but I've never wanted to live here, so I'm not taking this guilt trip.*

"You've got that look on your face again. Like you are fighting with demons," he said.

"Leaving town in one hand." She held up a palm. "Dry Creek in the other. Some days one is full of hope and the other one is lacking. Other times it reverses. I think about leaving and I think about staying. Most of the time leaving is the one that is most appealing."

"And tonight?" he asked.

"Tonight Dry Creek is winning. Tomorrow is another day, though."

When they pulled up to the Lucky Penny, the house was dark. Jud grabbed the big bag of diapers from the backseat and eased in the front door to leave them in the entryway before quietly locking up and returning to the car.

"I swear, it's colder here than it was in Wichita Falls, and that ground is so slippery that you could ski to work if we lived on a mountain."

Fiona giggled.

"What's so funny about that?" he asked.

"I'm imagining you in a cowboy hat and boots on skis."

He shut his eyes before he put the truck in gear and smiled. "Well, I'm imagining you in a hot pink bikini on skis."

"Silly cowboy." She swatted at his biceps. "Redheads don't wear hot pink."

"Oh, honey, in my mind you do and it looks almighty fine." He wiggled his head but did not open his eyes. "There you go down the mountain slope. Swoosh, swoosh. And the ice and snow is melting behind you because you are so damned hot in that pink bikini. Your hair is blowing in the wind and oh, there's a cameraman taking pictures for me."

"Did you get too close to that lady in the cart and breathe in some of whatever she'd been smoking?" Fiona asked.

His eyes snapped open and he backed the truck out, turned it around, and started down the lane. "Dammit! Why did you have to replace my beautiful picture with that one?"

"It's late and we've both got to get up early," she said.

"We still need to put those snow tires on Katy's car. We can pull it over into one of the barns on the Lucky Penny on Sunday and take care of it. You'll drive real careful until then, right?"

"I don't need you to tell me how to drive, Jud Dawson."

"Says the woman who ran through our barbed wire fence into a tree." Jud chuckled, taking the sting out of his words.

"Hey now!"

"Aw, c'mon, I'm just teasing you. You're even more gorgeous when you start to get all indignant."

"Are we flirting?" she asked bluntly. "It's been so long since I did any of that I'm not sure that I wouldn't have to drag out the *Flirting for Dummies* book to refresh my memories."

"Darlin', you don't need a book. All you have to do is flutter those pretty eyelashes and smile. Here we are. Want to make out in the truck or is it past your curfew?"

She opened the truck door. "No to both. Let's get inside and go to bed."

"Oh, I do like that idea much better," Jud said with a wicked grin.

"Rephrase. We should go inside and get some sleep."

She stepped out into the snow and her feet almost slipped out from under her. So much for slick-soled boots. Very carefully, she made her way from truck to porch and held on to the railing as she went up the three steps. She used her key to open the door, slipped inside, and flipped on the foyer light, then turned around to shut the door and ran right into Jud's chest. He wrapped his arms around her, held her steady until she could get her bearings, and then tipped her chin up with his thumb.

Every fiber in her body wanted the kiss. Every bit of her brain said that she should take two steps back. She listened to the loudest inner voice and moistened her lips with the tip of her tongue.

Lord have mercy! Sometime during the fourth long, lingering kiss—or was it the fifth or sixth?—she managed to shuck out of her coat and throw it on the foyer floor.

She was panting when Jud started guiding her backward up the steps. He lost his coat somewhere about the third step and by the sixth one, she gave a little tug on the top pearl snap and revealed a whole bed of soft light brown hair on his chest. Her arms left his neck and pulled the shirt free, then found their way to his muscular back. She'd never known that cold fingers on warm skin could make her forget everything, including her name and where they were.

Her shirt left her body and dropped not far from his on the landing right before she felt the cold bedroom door on her back. Jud pressed firmly against her front, leaving no doubt he was every bit as aroused as she was.

One hand found its way up under her shirt while he drove her absolutely wild when his mouth brushed the tender area right under her earlobe and worked the hooks on her bra. Her hand was deftly managing her belt buckle while the other one tried desperately to locate the doorknob behind her. The bed would be so much more comfortable than wrapping her legs around his waist and having wild sex against the wall.

A door slammed.

Fiona's breath caught in her chest.

Jud laid a finger over her lips.

"Damn kids!" Truman ranted. "Throw their coats on the floor. Leave the lights on and I'll be damned if they didn't leave the door unlocked, too. I bet they came home drunk and tomorrow morning Jud will have a beauty of a hangover. So much for him helping me."

The lock on the front door clicked shut.

"Guess I'll have to start waiting up for them to be sure things is locked up and we ain't wastin' electricity. Kids today ain't got a lick of sense."

The lights went out, throwing everything into darkness.

"Dammit! More snow and cold weather makes my bones hurt like the devil. Wonder if Dora June still has any of that liniment she used to brew up when we first married. Hell, no! It burned up in our house if she did have any."

The kitchen light sent a sliver of illumination up the steps but not much. Fiona giggled and Jud stifled it with a kiss but the mood had been broken and everything was funny.

"It's been a long time since I've been called a damn kid," she whispered.

He chuckled. "Last time I heard someone say 'damn kids,' it was a friend complaining that the kids had interrupted a well-planned evening of sex with his wife. I feel like saying 'damn old people' right now."

She raised an eyebrow. "So was this a well-planned evening of sex?"

"Hell, no! This was spontaneous, which is ten times better than planned. But now that you've mentioned it, it could be a night of wild passionate sex. The bedsprings could try to keep up with your moans and screams."

"Yeah, right. What about your moans of ecstasy, cowboy?"

"Want to see who can make the most noise?"

"Good night, Jud." She grinned.

"Good night, Fiona. See you tomorrow morning if that old fart wants to drop by the store for coffee." Jud gave her one more parting hug and in a couple of long strides disappeared behind his bedroom door across the hall.

Chapter Thirteen

The sunshine was bright and beautiful on Saturday morning. It was still cold enough that the dusting of snow that had fallen wouldn't melt except on the major roads where the traffic was heavier, but the sun took away the dreariness.

Either all that natural light or else the idea of a shopping trip the next day put a new spring in Dora June's step. And she talked nonstop all during breakfast. She started with how lovely it was to have a day with few clouds, went on to talk about her party the night before and what a success it was, and then segued into what she would buy when they went shopping the next day.

"A nice new Bible case for Henrietta, don't you think?" She stopped bustling around in the kitchen and wrote something on a list lying on the countertop. "I saw a pretty pink leather one last week with a Bible verse on the front. I think she'd like that. And a doll for Audrey."

"But, Dora June, Audrey is only a few weeks old."

Fiona finished her breakfast and put the plate in the dishwasher.

"She'll be big enough to play with a rag doll by this time next year. I saw an adorable Raggedy Ann in a cute little gift store at the mall."

Fiona slipped her arms into her coat and pulled a pair of gloves from her pocket. Suddenly she couldn't wait to get to the store where maybe she'd have a few minutes of peace. "Don't wait on me for supper tonight. I'll probably work late to get the bookkeeping business caught up."

"And a scarf for Ruby." Dora June picked up the pencil and waved.

* * *

The store was not quiet.

All day long, it bustled with folks coming in to visit around the table. Fiona had made eight big pots of coffee from morning until closing time and had sold six dozen doughnuts in addition to the prepackaged pastries right off the shelf. It had been a wonderful day for the store but a horrible one for catching up on her bookkeeping business.

It didn't matter that the clock above the cash register said that it was ten minutes past five. Six old guys were still gathered around the table discussing politics and the upcoming election while they polished off three more packages of chocolate cupcakes.

She did all the closing chores and swept the floor, but they did not take the hint and leave. Then again, what did she expect? They were men and they were used to women working around them.

"Well"—Herman Hudson finally stood up—"I reckon them cows of mine ain't goin' to drag a big round bale of hay out to the pasture and feed themselves. It'll be dark in an hour even if we did have sunshine today."

"Guess you heard that the weatherman is callin' for a norther about midnight," Truman said.

"But no more snow until the middle of next week." Herman nodded. "Then we're getting one big enough to run last year some competition. Never thought I'd see two hard winters in a row."

"It's them Dawsons over on the Lucky Penny that's caused all this," Truman fussed.

"Give it a rest, Truman," Herman scolded. "They ain't God and that's the only person who controls weather."

They meandered toward the door, taking their own good easy time, stopping to talk more about the weather and about the hay they'd put up for the winter. When they were finally outside, Fiona locked the door, turned the sign around to _Closed_, and flipped off the light switch.

Time had stood still for the past hour, but when she sat down in front of the computer, it moved much faster. She didn't realize how late it was until her stomach wouldn't be ignored another minute. A quick trip into the dark store netted two packages of peanut butter crackers, a pint of milk, a diet cola, and an iced honey bun.

She nibbled as she worked and didn't look at the clock again until her neck began to ache. Rolling it around a few times to get the kink out, she figured a couple more hours would put her up to date on everything. Then she looked at the clock and rubbed her eyes. Surely it wasn't midnight already, but the clock had no reason to lie to her, so she backed up all her files and shut down the computer.

The old guys had been right about that norther. In some parts of the country they called such a fierce, cold wind a nor'easter but in Oklahoma and Texas it was simply a norther. It hit with a force and dropped the temperatures by at least twenty degrees. Fiona ran from the store to her mother's car, slammed the door against the blasts of icy cold wind, and shivered all the way to her toenails.

Disappointment washed over her when she parked next to Truman's truck in the backyard. Jud's vehicle wasn't anywhere in sight. She'd hoped that they could have a few minutes to talk about the night before. She let herself into the house, made sure she locked the door, and went straight for the refrigerator. Dora June had made fried chicken and there were leftovers. She put a leg and a breast in a bowl and picked up a can of diet cola.

She didn't even turn on the foyer light but made her way upstairs in the dark. Once she was in her bedroom with the door closed, she lit up the room with a table lamp. Then she sat down in the recliner beside the window and bit into the cold chicken. Nothing had tasted so good in a very long time but it didn't take away the yearning to talk to Jud.

* * *

Jud was late to church that Sunday morning and slid into the pew right beside Fiona just as the preacher took the pulpit. Nudging Fiona on the shoulder, he whispered, "What time did you get home last night?"

"After midnight. Where were you?"

"At Deke's. I waited until ten for you and then got bored, so I went to Deke's for a beer."

"Shhhh." Dora June tapped them both on the shoulder from the pew right behind them.

The preacher cleared his throat loudly. "What do you want for Christmas? Are you thinking about a new car? A trip to a place where it's warm and you can put your feet in the sand? Or are you thinking about peace and happiness..." The preacher went on but Jud didn't hear a word he said.

What did he want for Christmas? For the better part of a year Jud had wanted to be at the Lucky Penny with his cousins by Christmas. He'd yearned to be there when Blake and Toby talked about the improvement they were making, the new baby calves last spring, and even putting up fence in the heat of a Texas July. From the moment he'd driven his truck onto the property a few weeks ago, he'd known peace. But what he truly wanted for Christmas was what his two cousins had. The start of a family and happiness with a woman they loved.

Fiona crossed one leg over the other and brushed his hip in the process. She did not bring happiness to him. Turmoil was more like it—that's what he felt every time she walked into a room.

She was family of family, and the awkwardness of a fling could cause more problems than he could count on his fingers and toes. He told himself for the thousandth time that she would be moving away as soon as she could and he was definitely staying on the ranch of his dreams.

Happiness might not be in Santa Claus's big bag this Christmas, but if Jud could ask for anything, it would be contentment. Fiona's shoulder touched his again when she fidgeted. He shut his eyes and imagined kissing that sweet spot between her shoulder and neck and moving up to taste her earlobe before settling his lips on hers for a series of kisses that left them both panting.

Every song, even "Jingle Bells," reminded him of her, every snowflake that dropped or cold breath of air he inhaled brought back a visual of her. Just one romp in the hay might put her out of his mind, but then what? Her sisters were married to his cousins and they would be thrown together forever. No, that would never work.

"So what do you want for Christmas?" Deke whispered on his left side.

"Haven't made my list yet. Have you?" Jud said from the side of his mouth.

"A tall blonde full of sass heads up the list or maybe a redhead so hot that she can leave burn marks on my mattress," Deke chuckled softly.

"Shhh." Fiona shushed them with a finger to her lips.

Lips.

A stirring behind Jud's zipper reminded him of how much Fiona affected him.

Think about something else other than the taste of those luscious lips. Think about what the preacher is saying. Think about pulling a calf, building fence in August, or drilling a new well.

"And now I'll ask Jud Dawson to deliver the benediction," the preacher said.

Jud stood and shook the legs of his Wranglers down over the tops of his boots, bowed his head, and said the shortest prayer of his life, thanking God for the day and the holiday season and asking that everyone be blessed with heavenly love, amen. It was not easy to talk to God when his mind was on the woman sitting to his right, looking like a billboard model in that red sweater hugging her curves and the green plaid skirt that barely skimmed her knees.

"I wish you'd do the benediction every week," Deke said the moment the rest of the folks in the church joined in with a hearty amen. "That was the shortest one I've ever heard, and Blake had to kick me awake to deliver it one Sunday so you can imagine how short that one was."

Jud clapped a hand on Deke's shoulder. "If I'd been sleeping, maybe I wouldn't have been thinking about things I shouldn't in church."

"I understand," Deke said seriously.

Dora June and Lizzy pulled Fiona out into the center aisle and Jud felt as empty as if he'd lost something. But he couldn't lay claim to what he'd never had, so he waved at Fiona as the women headed toward the nursery to collect Allie and Audrey.

Tonight, he promised himself, he would be home in time for them to visit. They needed to talk about what nearly happened Friday night and decide exactly where they stood with each other.

When he turned back around, Deke was gone as well as both his cousins and their wives. Truman was standing at the back of the line looking lost. He stepped out beside the old guy and threw an arm around his bony shoulders.

"Want to get some lunch at Nadine's? I'll buy if you'll keep me company," Jud said.

Truman's head bobbed up and down. "I wasn't lookin' forward to soup out of a can. Never did like that stuff. It don't taste like Dora June's."

"Her cookin' sure can spoil a man, can't it?" Jud removed his arm and shook hands with the preacher.

"Yes, it can. She can make something out of nothing when times is tough and she never puts anything on the table that disappoints me. I'm pretty much a lucky man," Truman said.

The norther that had hit the night before hadn't let up in intensity one bit. The wind whipped through the bare limbs of the mesquite and scrub oak, creating a strange music that said winter had arrived early and the human race couldn't do a thing about it.

"Colder'n a mother-in-law's kiss out here, ain't it?" Truman pulled his lined denim jacket tighter across his chest with one hand and used the other to keep his cowboy hat from flying south with the other.

"Ain't never had a mother-in-law. Are you speakin' from experience?" Jud laughed as he shortened his steps so Truman didn't have to run to keep up.

"Hell, yes. Dora June's mama hated me when we married and then when she found out it was my fault we couldn't have kids that put the icin' on the cake. Her last words to Dora June was that she wished she'd married someone else." Truman didn't waste a bit of time getting inside Jud's truck.

"What are you doing this afternoon?" Jud asked. "Want to play some dominoes while the girls are out shopping?"

Truman cut his eyes around at Jud. "You want to lose your money?"

"What are we playing for? If you are that good, maybe we'd best play for pennies." Jud contained the laughter but it wasn't easy.

"Quarters," Truman answered. "And I'm really good."

"Quarters, it is. Maybe I'll win back enough to pay for our Sunday dinner."

Truman chuckled for the first time since Jud met him. "I wouldn't count on it, son."

Jud wanted to do a fist pump and maybe even a little touchdown dance when Truman called him son but he kept his composure. They snagged the last table at Nadine's café, hung their jackets on the back of their chairs, and picked up a menu from the center of the table. Truman looked at it for less than a minute and put it back between the salt and pepper shakers and the napkin dispenser.

"Hey, boys." Sharlene set two glasses of water on the table. "What'll it be today?"

"I'll have the liver and onions special with mashed potatoes, corn, and an extra biscuit. Sweet tea and save me a piece of coconut cream pie," Truman said.

"And you?" Sharlene asked Jud.

"I'll have a bacon burger basket with gravy on the side for my fries."

"Sweet tea?" Sharlene asked.

"Yes, and save me a bowl of Nadine's blackberry cobbler with ice cream on the top," Jud answered. "I expect we'll both want a cup of coffee to go with dessert, right, Truman?"

"Sounds good to me."

A cowbell sounded at the back of the store and Sharlene hurried off to pick up an order to deliver. Truman tucked an oversized cloth napkin into his collar and spread it out over his chest. Jud opened his napkin and laid it on his lap.

"I wanted kids," Truman said bluntly. "It broke my heart for Dora June when we found out we couldn't have any. I told her she could leave me even though that would have killed me, but she said that she'd married me for better or worse."

"Is that when you bought the goats?" Jud asked.

A sad smile turned the corners of Truman's mouth up. "Dora June said they were her kids. We've had a little herd for years and she'd sit out there in her lawn chair in the spring when the babies are little and laugh at them rompin' around and headbuttin' each other. I always liked the sound of her laughter. It's like bells ringin'."

Jud sipped at his water and waited.

"I feel a change in the air and I'm not sure I like it," Truman said. "I thought it was because y'all had bought the Lucky Penny, but it's deeper than that. I can't put my finger on it yet, but I think it's got to do with me and Dora June instead of the whole county or even Dry Creek."

"Is it time for y'all to retire?" Jud asked.

"We don't know nothing but what we do and we like our life this way. I guess I need some kind of sign to show me that's what I'm supposed to do. Do I build another house? Do I sell my ranch? And if so, what do I do then?"

"I'm in the same boat only in a different way," Jud confided.

"Fiona?" Truman asked. "Don't look so surprised. I see the way you look at her. Same way I did Dora June back when we was young. But Dora June wanted to put down roots. Fiona was born with wings. You got a big job ahead of you if you set your mind for that girl."

"Yep, I sure do," Jud agreed, and changed the subject. "I should warn you about something, especially since it's Sunday and we should be honest on this day. My granddad taught me to play dominoes when I was barely able to see over the top of the kitchen table. He never let me win and when I did at the age of thirteen, I did a victory dance."

"Fair enough." Truman pursed his lips together. "My granddad taught me to play when I was about five years old. I won my first game when I was ten, so I'd say you best be real careful and think before you play."

Chapter Fourteen

Irene was sitting around a table with a group playing bingo when the girls all arrived that Sunday afternoon.

"Come on B twelve! Come on B twelve!" the little man beside her said.

"Willie, there ain't no B twelve on your card," Irene said.

"But there is on yours and it's all you need to bingo. Maybe you'd give me the candy bar if you win?" Willie said.

"And the next number is B twelve," the caller said.

Irene yelled, "Bingo," so loud that it made Fiona jump.

Irene pushed her card back, told the caller to give the candy bar to Willie, and hurried over to hug Fiona. "You were my good luck charm. And you brought everyone with you." Irene clapped her hands. "Audrey is here to see her great-granny."

Fiona hugged her grandmother fiercely. "I'm so glad to see you. I'll be home for a few months, so I can come see you real often."

"Did they tell you that sometimes I have trouble remembering things?" Irene whispered.

"Yes, Granny, they did." Fiona tried to swallow the lump in her throat but it was impossible.

Irene took Fiona's hand in hers and led her to the sitting room. She pulled her down on one of the two facing sofas and held her arms up to take the baby from Allie. "Dora June, what in the hell are you doing here?"

"The girls are taking me Christmas shopping," Dora June said.

"And they think *I've* lost my mind," Irene said sarcastically. "Why would my girls take you anywhere after the hell you gave Allie and Lizzy?"

Dora June crossed the room and laid a hand on Irene's shoulder. "I'm so sorry for that, Irene. I've been jealous of you my whole life. You got Katy and then three granddaughters and I wanted them all for mine."

"That's why you tried to drive them crazy with your meddling?" Irene crossed her thin arms over her chest and continued to frown.

"When you decided to live here, I..." Dora June paused. "I didn't know how to..."

Fiona very gently squeezed Irene's hand. "Granny, it's okay. Dora June and Truman are staying at Audrey's Place while Mama is on vacation. Their house burned down and they needed a place to stay."

"Now I know I'm either crazy or dead. Ain't no way Truman would stay there. He's too self-righteous. Who are these other girls you brought with you?" Irene cocked her head to one side and studied her other two granddaughters.

"This is Allie and Lizzy. My sisters, remember? Your

granddaughters. Allie is getting Audrey out of her coat so you can hold her," Fiona said softly. Her mother had warned her that Irene's memory could flash on and off like twinkling Christmas lights. "Remember when you came to Dry Creek last week and we put up the tree but it was too windy to put up the outside decorations?"

"I wish I had a tree," Irene said wistfully.

"I'll bring a little one and some decorations next Sunday and we'll put it right there in the corner. Maybe I'll even make a butter rum cake this week." Fiona winked but it was all she could do to keep the tears at bay.

Irene clapped her hands. "I love butter rum cake. Remember when we used to make them at Christmas for the church potluck and we never told anyone that it had real alcohol in it?" She glanced at Dora June. "I bought rum, didn't I? At a liquor store in Wichita Falls."

"You bought the rum because Truman would have pitched a fit if I brought liquor in the house and we made them at your place." Dora June smiled.

Irene frowned. "Who are these girls again, Dora? Did you and Truman adopt kids after all? Is this pretty little thing your grandbaby?"

Dora June wiped away a tear. "Got something in my eye. Yes, we did adopt all these girls. They've been our biggest blessing these past few days. You don't mind if we adopt them, do you?"

"Hell, no! Everyone needs kids. I don't know what I'd do without my Katy," Irene declared.

Allie put Audrey in her lap. "She's a good baby as long as she gets her way. Kind of like Lizzy."

"She looks like Fiona," Irene said. "My mother had red hair but she didn't like it so she put stuff on it. It stunk and I didn't like to be in the house when she did that." She frowned again and then smiled. "You are Allie and you are Lizzy and you belong to Katy, right? You aren't Dora June's kids?"

"Not really. We are your granddaughters and the baby is Audrey," Allie said.

"Audrey is the hooker that built our house. How can this be Audrey?" Irene was visibly confused.

"We named her after our great-great-grandmother," Allie answered.

"Well, ain't that a hoot," Irene giggled. "Where's Katy?"

"She's on a little trip with Trudy and Janie," Allie repeated.

"Oh, no! Those two are always up to no good. Tell her that I said she has to come home. They'll have her drinkin' and chasin' bad boys." Irene's voice shot up to just below yelling.

"I will call her soon as we get home," Lizzy said.

"Okay, now tell me, Dora, about your house burnin' down. Did it hurt any of your goats?" Irene asked.

Fiona didn't care if she had to hear about a fire and goats. It could be the last time she'd ever see her grandmother even in a semi-lucid state and she intended to capture every moment in a memory so she could visit it again when the dementia claimed Irene's mind forever. Dora June talked and Irene hummed as she rocked back and forth on the sofa with the baby in her arms.

When Dora June finished talking, Irene smiled sweetly. "I'm so sorry but I'm glad that you and Truman finally came to your senses and adopted some kids. Now you can have this baby back and I think maybe it's time for my nap.

This baby reminds me of a little girl I knew a long time ago but I can't remember her name today."

Dora June took Audrey and held her close. "It's okay. Next time maybe me and you will break out of this place and go to Frankie's to do some dancing."

Irene put a finger over her lips. "Shhh, don't tell the girls about that night. Our mamas would have sent us off to a convent if they'd known."

"Yes, they would have but it was the last night before I married Truman and we wanted to be wild and free," Dora June said.

Allie gasped.

Lizzy giggled softly.

Fiona grinned so big that her face hurt.

"Frankie's isn't a place for young ladies," Irene declared vehemently as she shook her finger at Allie, Lizzy, and Fiona. "Don't any of you go there."

"Yes, ma'am." Allie nodded.

"Now get on out of here and let me sleep. Sometimes I have the best dreams about a house and a bunch of little girls in it."

Tears streamed down Fiona's cheeks and dripped onto her shirt as they walked Irene down the hallway to her room. Lizzy's hand closed around hers and Allie hugged her from the other side. It wasn't fair that the grandmother who had lived with them her whole life was in that condition. Fiona's heart was heavy with guilt. She should have come home more often. She should have told her mother about the divorce when it happened rather than being so stubborn; then she would have been here the whole past year.

"It's okay," Lizzy whispered as she wrapped an arm

around her sister. "We still cry, too, but today was a good day. She knew all of us for a little while."

Irene went right to her bed and curled up like a little child. Fiona covered her with a crocheted throw and they all tiptoed out of the room. Allie closed the door behind them and Dora June put the baby in Fiona's arms instead of Allie's. "You need this right now."

"My heart is breaking," Fiona said when they were in the lobby again. "I had no idea that it would be this hard."

"Before we take another step, I owe every one of you an apology," Dora June said. "I wouldn't blame you if you kicked me out on the road halfway home the way I've acted in the past. Allie, I was beyond rude to you. Lizzy, I tried to run your life. Fiona, I gave you advice against Jud and I didn't even know him or Blake or Toby before I judged them."

"Accepted and you are forgiven," Lizzy said. "Now let's go get some retail therapy to make Fiona feel better. What store are we going to first?"

"Whichever one is closest to the front door at the mall." Dora June smiled. "Thank you all for everything."

"Merry Christmas to us all," Lizzy said. "Now that you are our friend, maybe Fiona won't be in trouble as much as we were."

"Not if she'll hang up her coat, turn out the lights, and lock the door. Truman fussed all day yesterday about that," Dora June said.

"You left your coat on the floor?" Lizzy whispered incredulously. "What…oh, my God…were you drunk or undressing on the way up the stairs?"

"Was Jud involved in this?" Allie asked.

Fiona widened her big green eyes, smiled, and told a

lie. "No, he was not." She did cross her fingers behind her back and since it was the Christmas season and everyone was in a forgiving mood, maybe God would let it slide. She changed the subject. "Next Sunday I am going to decorate a tree for Granny in her room. Who is coming with me?"

Three hands shot up in the air.

"Good. I'm holding you to it. We need to have presents to put under the tree. Candy. Cookies. Stuff that she'll enjoy. Let's wrap it all up so she'll have lots of presents."

"Chocolate," Lizzy said. "She loves chocolate on anything from doughnuts to ice cream."

They all nodded in agreement. Fiona felt a little better when Allie parked at the front entrance of the mall. She fully well intended to buy Audrey something first, but her mind was on what she'd like to get for Jud when she and the entourage entered the mall.

* * *

Jud was waiting in the chair on the landing when Fiona and Dora June came home that evening. Truman was snoring in the recliner in front of the television in the living room but he roused enough to fuss about all the bags Dora June brought into the house, his voice carrying up the stairs without losing a bit of its volume.

"What'd you do, buy out the whole store? We ain't got a house to keep all this stuff in anymore. All we got is one room," Truman complained.

Dora June fussed right back at him. "Oh, Truman, stop your bellyachin'. We got the whole corner of the living room to store it until I can get it all wrapped and put under the tree. Be thankful the girls wouldn't let me stop at that RV place and buy a travel trailer. I wanted to, but they laughed and said you'd never leave Dry Creek, not even to camp out on the Brazos. I think we should buy one and go see as much of the whole United States as we can before we die. Maybe even Canada. I always wanted to see Niagara Falls."

"You wouldn't leave your goats, so stop talking that nonsense," he continued to fuss.

"I'll barbecue every one of those little critters and serve them at the Christmas potluck if you'll buy me a big old RV and take me to see all the sights in this wonderful country," she said.

"You'd be whinin' to come home in less than a week."

"Damned if I would," Dora June said.

"You cussed on Sunday."

"Shows you how serious I am."

Jud kept the laughter to a chuckle. Truman in a travel trailer would take more than a Christmas miracle. It would take even more angel dust than heaven had on hand.

Fiona hung up her coat. "I'm taking my stuff to one of the spare bedrooms. I'm too tired to wrap presents tonight. Dora June about wore all of us out. And, Truman, she really did want to stop at the RV place when we passed it."

"She can shop the legs off a two-year-old who's had candy for dinner and supper," Truman said gruffly.

Jud heard a little pride in his comment. It was taking a while but Truman was coming around and his bark was a hell of a lot worse than his bite. He might just be willing to burn that Scrooge attitude by Christmas day after all.

"You are about ninety percent bluff, you old goat," he whispered as he got to his feet and met Fiona halfway up the stairs to help her carry her bags.

"I played dominoes with Truman all afternoon," he said.

"Really?"

The remnants of whatever enticing perfume added with the cold wind she'd brought in with her stirred Jud's desire to hold her, to kiss her again, and to go many steps on past that.

"I lost ten dollars in quarters to that sly old fart. He's got a poker face and I promise you one thing, I will never play cards with him. Where are we going with these?" he asked.

"Into Lizzy's old room." She slung open the door and set the bags on the bed before slumping into a chair beside the dresser. "Have a seat and talk to me. I'm exhausted. Can you believe it's only three weeks until Christmas day?"

He sat down on the end of the bed and picked up one of her feet, unzipped her black boot, removed it, and massaged her foot. "Poor baby," he drawled.

"God, that's wonderful."

"You looked stunning in church this morning," he said.

She pushed her hair back behind her ears. "But now I'm so tired that I look like the last rose of summer that the little dog pissed on."

"You do have a way with words." He put her foot down and picked up the other one.

"I'll miss this whole thing we have when I leave," she said.

"And you'll never come home again?" He dug into the heel of her foot, working out a knot.

"Sure I'll come home but you'll find someone else to give foot rubs to. Long distance never works," she said.

"So we would be in a long-distance relationship?" he asked.

"We'd have to be in a relationship first. And let's face it, Jud, with me leaving town, I don't see the sense in starting one. Anytime I came home to visit family, it'd be too weird."

"What if we go real slow and see where it leads?"

The words made a lot of sense, but the feel of her skin, even that on her foot, sure told him a different story. He wanted to treat whatever chemistry they had between them like a roller coaster. Go very fast! Scream! Wrap up in the afterglow that arrives after sex and cuddle until they were both rested enough get on the roller coaster for a second ride.

"Truman probably did us a favor on Friday night." She pulled her foot out of his hand and pushed up out of the chair.

He followed her across the landing to her room and put an arm on either side of her, caging her against the door. Her long lashes fluttered shut and fanned out on her cheeks. The tip of her tongue tempted him as she moistened her full lips. He lowered his face and shut his eyes, using his senses to guide him straight to her mouth. The electricity between them was so hot that he could hear sparks crackling all over the landing.

When the kiss ended, Fiona opened those fascinating deep green eyes and gazed past the bottom of his heart into his soul. "I thought we were going to take this slow," she murmured.

"This is slow, darlin'. Fast would be a walk backward to your bed or maybe I'd pick you up and carry you to mine."

She tiptoed and brushed a quick kiss across his lips. "I can do slow—for a little while."

Chapter Fifteen

Truman fussed and fumed but he kept feeding the lights up the ladder to Blake, who then sent them on up to Judd, who snapped them into place around the porch roof. "Craziest damn thing I've ever seen," Truman grumbled. "Put up lights on the sixth day of December and take them down on January second. All this work and energy for less than a month and just think of the electricity they use. Why, I could buy two new goats or a nice bull calf for the price of what the utility bill will cost."

"Come on, Truman, all that complainin' ain't foolin' us one bit. You really like Christmas but you just like to bitch about it." Toby finished the last string of lights around the porch railing.

"I like Thanksgiving. Make a turkey and dressin', watch a parade on the television, and then it's over. This blame holiday lasts a month and costs a fortune. And women are the ones who do the bitchin'. Men just state the way things are," he protested.

"Well, you are really going to hate what I'm about to tell you, then," Jud said. "We've decided to have a Christmas ranch party and you're going to be Santa Claus and give out presents to all the kids. You reckon Katy would mind if we borrowed her pillows to make you a little fatter?"

Truman shook a bony, veined finger at Jud. "What kind of funny weed have you been smokin', boy? I ain't doin' no such thing! I wouldn't even be out here now, but Dora June said if I didn't help y'all she was going to burn the ham for breakfast tomorrow mornin'. But I will not be Santa Claus, skinny or fat."

Blake handed the last light up to Jud and crawled off the ladder. "Then we'll go to plan B. Herman said he'd be glad to wear the red suit if you wear your normal stubborn jackass self."

Jud came down the ladder and carried it around to the side of the house. "He even said he'd ask the preacher to borrow the suit from the church."

"Where are you going to have this thing? Your biggest barn is full of hay," Truman said.

"Katy said we could have it here at the house since the weather is supposed to be cold all month," Blake answered. "Dora June has promised to help cook for it, but we understand if you choose to stay in your bedroom and not even come out. Herman don't like you so much anyway, and you can be sure he and Lucy will be here."

Truman shoved his hands into his pockets. "How long would I have to stay in that monkey suit?"

Toby hiked a hip on the porch railing. "Depends on how many kids show up. We're making it an open house, so folks can show up anytime during the evening and stay as long as they like. Children normally are in bed by about nine, so we figured that Santa Claus would show up about seven, give out some presents. Probably thirty minutes at the most."

"But don't worry about it," Blake said. "The preacher said that Herman could use the suit."

Truman crossed his arms over his thin chest and glared at Blake. "I give that church more money than Herman does, so if I want to wear that suit, I'll damn sure wear it. Herman ain't got no more right to it than I do. Let's get in out of this cold. Ain't showin' that we got a lick of sense standin' out here when there's a blaze goin' in the fireplace and our job is done out here."

"You going to come down the chimney at the party?" Blake opened the door for Truman.

"Hell, no! I'm goin' to get ready in one of them empty bedrooms upstairs and come down the steps. I might even slide down the banister just to show Herman that I ain't old as dirt like he is," Truman said. "Is Dora June going to be Mrs. Claus?"

"She said she'd be glad to dress up and serve cookies and punch to the guests." Jud followed him into the house.

"I'll show Herman that he can't run things. I'll even help her." Truman's bony chin shot up three notches. "That is, after I hand out the presents. And a ranch party ain't a sissy party. You need a corner to set up for drinks. Ranchers like beer and whiskey."

"You going to be the bartender, too?"

"I am not. I might cuss and take a nip when I'm sickly, but I ain't goin' to be fixin' nobody drinks. One of y'all can do that. It's your party, not mine. I'm just Santa damn Claus."

Dora June and the three Logan sisters were at the table

with notebooks spread out when Jud reached the dining room. Audrey had begun to fuss about being left alone in her swing too long, so he took her out and carried her to the nearest rocking chair.

Blake stood behind Allie's chair and kissed her on the top of her light brown hair. She looked up at him adoringly with the darkest brown eyes Jud had ever seen. That's what he wanted to see in a woman's eyes when she looked at him. Pure adoration and love with nothing held back.

Toby pulled up a chair close to Lizzy's and looked at the figures she was writing down. He frowned but she patted him on the shoulder.

"Do you really think we need that much liquor?" Toby's eyebrows shot up.

"It's a ranch party, not a church social. Ranchers expect something more than watered-down punch. If the Lucky Penny is going to get its name in the pot with the big ranchers in this area, you'd best give the folks who come to this party good booze," Lizzy answered.

"And good food," Allie said. "We'll make the desserts, the Christmas cookies, and the candies, but we're getting barbecue from a really good caterer in Throckmorton. We'll set up a table with punch and cookies in the foyer. If we move the furniture out of the living room, we can set up small tables for four."

"Y'all really got busy with this," Jud said.

"We did our part." Fiona winked.

"So did you call Herman?" Dora June asked.

"He did not!" Truman said loudly. "That rotten old fool would scare the kids with his big booming voice. I'll be Santa Claus, and then after I give the presents to whatever kids are here, I'll help you with the punch table, Dora June."

Dora June's eyes came close to popping out of her head and rolling across the floor. "Well, Truman O'Dell, I think you'll make a much better Santa Claus than Herman, and Lucy is going to be so jealous of me."

"Good. That meddlin' woman needs to be jealous of you. I'm going to take a nice warm bath and go to bed. All this decoratin' crap done wore me out," Truman said gruffly, and headed toward his bedroom.

* * *

Fiona took a quick shower, checked the hall, and then trotted to her bedroom with nothing but a towel around her body. She dried off, then slid on a pair of cotton bikini underpants and an oversize red plaid flannel shirt that hung to her knees. She was brushing the tangles from her wet hair when a gentle knock on the door drew her attention from the vanity mirror.

"Come on in," she said.

"You sure?" The door swung open and Jud stood there like a blond Greek god in a pair of red flannel pajama pants and a white tank top that hugged his body like a glove.

"Of course. We're over twenty-one and I expect we can be trusted since the door is open." She smiled. "You can have the recliner. Soon as I got my hair brushed out I was going to come over to your room. I'm dying to know how you got Truman to be Santa Claus."

When he sat down in the recliner, the overhead light lit up the water droplets still hanging like diamonds on his hair. The stubble on his face was downright sexy.

"It was kind of funny." His smile lit the room up far more than any artificial light could do, and then he went on to tell her word for word what he could remember of the conversation.

When he finished, tears were rolling down her cheeks. "My sides hurt and I can't breathe. That is priceless," she said. "He and Herman Hudson have never gotten along. I bet it's because Herman and Lucy have all those kids. You did a bang-up job by baiting him with Herman."

He stood and held out a hand. "Well, thank you, Miz Fiona. Now give me that brush and I'll work on the back of your hair."

She put the brush in it and he gently ran it through her hair. When it hit a snag, he laid the brush aside and worked the tangle out, one hair at a time. When there were no more rats, he dug his fingers all the way to her scalp and massaged. She thought that his foot rubs were a turn-on but her body turned into a quivering mass of jelly when he worked on her scalp.

"Sweet Lord! If all the Dawsons are as good as you, no wonder my sisters fell head-over-heels crazy in love." She shut her eyes and enjoyed every hot little quiver that shot through her body.

Jud bent forward, swept her hair to one side, and planted a kiss on her neck that sent her hormones into a spiral. Slow be damned. She wanted him.

Pretty, brilliant sparks danced around the trailer and Lizzy's knees went weak. She leaned into him and the second kiss was even more sensational. Hormones whined. Her heart thumped so hard that her chest hurt. Her hands were clammy and his hands on her back were like fire. She wanted him and nothing was going to fill the aching void but Toby.

Jud caught her gaze in the mirror, his brown eyes boring into hers with questions. "I should leave now before we go from low gear to high and have regrets later," he whispered huskily.

His tone said that he was every bit as affected as she was. His eyes said he wanted more like she did. His hand on her shoulder was warm even through her knit shirt. The world stood still in that moment. The moon didn't rise. The stars held their breath.

She put a hand over his. "Shut the door and stay."

"I thought we were going to go slow," he whispered.

"The second time, we will. It's been a very long time for me, so if I get in a hurry the first time, I promise I'll slow it down to low gear the second time around," she said.

"But, Fiona, you are..."

"This is tonight, Jud. Not tomorrow. Not next week or next spring. Just tonight between two consenting, very hungry adults. No questions. No promises. And I don't think Dora June can hear the squeaky springs all the way in her bedroom."

She flipped around and tugged his shirt up over his head, tiptoeing to kiss his Adam's apple before digging her fingertips into his thick hair and pulling his face toward hers. His lips were pure honey to her starving heart. She pressed her whole body against his, feeling the effect below the elastic waist of his pajama pants. She pulled away from him, their lips making a sucking noise when the kiss broke.

Running her hands through the soft brown hair on his chest, she felt his big hands fumbling with the buttons on her shirt. Finally, he got them all unfastened and tossed it to the side. He held her breasts, one in each hand, staring at them as if they were gold.

"You are so beautiful," he said.

"And you are so sexy it takes my breath away," she whispered as she tugged his pants down over his firm hips.

"Oh, my!" she gasped.

"And so ready." He pulled her pants down and then slowly bit at the side of her bikini underpants. Taking them down an inch at a time, his hand barely brushing her skin, teasing, tempting all the way down was far hotter than massaging her feet or her scalp. Her insides vibrated with desire.

When her underwear was on the floor, he feathered kisses so light that her skin ached for more all the way from toes to knees to the outside of her thighs and up to her breasts. He stopped to run his tongue over each one and then quickly moved on up to her lips, where he brought the game home with a kiss so passionate and filled with promise that she leaned into him, pressing her naked body to his. With a hop, her legs were suddenly wrapped around his waist, her body pressing against his erection. With a few deft movements, she could have all of him inside her, but she waited to see what was next.

He carried her toward the bed, shut the door with the heel of his bare foot, and laid her head on the pillow. He hovered over her, his eyes never leaving hers for several seconds and then their lips met again. The excitement of their tongues touching, the feel of his body heat so close that she could actually see the flames in her imagination, the tightness of the erection; it was more than she'd ever experienced and she wanted it all. Tomorrow didn't matter. Tonight she wanted to be satisfied and the only person who could do that was Jud Dawson.

"You make me so damned hot that I can feel the blaze and still I'm willing to walk right into the fire to have you." He ran the tips of his fingers down her rib cage, passed the curve of her waist, crossed over, and back up the other side.

"I like the way your eyes go all dreamy when you touch me," she said.

"So do yours. They remind me of the green water of the ocean down in Florida. They're inviting me to dive right in." Tucking his fist under her chin, his eyes fluttered shut and his mouth covered hers, his tongue touching her lips, asking permission before he entered.

"Yes, they are. The water is so warm that it's about to boil," she gasped when the kiss ended. She traced his lips with her fingers, letting them roam from there down his chest to his erection. Then suddenly she pushed him backward and flipped over on top of him. In an instant, ready or not, he was inside her and she'd taken over the whole game. They rocked together until she was panting. He pulled her closer to him and with a fast roll he was on top and the tempo increased until there was an explosion like she'd never felt before. The glazed look in his eyes said that he was every bit as satisfied as she was.

"Oh my God, Fiona." One word at a time came out because that's all the air he could muster up from his lungs.

"I know." She cuddled next to him, her ear pressed to his thumping heart and her legs still quaking. Nothing at any time had prepared her for what she'd just experienced. Not her ex-husband, not the boys in college—no one, ever!

She'd said no regrets and that tomorrow didn't matter. If she stood by her word, then all she'd have would be the memories of that night. But dear Lord, what memories they were.

He pulled her even closer. "I should go."

"Not yet. Stay a little while longer."

They fell asleep in each other's arms, totally exhausted and absolutely satisfied.

Chapter Sixteen

Fiona awoke slowly and reached for Jud but he wasn't there. She was wrapped up inside the white chenille bedspread like a caterpillar in a cocoon. The fringe from the edges tickled her nose and she sneezed three times in rapid succession before she finally broke free from her bindings.

Something between freezing rain and sleet beat against the windowpane when she slung her legs off the bed. Jud's scent was on her body, so she gathered up her nightclothes, checked the hall, and jogged to the bathroom for a quick shower. If she could detect that wonderful smell of shaving lotion and pure sex, then Dora June would take one sniff and the questions would start.

Instead of the plain old shower soap she usually used, she chose a rose-scented body wash and just in case there was anything left of Jud lingering behind in her hair, she washed it, too. Tingles shot up and down her spine when she shut her eyes and thought about him brushing the tangles from her hair and then massaging her scalp. Then she flashed on his naked body on hers and she had to remember to breathe.

Warm water sprayed over her back for a full minute after she'd rinsed the last of the conditioner from her hair; then she turned off the water and stepped out of the tub. One towel was wrapped turban style around her head and another around her body as she went from bathroom to bedroom, where she dressed before padding downstairs for breakfast.

"Looks like we're in for a nasty day," Dora June said.

"Yes, it does and I still didn't get those snow tires put on the car like Mama wanted me to do. I'll take it easy," Fiona answered.

"You might as well close up the store and stay home."

"There may not be a lot of customers, but I could get all caught up on my bookkeeping work." Fiona removed a lid from a pot on the stove and took a big sniff. "I love your oatmeal, Dora June."

"It ain't nothing special. I just add some granola to it, lots of butter and cream, right off the top of the milk that Truman brings in every morning, and a touch of cinnamon. Oatmeal is kind of bland without some help." Dora June beamed at the compliment.

Fiona listened with one ear as Dora June talked excitedly about the upcoming party, about doing some more Christmas shopping on Sunday if the weather was fit, and how happy she was that Truman had decided to play the part of Santa. "Although I'll never understand how them boys got him to do it. Why, you'd think it was his idea." She went from one tangent to another.

Fiona nodded at the right moments. When she'd swallowed the last bite Fiona pointed at the clock on the microwave. "Oh my! It's already seven o'clock. My coffee drinkers will think I've died. I've got to get going. Save all the ugly cookies for me." She took the stairs two at a time with Dora June's voice following her.

"You wear something warm. Your mama will be disappointed in me if you get sick. And drive safe!"

"Yes, ma'am," Fiona threw over her shoulder.

* * *

Dora June was a prophet. Not even the regular coffee drinkers came by the store that morning. The sleet had stopped, but the freezing drizzle coated every twig on the mesquite and scrub oaks in that part of Texas. Even the cow tongue cactus got a blanket of ice on the spiny little needles protruding from their thick leaves.

Nadine came by in the middle of the morning to drop off the week's journey tapes and the business from her café. "I've hung a sign on the door that I'm closing early and won't be in tomorrow or Friday. I hate winter. This didn't start until you came back. Did you cause it?"

"Not me. If I would have brought anything, it would have been heat. It never does this in Houston."

"Well, crap! I was hoping I could blame you for this." Nadine sighed.

"Maybe it would warm up if you'd go home and spend the whole afternoon in bed with your new husband," Fiona teased.

"I tried that last night and look what happened. We got freezing rain. I'm afraid to do it again for fear we'll have a downright blizzard. Maybe you need to help out and take that sexy man you're livin' with to bed."

Fiona fanned herself with the back of her hand. "Oh, darlin', there would be a heat wave come through here that would fry the whiskers off Truman's goats if I did something that wild."

"I don't have a doubt that you are right, so go home and try it. I'll see you Friday unless this keeps up. I don't mind a white Christmas, but I hate ice." Nadine ducked her head against the driving wind trying to push her back into the store.

At noon, Lizzy popped inside the back room. Ice crystals covered her brown suede jacket and stuck to her stocking hat. "God almighty! What did we do to deserve another hard winter?"

"Should be good for business. Don't farmers and ranchers need more cattle feed when it's this cold? Fix us both a cup of hot chocolate and pull up a chair. Are you closing, too?"

Lizzy filled two mugs and swiped two maple-covered doughnuts from the glass enclosure. "Too? Did Nadine close the café?"

"She just left. The beauty shop and the day care have signs on the doors so I guess I'm the only person in town who's still open." Fiona reached for a doughnut. "What are you going to do all day if you close up?"

"I'm going to help Dora June make cookies for the party."

"Hey, where's Lizzy…Oh there you are." Allie pushed her way through the back door with Audrey in a carrier covered with a bright colored baby quilt.

"Holy crap, Allie! What are you doing out in this with a baby?" Fiona scolded.

"Dora June said to bring three dozen eggs and a bottle of vanilla extract with me. I didn't have that at the house so I ran by to get it. Audrey is fine. See." Allie whipped the quilt off to show Fiona a smiling baby girl all bundled up in pink fleece.

"Come here to Aunt Fee-Fee, darlin' girl," Fiona crooned as she unhooked all the buckles and took the baby from the carrier. "Aren't you the cutest thing ever? You look like a princess in all that pink. I believe you need a tiara with pink rhinestones in it for your Christmas present."

Lizzy's brown eyes twinkled. "You look good holding that baby."

"She really does," Allie agreed.

Fiona's full lips curled in a smile and then it hit her like a wrecking ball. She hadn't even thought of protection the night before. Jud had most likely thought she was on the pill, but she hadn't used them in a year. Why buy something that cost a fortune without the help of insurance when it wasn't necessary?

"Are you okay?" Lizzy asked worriedly. "You look like you just saw a ghost."

"I'm fine." Fiona managed a tight smile. "Don't start trying to fix me up with every eligible bachelor in the county."

"Wouldn't dream of it," Allie laughed. "But give the baby one more kiss because if I don't get the eggs and vanilla to Dora June soon, she can't make any more cookies. According to her, it won't matter if the ranchers have to use sleds and mules to pull them, the party will be huge and a success."

"Oh, yeah?" Lizzy asked.

"She says that no rancher would stay home when Bubba Joe's catering barbecue and when there's free booze on a cold night," Allie said. "Besides, everyone in this part of

Texas will turn out just to see Truman dressed up like Santa damn Claus."

"Who's going to Wichita Falls to buy the liquor?" Fiona asked, but her mind was still on unprotected sex.

"Jud volunteered to pick it up next week. You going with him?" Lizzy asked.

"Depends on how many cookies y'all get made. I might need to stay home and help cook." Fiona kissed Audrey's chubby cheek once more and handed her off to Allie.

"What's going on with you two?" Allie asked bluntly.

"We're friends, I guess." How could she answer that honestly when she wasn't sure what they were or what she really wanted them to be? How would last night affect anything they might or might not have? She mentally calculated how many days until she'd know for sure if the night had produced a positive sign on a pregnancy test and came up with the lucky number seven.

In one week, just two days before the party, she would know because she'd never been a day late in her life. Regular as clockwork and hopefully this wasn't ovulation time.

"He looks at you like you could be more than friends," Allie said.

"That's because there's not an abundance of eligible women in Dry Creek. When we have the party, you can bet all the women will come out of the woodwork to get a chance at him and he'll look at me a hell of a lot differently then."

"Will that make you jealous?"

Fiona shook her head. "Hell no! We'd never—"

Lizzy cut her off. "Never say never. I said it and Allie said it and look what happened. Not that I'm complainin' one bit. If you get tired of book work, come on home and we'll let you play with the baby if you don't want to cook with us."

Ten minutes later, Fiona was alone with nothing but her scary thoughts and numbers on the computer that wouldn't stop blurring when she looked at them.

* * *

The truck tires slid to one side of the slippery road before Jud got control of the steering wheel. The wipers worked as fast as they could, but the sleet and snow mixture fell faster than they could swipe the windshield clean. Stupid! Stupid! That's what he was. He never had unprotected sex. It didn't matter if she was on the pill or swore she'd had a hysterectomy; he took precautions of his own.

He slapped the steering wheel, went into another long, greasy slide, and grabbed the thing like a long-lost brother, straightening up in a few seconds. If only it were that easy to get control of his irresponsibility, the world would be right.

There wasn't one single car or truck on Main Street. Of course not: All the smart people were home counting their condom supply. He circled around behind the convenience store. Katy's red car was right next to the back door and the lights from the store cast a yellow glow out the window through the driving winter storm.

He slid in beside the car and ran from truck to the back room of the store. Without knocking, he rushed inside, stomped the white stuff from his boots onto the rug in front of the door, and looked around for Fiona. The desk chair was empty. The lights in the front of the store were turned off and her computer screen was dark.

"Fiona," he called out, and heard the sound of her boots on the tile floor.

"I was making sure everything was locked up for the weekend," she said. "What brings you to town? Does Dora June need something else? Good thing you got here when you did because I'm sure not coming back out in this miserable weather once I get home." She paused. "About last night..."

"I'm so, so sorry. I always, always..." His chest tightened.

Fiona hiked a hip on the desk. "It's not just your fault. I didn't think of it, either."

Those green eyes drew him to her. He should take her into his arms and assure her that if their unprotected sex had caused a problem he would share in the responsibility. But his feet were glued to the floor.

"You've got that deer-in-the-headlights look in your eyes." She managed a weak smile.

She was right. He felt like a big buck whitetail deer standing in the middle of the road with a semi coming right at him. What in the hell had he been thinking? He hadn't been! That was the whole problem. He wanted Fiona; she wanted him. They were consenting adults.

"I wouldn't marry you, even if I was pregnant," she said softly.

"Why?"

"Because of the way you look right now and because you are going to live in Dry Creek and I'm going to move away. Those are the facts that can't be changed. Life is more than a brand of cereal. If it was meant that I'd be a single parent, then so be it. If not and according to the calendar, the time of ovulation should be over, then so be that, too. I'm learning to deal with the problems life throws at me, Jud."

"Well, I want you to know that if a baby happens, you won't have to deal with it alone. I would never..."

She smiled. "I know."

"Are we good, then?" he asked.

"We're good." She nodded. "Front door is locked. Lights are out. Thermostat is adjusted. Book work is all caught up. Can we go home now?"

He nodded and held the door open for her.

She'd said the words, but he hadn't felt them—not at all. Instead of instant relief, his heart was a stone in his chest. The wind blew freezing rain across his face with such force that he ducked his chin and jogged to his truck. He was inside with the wipers on and the truck engine running when he noticed that Fiona was frantically scraping at the layer of ice on her windshield.

Leaving his engine running, he grabbed his scraper and hurried over to help her. Some boyfriend he was, not even giving her a thought.

Wait, boyfriend?

Why not? asked a little voice in his head.

Because they were too different, wanted different things. Roots. Wings. Country living. Big city life. Oil did not mix with water.

"Another reason I don't like north-central Texas," she yelled above the howling wind.

"Get in the car and I'll finish this. You don't even have gloves. Your fingers will freeze. We have got to get those other tires on this car," he shouted.

She didn't argue, which was a miracle. He'd expected a dirty look that would melt the ice and scare away the gray skies but she nodded and got into the car. He could see her blowing on her hands to warm them and mentally kicked himself for not taking care of this sooner.

Boyfriend?

The word popped back into his mind.

Friends?

He argued with the voice in his head.

With benefits?

He shook his head. He couldn't do that because Fiona deserved so much more.

What if she finds someone like a fancy lawyer?

A wave of hot jealousy covered him. With every jab of the scraper against the layer of ice, he gave himself another lecture on how he had no right to be jealous because she'd been up front and honest about her future. And that did not have a rough old cowboy in the picture.

He finally finished the job, waved at her, and trotted back to his truck. He waited for Fiona to back the car out and start moving slowly toward home before he followed at a safe distance behind her.

Déjà vu!

He held his breath when she went into a long, greasy slippery ride toward the ditch at one point, but she got control and made her way around the next turn into the lane to home. She applied too much brake when she reached the yard, but it was far enough back that when the wheels came to a stop, she was still two feet away from the white picket yard fence.

"That was close," she yelled as she crawled out of the car and started to run toward the porch.

He slammed the truck door and was only a few steps behind her when she slipped on the slick sidewalk and went down, arms flailing as she tried to latch on to anything to break her fall. Before she hit the ground, he reached forward to scoop her up in his arms like a bride, but leather-soled boots and ice do not make for a perfect situation. He managed to pick her up but then he went down in a sideways roll where he landed on his back with her on top of him.

His cowboy hat sailed through the air, landing on a fence post and twirling several times before it stopped to hang there, waiting for him to reclaim it. He became the sled and she was the rider as they slid across the ice-covered yard toward the post where the hat had come to rest. They came to an abrupt stop when she threw out her hands and grabbed the trunk of an old pecan tree in the front yard. With the speed they were picking up in another five seconds, his head would have brought them to rest on a fence post.

"I think you might have saved me from a fractured skull," he said breathlessly.

"You probably saved me from a broken arm or neck," she panted as she rolled to one side.

"Are we going to attempt standing up or just lie here and turn into Popsicles?"

"I was thinking icicles," she huffed. "But if you want to get up real slow like and brace your back against that tree trunk, I might let you help me to my feet."

He chuckled as he eased up, one tiny bit at a time.

"What's so funny?" she asked.

"That was one wild ride, but it wasn't as wild as last night," he answered.

"Honey, if it had been as hot as last night, we would have melted this ice and stopped a lot sooner. Look, it's snowing again." She brushed a flake from his hair.

He grabbed her hand and held it against his face. "I can't believe you are so calm about us not using birth control. I was freaking out."

"So was I at first, but what's done is done and can't be undone. I did stock up on condoms while I was cleaning the bathrooms at the store this afternoon, though." She grinned.

"So does that mean..."

"What in the world is going on out here?" Dora June called from the open door. "Lord, I'm glad we don't have close neighbors or the gossip would run rampant by morning. Get on in out of the cold. Supper's ready."

"What the hell?" Truman yelled over her shoulder. "Good God almighty. Kids these days! Shut the door, Dora June, before you let all the warm air out."

Jud rolled to one side and sat up. "You think they're going to ground us?"

Fiona used the tree to pull herself to her feet. "I hope they let us eat supper before they send us to our rooms, but I don't mind being grounded for a week or even more."

"How many condoms did you buy?"

"Plenty enough for even you, cowboy."

It was a bad idea. No, it was a damn horrible idea to continue on this path they'd started, but he could no more stop it than he could a mad Angus bull coming at him at full speed. He'd suffer the consequences later, but right now, he wanted nothing more than to be grounded to his room for the next week.

"I expect we'd better get started early, right?" he asked.

She pointed toward the porch where her hobo bag had come to a stop when it stopped sliding.

"Thank goodness nothing flew out," he teased. "It would put a whole new meaning to 'a cold one.'"

She giggled. "Let's get inside before we freeze to death and Truman has to dig two graves."

"I bet he'd bitch us back alive," Jud laughed as he slung an arm around Fiona's shoulders, grabbed his hat, and then slowly walked with her to the porch where she retrieved her purse.

"Let me see," he whispered.

She opened the cloth bag and he gasped. It was half full all right, but they were all glow-in-the dark condoms and even through the wrapper, they lit up the whole inside of her purse in neon green, yellow, pink, and blue.

"What's wrong? Does the big sexy cowboy not like pink?" she asked with a slight giggle.

"Hell no, I've just never been real partial to yellow," he answered.

Chapter Seventeen

Only sixteen more shopping days until Christmas," the DJ on the store radio said. "For all you folks on the road trying to get some shopping done this morning in central Texas, drive safe and keep your radio tuned to..."

Fiona blocked out the DJ's voice and tried to decide if she liked blue or green better, or if one color made hotter sex than the other, when Sharlene came out of the women's bathroom at the convenience store and threw her hands up in anger. "Are you aware that the condom machine in there is empty?"

"Try the men's bathroom," Fiona said without taking her eyes off the coffee stains she was washing from the table.

"I did and it's empty, too."

"Must be this weather. Folks got to stay warm somehow," Fiona laughed.

Maybe she should ask the man who filled the dispensers once a week if he had some in Christmas red and green.

"Well, dammit!" Sharlene huffed. "I'm out and my boyfriend is planning to be here tonight and tomorrow. I've closed down the day care until Monday with this weather and that leaves us lots of time to play around in the bedroom. Don't suppose you'd share any of your personal stock, would you?"

"Why would I have any? I don't have a boyfriend." Fiona skirted the issue. "And why doesn't he buy them?"

"He usually does, but I've always kept a backup stock on hand. Oh! Oh! I forgot about Nadine's. There'll be some in the machines in her bathroom and I have a key." Sharlene wiped her brow in a dramatic gesture.

"Well, aren't you lucky?" Fiona said at the same minute the bell above the door let her know someone was entering the store. She glanced over her shoulder and caught Jud's gaze and wicked little crooked grin. The blush started at the base of her neck and rapidly traveled to her cheeks.

"You are flushed," Sharlene said. "That heater vent right above you has made you too hot or maybe"—she lowered her voice—"it's the customer. You want me to buy a few extra things from Nadine's bathroom so you'll be prepared?"

"No, thanks," Fiona whispered.

"Hey, Jud Dawson, what are you doing in town?" Sharlene asked.

"On my way to Lizzy's for a pickup load of feed and thought I'd take her a cup of hot chocolate," he said smoothly.

"I'm amazed that she's keeping the store open in this weather," Sharlene said as she dropped her hand and reached for the doorknob. "Does she have a machine in her bathroom, Fiona?"

"Of course. The deliveryman has to have at least two stops to even drive all the way up to Dry Creek. You should put one in the bathroom at the day care," Fiona said.

"I'm sure that would go over real well with preschoolers." Sharlene left the store and hurried on down the street to Nadine's café.

"I don't think she's talking about a candy dispenser, is she?" Jud continued to grin.

"I think you know what kind of machine she needs." Fiona started toward the front of the store and he opened his arms.

She walked into them and inhaled slowly, taking in the remnants of that morning's shaving lotion on his face, the cold air still lingering on his coat and the smell of coffee on his breath.

"Last night was amazing," he whispered.

"I think we need some red and green for Christmas day. I could wrap them and put them under the tree," she teased.

"When I open them, will you blush?"

"Probably but then so would you." Fiona took two steps back when a truck pulled up to the gas pumps. In a minute, she was at her place behind the counter and Jud was heading back to the coffee machines. He pumped out two cups of hot chocolate and took them to the counter.

He was putting the change from a five-dollar bill into his pocket when Deke pushed his way into the store.

"Man, this warm feels good. I'm never complaining about the heat of summer again. This chills a grown man to the bone. At least in the summer, we just sweat a lot and drink more beer. I want a big cup of hot chocolate," he said. "And I need to make a run through the bathroom."

"Machine is sold out. Sharlene tried both bathrooms and said there's none left," Fiona said.

"Looks like folks are finding one way to stay warm," Deke chuckled. "I'll just have to leave early tomorrow night and drive into Wichita Falls to a drugstore and stock up. Y'all want me to get you a box while I'm there?"

One of Jud's sexy eyelids slid shut in a sly wink. Fiona could feel the high color in her cheeks but there wasn't a thing she could do about it.

"I cannot believe we are discussing condoms like we would doughnuts and coffee. And the answer is no. I do not need a box." She hoped that her comment would justify the crimson in her face. She hadn't blushed in years, so it had to be living in Dry Creek that brought it on so often.

"You should stock some on the shelves. I bet you'd make a lot of money." He pulled out a couple of dollars and handed them to her to pay for the hot chocolate that he'd drawn up.

"And get sued for causing the old ladies in town to drop dead with heart attacks in my store," Fiona said. "It's a wonder any of them even use the bathrooms."

"Maybe they don't know what those machines are dispensing," Jud said.

Deke chuckled. "Don't fool yourselves. I bet they're the ones guilty for the machines being empty. Can't you just see Truman wearing one of those new glow-in-the dark—"

Fiona leaned all the way across the counter and put her hand on Deke's mouth. "Enough! It'll take all day to get that image out of my head." She shivered.

"I was thinking about Dora June's face if he rolled on—" Jud started.

"Both of you"—Fiona pointed at the door, her face burning red hot—"out, right now!"

Their laughter still echoed in the store five minutes after they'd gone. She refilled her coffee cup and carried it to the back room, where she turned on the computer and went to work on her second job.

* * *

The weather in Texas is as predictable as a seven-month pregnant woman. It changes its mind constantly and is never happy, so when the sun came out that Thursday afternoon, no one was surprised. There was more than one sigh in Throckmorton County and lots of hopes that they'd seen the last of snow, sleet, and ice for a long time.

In spite of the sun, no one else came into town that whole day after Deke and Jud had been thrown out of the store, so Fiona got completely caught up on her work by closing time. The roads were still slick, so she drove home slowly, glad that she'd be there in time for supper since she'd missed lunch and was starving.

The sweet smell of cinnamon welcomed her into the house, but neither Dora June nor Truman were anywhere in sight. She sniffed the air again and sure enough, it was cinnamon, so she followed her nose to the dining room where she found a note propped up beside a platter stacked high with snickerdoodles.

"They've gone to a Christmas party at Henrietta's, whoever that is, and we have the house all to ourselves for about two hours," Jud said from the shadows.

Her heart leapt into her throat and the note fluttered to the floor. "You scared the hell out of me."

In a blur he was across the room. He scooped her into his arms and carried her up the stairs. "I had something better in mind for our time than scaring you," he whispered.

She laid her head against his chest and listened to the steady beat of his heart. She gasped when he opened the bedroom door. Curtains had been drawn, a dozen jar candles were burning around the room, casting their yellow glow, and there were rose petals strewn on the bed—there was no way in hell she could back out of a deal like that. She could hardly even hear for the humming noise her hormones made in her ears. When he laid her on the bed, the fresh smell of roses washed away every sane thought in her head.

"How did you do that? These smell like roses but they are silk."

"Magic." He kissed her long, lingering, and hard. "Only our lips can touch."

"Who said?"

"We are going to make love, Fiona Logan, not have sex," he whispered.

"Is there a difference?" she asked.

"You tell me in two hours."

"How many times have you made love instead of having sex?" she asked.

"Never, and this time we are going to take it slow. It's going to last all night," he said in a husky voice as he bent forward to kiss her on the lips.

Her hands ached with desire to tangle themselves in his hair. Her body wanted his hands to roam over her like they had two nights before. She promised she wouldn't even laugh at glow-in-the-dark protection if he'd take her clothes off and satisfy the deep need threatening to devour her.

"One article of clothing at a time," he said. "You first."

She thought about it, wanting it to be his jeans, but she'd never get them down past his boots. She decided to start with his shirt. Two could play this game even if she was a beginner.

She undid the three buttons at the top of the oatmeal-colored thermal knit shirt and slowly tugged it free of his jeans. Then she pulled it up over his head, stopping to kiss each nipple and his neck on the way. When it was fully off his body, she took time to fold it perfectly and lay it on the end of the bed.

"Aha!" He grinned. "Trying to torment me?" He flashed one of those devastating, heart-stopping smiles that heated her insides. "Just remember, darlin', don't dish it out if you can't take it."

He removed one of her boots and then the other and was starting to take off her socks when she shook her head. "That would be two articles, so only the boots."

"Okay, darlin', if that's the way you want it." He massaged her calves through the fabric of her skinny jeans and her feet through her socks.

She'd had massages of all kinds. Full body, hot rocks, the whole works. But nothing affected her like sinking into the depths of his brown eyes as he worked all the kinks from her lower legs and feet. Lord, if the look in his eyes really held the promise of what was to come, they might really wake Dora June with all the noise. Her soul hovered up there near the ceiling somewhere and her heart told her repeatedly she was a fool if she ever let this man get away from her.

"Do we have a time limit between takeoff and the next turn?" She gasped when he bent and strung soft kisses from the top of her sock to below her knee.

"Three minutes or we'll lose too much time," he drawled.

"My turn." She sat up, pushed him back on the bed, and straddled his waist. The silver buckle of the leather belt hooked into a hole, so it was easy to undo. Getting it through the loops with him lying on his back was another thing but she managed with thirty seconds to go. She covered the bulge behind his zipper with her hand and massaged gently.

"Oh. My. God. That's not fair," he groaned.

"All's fair in love and war." She leaned forward and claimed his lips with a long, hot kiss.

"Love and war?" He teased his tongue between her lips.

"Right now the lines are pretty blurred," she said breathlessly when the kiss ended.

He chose her shirt next and proceeded to kiss every inch of flesh above her bra. She fought the urge to shuck her bra and throw it across the room. A few more minutes of that and she was fully well ready to forget about making love and go back to plain old cowboy hot sex.

By the time they were both fully naked, every nerve in her body tingled. Every hormone hummed.

"Please," she said.

"Now?"

"God, yes."

He pulled a condom from the nightstand and she watched him unroll it onto his erection.

She slid into position and locked her legs around him. "I want you, Jud."

With a firm thrust, he entered her and they rocked together in perfect tempo to the buzzing in their ears. Then, just as she was ready to dig her fingers into his back and squeal his name, he slowed down.

"No!" she whimpered.

"We still have thirty minutes." He smiled.

"I'll be nothing but a pile of ashes on your sheets in thirty minutes," she said breathlessly.

The tempo sped up. The noise in her ears got louder and louder. Sparks bounced off the walls and then he said something that had the word *love* in it, or did he? She might have imagined that part in her flight to the top of the sex mountain, where she plunged off the side of the cliff into the cool lake below.

"Holy shit!" she muttered.

"Beats the hell out of sex." He rolled to one side but kept her in his arms.

All the sparks in the room blended together to make a blanket of satisfaction that surrounded them like the warmth of a hot summer night under the stars.

"I've never...," she said.

"Me neither." His lips closed over hers.

Her last thought as she fell asleep in his arms was that she never wanted to leave, not this bed, this house, or Dry Creek.

* * *

On Friday, Jud awoke and watched Fiona sleep for several minutes before he eased out of bed, took a quick shower, dressed, and went to breakfast. He would have far rather spent the whole day in bed with her than have breakfast with Truman and Dora June and then go feed goats.

This thing he felt for her went deeper than anything he'd ever experienced. If this was love, no wonder his cousins were willing to hang up their party boots and settle down. He wanted to awake every morning with Fiona curled up beside him. He wanted to talk to her every night before they went to sleep. Did that mean he was falling in love?

Love!

His fork stopped midway to his mouth.

"What's the matter with you?" Truman asked gruffly. "Got something stuck in your craw?"

Jud downed half a glass of orange juice before he stopped. "Yes, sir, I did but it's better now."

"Well, don't go gettin' sick on me just because the sun is out a little bit today. That don't mean it's not cold as ice cubes out there."

Dora June giggled softly. "You are spoiled, Truman. In two weeks you are spoiled rotten to having someone help you and listen to your stories while y'all work."

"I am not," he protested loudly.

"Yes, you are, whether you admit it or not. Frankly, darlin', I like you better and better." She dropped a kiss on the top of his near-bald head.

Jud bit back the laughter when high color filled Truman's cheeks.

"Hmmph!" The old guy grunted and kept his eyes on his plate until his food was totally gone.

After breakfast, they bundled up and set about doing Truman's chores before Jud went over to Blake's place to work on his own property. Truman acted as if nothing happened and prattled on about the weather, the new president who'd be taking office in a few weeks, and the state the world was in. Jud nodded at the right times, took care of the goats and fed the cattle, chipped ice from the watering troughs, and listened sporadically so if Truman asked a question, he might be able to answer it.

But his mind was on that one word that stunned him

that morning as well as sleeping with Fiona. Not having sex or making love but sleeping with her in his arms all night. He'd slept with women before on occasion when he couldn't figure out a tactful way to leave, but not a single woman in his past had stirred him like Fiona. And it wasn't just the amazing sex. She was dependable, kind, hardworking, loved her family, and then there was the way her smile lit up the whole room and that cute temper when something like a tire blew out. Just exactly the kind of woman Jud needed: sass and love all rolled into one beautiful woman.

"Where's your mind? I asked you three times if you wanted to go have some dinner with me on Sunday. Seems the womenfolks is goin' to see Irene again and then they're going to buy a bunch of shit for this ranch party next week," Truman said.

"I'm sorry. I was—"

"Thinkin' about Fiona. I know. I know," Truman interrupted. "But you got to get a hold of yourself, son. That woman wasn't never the settlin' type and if you are ever goin' to make a go of the Lucky Penny, you'd damn sure better not tie yourself up to a woman who's half bird."

"Bird?" Jud asked.

"You heard me. Soon as she can she'll fly out of this nest again. Ain't nobody, not even her mama, been able to clip her wings for very long. One time when she was about eight years old, she packed a bag and made it to the outskirts of town before they found her."

"What happened?"

"She told Katy that she was going on an adventure. That was Fiona, always looking for something out there beyond

Dry Creek. Now, are we goin' to eat at Nadine's together on Sunday or not?"

Jud cut his eyes around to Truman and rubbed his chin with the palm of his hand. "You buyin' or am I?"

"This time it's my turn. After we get done, we'll have us another go at dominoes and you can invite your two cousins if you've a mind to. They might be getting tired of all this Sunday shit, too."

Jud could hardly sit still and drive. This was a big step for the old scrooge. He might turn Truman O'Dell around by Christmas yet. "Well, I ain't never turned down a free meal yet, so I'll go with you. Reckon we could ask Blake and Toby to meet us there."

"That'd be okay, but I ain't payin' for their dinners, too," Truman said.

* * *

Fiona and Dora June watched reruns of *NCIS* that night on television. Truman had voiced his opinion about folks who watched those crazy cop shows and spent the rest of the evening in his room, probably watching a fishing show and wishing it were summer.

At ten o'clock, Dora June yawned and stood up. "It's an hour past my bedtime, but I wanted to see one more. I expect Truman is already snoring like a grizzly bear, so I'll get on to bed. Wonder what's kept Jud out so late?"

"He called a couple of hours ago and said they had a heifer giving birth out of season. They've got her in the barn and all three of them are out there with her, trying to save the calf," Fiona said with a long sigh.

"Y'all talk up there a lot at night, don't you?"

If you only knew what we do up there at night, Fiona thought.

"Sometimes."

"You like him. I can see it on your face when he's around. I ain't meddlin', but be careful, honey. He's slicker than his cousins. He comes across all sweet and sensitive, but he probably don't even know that he's leadin' a woman on until she gets serious and then he bolts like a jackrabbit in huntin' season."

Fiona frowned. "You think he's leadin' me on? I'm the one who's been ready to bolt. He's the one who wants to put down roots."

Dora June shook her head slowly and pursed her mouth tightly. "Lord knows I love that boy, but that's what he'd have you to believe. Maybe he even believes it himself. But if you told him that you'd changed your mind and was goin' to stay on here in Dry Creek, he'd be livin' in that travel trailer in half an hour."

One corner of Fiona's mouth turned up slightly. "You really think so?"

Dora June patted her on the shoulder as she passed by. "I know so. I know men folks. Good night, Fiona. You'll unplug the Christmas tree lights before you go to bed, won't you?"

"Yes, ma'am, and good night, Dora June."

"There's snickerdoodles on the cabinet if you want a snack."

"Thank you," Fiona called over her shoulder.

* * *

On Saturday morning, Jud opened the kitchen door to find Dora June at her regular business of making breakfast, Truman sitting at the table with a cup of coffee, but Fiona was nowhere in sight.

"Where you been all night? Out with some old hussy?" Truman grumbled.

"Truman O'Dell!" Dora June popped her hands on her hips.

"I stayed over at Blake's. Didn't want to wake y'all. Is that pancakes and sausage?"

"It is and omelets so you have some protein to stick to your ribs," Dora June answered.

"You up to helpin' me or do you need to get a rest?" Truman asked.

"I've had five hours of sleep, so I'm good," Jud said, keeping the smile off his face. They'd both have an acute coronary if they knew he and Fiona had been running on about that much sleep all week.

"Well, sit down and eat your breakfast so we can get goin'. That calf a good one?" Truman asked.

"Fine-lookin' bull calf. Want to go see it once we get the chores done?" Jud asked.

"I might. Why'd you breed a heifer so she'd birth in December? Ain't you got any sense about cows?"

"Didn't do it on purpose. Sometimes those hussies get around the best rancher. You ever had one calve in the middle of the winter?"

"Couple of times, but I sure don't like it. Spring calves are the best and that's when we're ready for them. Not in the winter when we got to keep them in the barn for fear of 'em freezin' to death," Truman answered. "Is it goin' to be a good breeder or just another one to throw in the auction this next fall?"

"A bit hard to tell so early but looks like a breeder. Maybe you could give me your opinion. But if you don't want to set foot on the Lucky Penny, I could ask for Herman's thoughts on it," Jud said as he poured warm maple syrup on a tall stack of pancakes.

"Hmmph." Truman almost snorted coffee out his nose. "Herman might raise cattle, but he ain't got as much sense about breeders as I got. I'll look at that calf. You don't need to be askin' Herman Hudson a damn thing."

Jud tucked his chin and set about eating breakfast. Laughter was not an easy thing to keep in when it was determined to escape, but Jud managed to keep it contained. It had to be the spirit of Christmas had finally gotten past that tough exterior and found Truman's heart.

"When you get done, Jud, will you plug in the Christmas lights for me?" Dora June asked. "It's awful hard for me to get down on my knees and do that."

"Sure thing." Jud finished off the last of his coffee and carried his dirty dishes to the sink. "You about ready, Truman?"

"Been ready for ten minutes. Dora June, why in the devil do you want lights burnin' on that tree when the sun is coming out and it's daytime? It's a waste of electricity," Truman grumbled.

"I'll pay the electric bill if that's what's worryin' you." Dora June patted him on the shoulder. "You can hate baby Jesus if you want, but I love him and I'm having Christmas every minute that I can."

"I don't hate Jesus," Truman argued.

"Actions speak louder than words," Dora June said icily.

Truman slapped his forehead. "Well, go plug in her lights so we can get on with our business. Women! Can't figure them out and it's against the law to shoot 'em."

Jud managed to have his back turned before he grinned and he made it to the living room before a chuckle erupted. Next time he got to town, he intended to buy a cord that had one of those on/off switches attached to it. He would affix it to a tree branch at the right height for Dora June to reach. That way she could turn it on and off at whim.

When the lights were all shining brightly, he heard a slight noise behind him and whipped around to find Fiona curled up on the sofa. He drank in the sight of her for several seconds, red hair flowing over a throw pillow under her head, thick eyelashes resting on her cheekbones, one arm under her head, the other one clutching a second throw pillow. She was so damn cute that it took all his willpower not to awaken her with a kiss. But it wouldn't be right to deprive her of another hour's sleep, so he gently tucked a throw blanket around her. Tonight, he promised himself, they'd have some time together.

Chapter Eighteen

Saturday was one of those days that started out fast and built speed until the sunset. With the sun shining and the roads semi-clear, folks were in and out of the convenience store all day. Fiona sold more gasoline that day than she'd sold in the two weeks her mother had been gone. She was tired and ready for an evening in Jud's arms when she headed home.

She turned on the radio, hoping to catch a weather report, and listened to country music. Every song reminded her of Jud and the situation she'd landed in with him. Her phone vibrated in her hip pocket just as she parked in front of a dark house. She fished it out and answered on the third ring.

"Hey, Jud," she said. "You working late, or are you sittin' in the dark?"

"Working. Another one of our heifers that we've been worried about has decided to calve tonight," he said with a sigh. "Remember Blake and Allie are up in Muenster for the day so the grandparents there can have a little time with Audrey. They're on their way home, but it'll be after eleven when they get here. Lizzy and Toby are in Throckmorton for a Christmas party, something about one of the products she sells," Jud answered. "Oh, and another thing. I got that extra set of keys from the hook by the back door this afternoon and stole your car for an hour this afternoon. I got the snow tires put on it and brought it back. I planned to come inside but the store was full and I was in a hurry."

"Thank you but I was going to do that tomorrow afternoon after church," she said.

A picture of Jud's big biceps bulging as he removed one tire at a time and replaced it with a snow tire popped into Fiona's head. In spite of the bitter cold outside, the car was suddenly too hot, so she rolled down the window an inch.

"Maybe we can do something more fun after church," he teased.

Fiona couldn't keep the smile off her face. "Pink, yellow, or blue?"

"None of the above. I rather like the plain love more than the playful sex," he said.

"I missed you last night, and tonight Truman and Dora June are at Ruby's place to play dominoes, probably until after ten. That's why you asked about the dark house, isn't it?"

"Yes, it is."

"Dammit!"

"What?" she asked.

"I'm in the barn and my phone is going dead," he answered. "If I don't see you before then, I'll see you in church tomorrow morning..."

She held the phone out but the screen was blank. An

empty house. Leftovers warmed up in the microwave. Depression set in as she remembered other evenings just like that in the shabby little apartment in Houston.

The DJ on the car radio broke the silence surrounding her. "And we have a request from Diana this evening, so here's a little Sara Evans for all y'all out there in north-central Texas."

"Suds in the Bucket" started off with the twang of guitar music. The lyrics didn't match her exactly, but it sure made her antsy to get out of Dry Creek. The lyrics about not being able to fence time reminded Fiona of when she'd packed a bag and started walking out of town to go on an adventure. That same antsy feeling hit her as she sat in the car with new snow tires and looked ahead at a dark house.

"I need an adventure tonight," she said.

Every song on the radio reminded her of Jud or something about Dry Creek as she drove north. When she was out of range of that station, she hit the search button and a DJ with a voice almost as deep as Jud's filled the car. "And now for an hour of Christmas music starting with Vince Gill's 'Peace on Earth,' " the DJ said.

Tears flowed down Fiona's cheeks as the lyrics asked for peace on earth and for it to begin with her. She tried to clear her mind and think about nothing but the joy of an adventure as she drove, but when she reached Claude, Texas, at nine o'clock, she realized that every single thing she'd thought about on the journey that evening had circled right back around to Dry Creek, to her family and to Jud. Maybe it was time to hang up her adventurous nature and go home.

A convenience store was still open, so she stopped to put gas in the car and get a cup of coffee. The small motel down the street beckoned to her, but she was reluctant to shell out any more money, so she got back in the car and started toward Amarillo. Then she saw a sign that pointed south down through the Palo Duro Canyon and she made a left-hand turn.

Suddenly, the flat land where dirt met a sky full of bright twinkling stars disappeared as she fell into a deep canyon filled with shadowy formations on either side of the narrow two-lane road. Somewhere in the middle of the journey, her eyes grew so heavy that she dozed and awoke with a jerk to find that she was on the wrong side of the road headed straight toward a barbed wire fence. With adrenaline pumping, she whipped the steering wheel, over-correcting to the point that she just missed another fence on the other side of the road. Finally getting it under control and back on the road, she let out all the pent-up air in her lungs in a long, loud *whoosh*.

She pulled into a short lane with a locked gate right ahead of her. Hands shaking, her heart still pounding, she looked up past the canyon walls at the sky above her where the moon hung weightless with a billion stars around it. She remembered the song from a couple of hours before and nodded. She wished that Jud was with her and that all those stars were shining on them as they cuddled up and slept together in the backseat of the car.

She turned off the engine but wasn't sure what to do next, so she laid the seat back and gazed at the sky through the top of the windshield. She'd wait until her pulse settled back to normal before she got back out there on the road and drove up to Silverton. According to the last sign she'd seen, it was probably only half an hour at most from there and then she'd get a motel, no matter what the cost.

She wrapped her coat tightly around her chest and shut her eyes. Just for a minute until her heart stopped racing, but the adrenaline left as suddenly as it had flashed through her body and she fell asleep.

* * *

Jud slipped into the house a little after midnight. He grabbed a fistful of cookies from the countertop and poured milk into a quart jar. There was no light under Fiona's door, but he knocked very lightly in case she was still awake.

She didn't answer, so he eased the door open. Her bed was unmade, her spotless room every bit as empty as the feeling of emptiness in the whole upstairs portion of the house. Come to think of it, her car hadn't been outside, either. Leaving the door open, he quickly went to his room, put the cookies and milk on his nightstand, and got his phone attached to the recharge cord. Not waiting until it even had one bar, he hit her number and it went straight to voice mail. Either her phone was turned off or she was in a place with no service. She hadn't mentioned going anywhere, but then their conversation had been cut short when his phone went dead.

He headed toward the bathroom for a quick shower. When he returned, he tried calling her three more times but it still went to voice mail. Finally, at one o'clock, he crawled into bed and slept fitfully until morning.

* * *

Dora June wore a bright red robe and a very worried expression when Jud reached the kitchen for breakfast. "You heard from Fiona? Allie and Lizzy both called this mornin'."

Jud shook his head.

Truman sat at the table with his breakfast before him.

"Quit your fussin' and carryin' on, woman. Fiona is a grown woman and she don't have to answer to you. If she wants to lay out all night in some dive motel with God knows who, it ain't none of your business." He stopped long enough to sip his coffee. "I keep tellin' both of y'all that girl won't never have roots. Her wings have probably carried her away and we might not see her for another year."

Jud's heart skipped a beat. He'd never thought about her leaving permanently. His wildest idea was that Mary Jo and Sharlene had talked her into going back to that bar with them and that some other two-steppin' cowboy would take her eye.

"The girl has run away again. Get that through your heads. Now eat up, son, so we can go see if that new calf is as good as the one you got the day before," Truman said grumpily.

Jud ate breakfast, but he might as well have been eating sawdust. He helped Truman with chores, but that morning he didn't care if he changed Scrooge into a nice person or not. He just wanted to know that Fiona was safe. He tried several more times to reach her and got the same results every time. At least Truman didn't harp on the issue anymore. That much was a blessing. When they finished at Truman's place, they went straight to the barn where the two calves were penned up with their mothers.

Blake was already leaning on the stall door, a smile on his face. "I believe this one is even better stock than the last one. He's got good heavy bones and look how alert he is."

Truman climbed up on the first slat and tilted his head to the left, frowned, squinted, and nodded. "You're right. That's a breeder. You'll have to watch Herman. He'll try to tell you that it ain't so he can get a chance to buy him."

"What about you, Truman?" Blake asked. "Would you buy him if you had a chance?"

Truman shook his head. "Sorry, boys, but I'm not real sure that this time next year I'll be in the cattle business. I been doin' some real hard thinkin'. I ain't through yet, but seems like God is tellin' me what I need to do. I just got to figure out if I want to listen to Him."

"You plannin' on arguin' with God?" Blake asked.

"Wouldn't be the first time," Truman answered.

"How does that work out?" Jud asked.

"Okay, if I let him win. If he lets me win, then not so good most of the time."

"What're y'all fightin' about this Sunday mornin'? Where Fiona is or isn't?" Blake turned around and sat down on a hay bale.

"You heard anything about that flighty girl?" Truman stepped down from the slat and leaned against the stall.

"Not a word. Allie has sent a dozen messages and she called Sharlene. Neither she nor Mary Jo have seen her. I keep tellin' Allie that Fiona is a big girl and she's promised her mama she'll run the store, so she'll be home by tomorrow at the latest. And she's supposed to go shopping with the ladies after church, so if she can't make that, she will call."

With every fiber of his being, Jud hoped his cousin was right. What if she was mad at him for stealing the car and putting those snow tires on it without waiting for her to help him? What if she'd planned something special for the evening and thought he was making excuses not to be with her?

"I expect we'd all better get on about the church business now. Dora June has to teach that Sunday school class, so we have to go earlier. I envy the lot of you that," Truman said.

Blake shook his head. "Would you say that again? You envy the guys who bought the Lucky Penny? Never thought I'd see you on our ranch or hear you say that."

Truman pushed away from the stall. "Maybe I was wrong. I'll admit it if I decide I was."

"Is that what you and God are in a fight over?" Jud asked.

"Hell no! That's my decision, not God's."

*   *   *

A hard shiver awoke Fiona. Somehow during the night she'd kicked all the covers off her bed. She reached for them, but got the steering wheel instead. That popped her eyes wide open as the realization of where she was and what had happened washed over her like baptismal waters.

Sleet made little popping noises as it hit the roof of her car. She quickly brought her seat upright, started the engine, rubbed her cold hands together until the circulation was better, and shoved the gear stick into reverse.

The roads were clear when she started back south, but they were getting slick when she started climbing to the top of the canyon's edge not far from Silverton. Even though the sky was gray, when she reached the tiny town, the sleet had stopped and the roads were clear again.

Her phone vibrated and she picked it up to find a dozen messages from Jud, five text messages from each of her sisters, and one from Sharlene asking why she'd gone out to have a good time and hadn't invited her or Mary Jo to go along.

She knew she needed to call her sisters first, but she wasn't ready to talk to them. So she sent Lizzy a short message: *See you in church.* Then her phone screen went blank and there were no more bars.

Lights were shining from a little restaurant on the north side of the street in Silverton, and she pulled the car into the parking lot. A cup of coffee was all she intended to buy, but when she stepped out of the car, a wave of light-headedness swept over her. That little niggling voice in her head said that if she didn't eat something, she might see her sisters in church, but it wouldn't be today and she'd most likely be lying in a casket instead of sitting beside them on the Logan pew.

At 5:00 a.m., she wasn't surprised to find she was the only person in the café, so it didn't take long for the waitress to bring out her order. She was busy cutting up her fried eggs when the waitress asked if she was just passing through or looking for a job.

"What kind of job are you talking about?" Maybe this was Fiona's answer. She'd have never thought she'd find it out there in the flattest part of Texas but stranger things had happened.

"I need a waitress. You just looked kind of lost, so I thought I'd offer."

Fiona looked up at her name tag. "Thank you, Macy. I am lost, but I think I'm about to find the light at the end of the tunnel."

"If you change your mind, write down the numbers on the bulletin board in the foyer," Macy said. "Here comes my early morning coffee drinkers with a fresh crop of bull-shit to spread this Sunday morning."

Fiona laughed with her as she hurried off to get four old men seated by the window. When she'd finished her break-fast, Macy brought a to-go cup full of coffee and the bill to her table. Fiona handed her a ten-dollar bill and told her to keep the change. She walked right past the bulletin board, out into the cold winter air, and headed home.

She was driving through Floydada when a song on the radio made her pull off the side of the road and listen to it more intently. The song had been popular when she was in high school, but it made more sense to her that morning than it ever had.

Strange, that Sara Evan's song "Suds in the Bucket" had put her on this trip and now it was Sara's song "Three Chords and the Truth" that put her mind and heart in perfect harmony. She kept time to the music with her thumbs on the steering wheel. The song was about a woman who thought she was over a man but a song on the radio had changed her mind with three chords and the truth. Fiona missed Dry Creek and she didn't want to leave in six months.

"I'm ready to go home," she whispered as she pulled back out onto the road.

Chapter Nineteen

Fiona slid into the last spot on the pew that Sunday morning, right next to Jud, who kept his eyes straight ahead and didn't even acknowledge her presence. Lizzy leaned forward and shot her a dirty look. Now wasn't this just the cherries on the top of a triple fudge brownie sundae?

"Where have you been?" Lizzy mouthed.

"Later," Fiona said.

"Good morning," the preacher's loud booming voice cut through the low buzz of whispers.

Fiona wondered how much of the conversation was about her that morning. If Sharlene had already found out that she'd been out all night, then the whole town knew. Suddenly, she could feel the whole congregation plus the preacher staring at her. It didn't matter. She didn't give a damn what they thought, what they imagined, or what was truth or rumor. She'd found peace and that was worth every hour she'd spent driving half the night.

She nudged Jud. "We need to talk."

He nodded but didn't glance her way.

She'd recharged her phone while she'd taken the quickest shower in her life, then changed from her jeans and sweatshirt into a nice straight denim skirt and a pretty red and green plaid sweater. She had kicked off her work boots and put on a pair of red leather ones that she hadn't worn in years, but they felt comfortable.

"I'm going to read from Luke about the birth of Jesus," the preacher said.

She tried to listen, but the vibration in her purse that sat between her and Jud let her know someone had sent her a text message. She looked over at Jud, but his hands were crossed over his chest. Leaning forward, she could see that Lizzy and Allie both had phones tucked inside their Bibles and their thumbs were flying.

It's a good thing Dora June couldn't see them or she'd be tapping them on the shoulder and giving them one of her meanest come-to-Jesus looks. Fiona eased the phone from her purse, opened a hymnal, and laid it inside. Instantly, a message from each of her sisters popped up, asking the same thing: *Where in the hell have you been?*

She typed in: *I was driving alone all night, except for a few hours when I fell asleep at the bottom of the Palo Duro Canyon. It was worth every hour because I found what I was looking for.* She sent it to both of them with the flick of a fingertip.

"And that was?" Jud whispered.

"You were reading over my shoulder."

He nodded.

"That's not nice."

He tilted his head to the side. "I was worried."

She turned her phone off, returned it to her purse, and

sat up straight, determined to hear the story of baby Jesus again. Her sisters would have questions. Jud would have questions. Even Dora June would grill her, but right then Fiona didn't want to answer any of them. She wanted to enjoy her decision because it seemed right. Every other plan she'd made felt as if she had to work at it. She'd decided this morning that there was no plan. She would enjoy life wherever she was, take what it offered and make the best of it and hope that Madam Fate or Lady Destiny would lead her in the right path.

If Jud Dawson was part of that future, then so be it. If he wasn't, well, it had been an interesting two weeks and she'd always be grateful to him for what they'd had, no matter what it had been. It was the unrest that he'd brought into her life that had caused her to find harmony in her soul.

"Now I'll ask Truman O'Dell for the benediction," the preacher said.

Fiona jumped back to the present and wondered where the thirty minutes had gone. She hadn't heard anything the preacher said. Maybe he'd talk more about the birth of Jesus next week and she vowed she'd pay more attention.

"Where have you been?" Dora June caught her at the end of the pew.

"Driving and soul searching," Fiona answered honestly. "Are we ready to go see Granny and do some shopping this afternoon?"

"Did you do any good by driving all night?" Dora June's expression left no doubt that she was serious and that she would have answers.

Fiona nodded. "Yes, ma'am, I did."

"Good. We'll talk details later. For now let's gather up

the family and go shopping. I could get used to this kind of lifestyle." Dora June smiled.

"Yes, we will talk details later," Lizzy said right behind her. "You scared the hell out of us."

"I lived in Houston for years. You didn't know where I was for a whole week, maybe more, at a time and you didn't act like this," Fiona said.

"Things were different in those days," Jud whispered close to her ear. His breath on her neck sent shivers down her spine.

"Hey, if you're through whisperin' sweet things in Fiona's ear, I'm ready to go eat. If we slip out the back door, we can beat the rest of these people to Nadine's and get our dinner quicker," Truman said.

"Truman O'Dell," Dora June gasped.

"Y'all could be about your shopping trip sooner if you'd do the same thing," Truman told her.

"Do what?" Allie returned from the nursery with Audrey.

"Sneak out the back door to go shopping," Fiona laughed.

"I will if Dora June will," Allie said.

"I reckon the preacher has plenty of people to shake his hand." Dora June nodded. "Lead the way, Truman. I feel like a kid again. Remember when we was dating and we'd do this so we could have a little bit of time together?"

"Shhh." Truman actually blushed. "You'll be givin' these kids ideas."

Jud touched Fiona on the arm. "Tonight?"

She nodded.

Tonight might not be sex or making love, and when she was done telling him what she intended to say, he might not even want to talk to her again. Thinking of the talk they were going to have, she decided it would occur while sitting in the two wingback chairs and not in either of their bedrooms.

"I want to eat at that little family restaurant in Seymour," Dora June said on the way to Allie's van. "I'm buying today and there'll be no arguments. I hear they've got fried chicken on the all-you-can-eat buffet and it's been a long time since I got to eat fried chicken that I didn't cook." She opened the door and crawled up into the front passenger seat.

Allie tossed the keys to Lizzy. "You can drive. Baby girl is fussy today."

Lizzy caught the keys, got inside, and buckled the seat belt.

"I do hope Irene is herself today," Dora June said. "I'd love to sit and talk to her like we did for that little while when we decorated the tree." She fixed her big black shiny purse just right in her lap and wrapped her arms around it. "Do any of y'all know what's going on with Truman? He's actin' strange lately. Talkin' to himself and frownin' like he's arguing with someone."

"Blake told me this morning that he's arguing with God over something," Allie said. "We're all ready, Lizzy. You can go now."

Lizzy started the engine, backed out, and headed north toward Seymour. "Okay, Fiona, start talking."

"About what? I told you I drove most of the night and most of the morning to get to church on time." This feeling was all so new that she didn't want to talk about it right then. Selfishly, she wanted to hug it close and let it all sink in before she tried to explain what she'd figured out. Besides, what if she was wrong? Why give them false hope if in a few days the aura of peace disappeared?

"Why did you drive all night and where did you go?" Allie asked.

"Y'all ever hear that song by Sara Evans called 'Suds in the Bucket'?"

"What's that got to do with anything?" Lizzy asked. "Don't change the subject. We want details and we aren't going to talk about old songs."

"It is a detail," Fiona said. "I think it was a detail before I ever left home to go to college. I left the suds in the bucket and the clothes hanging on the line."

"You did not," Allie said.

"Figuratively speaking, I did. I left behind all the things that I did back then. My boots and my country girl clothes. I didn't leave them on the line but hanging in my closet and in my dresser drawers," she argued.

"Go on," Dora June said.

"Last night, I left the store and when I got home the house was dark. Jud was delivering another calf and that song came on the radio and I got that same feeling I had back then. The same thing that I felt when I was a little girl and decided to leave Dry Creek and go on an adventure," Fiona said. "I wanted to run away. It didn't matter where or how long. I could not go in that house. It reminded me of all those times I went home to that depressing little apartment in Houston."

"Okay, then what?" Allie asked.

"I drove to Seymour and then to Vernon and all the way to Claude, right on the edge of the Palo Duro Canyon. I stopped and got coffee because I was getting tired. Every single song on the radio reminded me of Dry Creek." She wasn't going to tell them that most of them reminded her of

Jud. "On a whim, I turned down into the canyon rather than going on to Amarillo, which was my first plan. I got sleepy, almost ran off the road and..." She went on to tell them the rest of the story, leaving out the part that Sara Evans's other song played in settling her mind.

"So now what?" Dora June asked.

"So now I'm through making plans. They always fail me and I'm going to see what each day brings. It's not easy for me because I've always had a plan but knowing that I don't have my life mapped out for the next ten or twenty years brings me a certain amount of tranquility."

"Good," Allie said.

"Does that mean you aren't leaving Dry Creek?" Dora June asked.

"It means that I'm not closing the door to anything, even living in Dry Creek. Seems like the harder I fight against living here, the more miserable I get and the more trouble it gets me into," she said. "And now can we please talk about the ranch party and Christmas?"

"Not until I fuss at you for sleeping in your car. You should have stopped in Claude and rented a room," Dora June said sternly.

"Sleeping in the car and my near brush with an accident is what brought me to my senses," Fiona said.

"Well, I'm glad that I didn't know that's what you were doing. I wouldn't have slept a wink. Okay, now, girls, I expect you all to get your ten dollars' worth at this buffet dinner," Dora June giggled.

* * *

Before she took their order, Sharlene leaned close to Jud's ear and whispered, "What in the hell is going on? Did y'all drug Truman?"

Jud cupped a hand over her ear and said softly, "No, he's here of his own free will."

"With all y'all Dawsons? He hates you," Sharlene said.

"Not anymore." Jud smiled.

"Good God, man! Do you whisper sweet things in all the women's ears?" Truman asked.

"Most of them," Blake chuckled. "It's the Dawson in us. Be careful or you'll be whispering in Dora June's ear. Our bad habits are contagious."

"Lord, I hope not," Truman sputtered. "Do y'all have to play Christmas music in here? I swear it's all a man hears from Thanksgiving until after the twenty-fifth of the month."

"Well, it is the holiday. Don't be an old scrooge, Truman. What can I get you?"

"I'm sick of turkey and dressing already, so I want a big old greasy hamburger basket with a double order of French fries and a piece of Nadine's apple pie for dessert. And I'm paying for Jud's dinner but not these other two."

Blake held up a finger. "I'll have the same and I'll take the ticket for all of us."

"Bullshit! I ain't acceptin' no charity from you." Truman's eyes narrowed and his jaw set so hard that Jud thought he might break the bone.

"It isn't charity. I intend to take all your money when we play dominoes and I don't want you to run short and quit playing after the first game," Blake said. "It would be a shame for you to have to go pout in your room and for us to have to call Herman in to finish up the afternoon game."

"Y'all best stop threatening me with him or I'll go over there and eat all by myself," Truman said. "Besides, he can't play dominoes worth shit. So you can buy my dinner but don't you think for one minute you'll come out the winner when this day is done."

"That true, Jud?" Toby asked. "Is he really that good?"

"He's tellin' the truth." Jud nodded.

"Okay, then Blake is paying, right?" Sharlene asked. "And just for the books, if I was bettin' on who'd win the most games today, I'd put my money on Truman. He won the competition last summer at our first annual summer festival. They set up tables over there in the corner and he beat the socks off everyone."

Truman nodded curtly. "Herman was the first one to fall. Too bad we wasn't bettin' that day or I'd have taken all his money, too."

"I'll have the same thing he's eating," Toby said. "Maybe his luck is in the dinner."

"My luck, son, is in my skill," Truman told him.

"Just make it four," Jud said.

"Will do. Sweet tea all around?" Sharlene asked. "And apple pie after?"

"Pecan pie for me," Blake said.

Sharlene nodded and hurried off to give Nadine the order and the gossip before the next group of church folks came into the café.

"So y'all goin' to take my advice and keep them two bull calves?" Truman asked.

"I think we are," Blake said. "You've got a good eye for cattle, Truman. Why would you ever raise goats?"

"Them is Dora June's goats. She says them kids that come along in the spring is her babies. She don't seem as took with them the past couple of weeks since she's got your wives to tear around the country with on Sundays."

He sat back in his chair so that Sharlene could unload four glasses of sweet tea on their table.

"Maybe Audrey has replaced them," Blake said. "That little girl's going to be a charmer."

"She already is," Toby said.

"I need some advice and I reckon you three can keep a secret, can't you?" Truman blurted out.

"I don't know about these two"—Jud pointed in either direction—"but you can count on me."

"Come on now," Blake said. "I never did tattle on you, not one time."

"You got to promise me you won't breathe a word," Truman leaned in and whispered.

"Promise," they said in unison.

"I'm tired of arguing with God. He wins. Dora June has stood beside me for fifty years, and I think she was serious about seeing the whole United States in an RV. So I'm thinkin' about buyin' her one for Christmas as a surprise."

Jud came close to spewing tea across the table. "And you're going to live in it on your property until you get things sold?"

"Hell no! This is where I need you boys. I ain't got the time to get rid of my livestock, and that's all I got left on my place. I'm not even sure I want to sell the ranch until we see if we want to keep livin' like hoboes or if we want to come back home and rebuild." He paused.

The silence at the table was so pronounced that it reverberated in Jud's ears. "When are you going to buy this thing?"

"One day next week when me and you is doin' our chores. She saw one up in Wichita, so we could go up that way and pick out a real nice one and pay for it. Then if one of y'all would help me, I'd—"

"Hey, y'all mind if I sit with you?" Deke asked.

"Drag up a chair," Blake said.

"I reckon he'll have to know now," Truman sighed.

"Know what?" Deke motioned for Sharlene to bring him a glass of sweet tea. "And I want the turkey and dressing special," he said.

She nodded and brought the tea right over to the table.

"You want to tell him?" Blake asked.

Truman brought him up to speed.

Deke's eyes were about to pop out of his head when the old guy stopped talking. "You serious? If you are selling, I want first chance at your cattle."

"Get in line behind these boys. You want my goats?" Truman asked.

"If you'll let me have first choice of the cattle, I'll take all those goats."

"What do y'all think?" Truman asked the other three. "You want the goats to get the cattle?"

Blake shook his head. "Allie will want to bring every kid in the house in the springtime. I'll stand back and let Deke have the cattle if he'll take the goats."

"I'll make you a deal on the whole lot of them and throw in all the hay in my barn as a bonus," Truman said.

"You be sure about this before we shake on it, Truman," Deke said. "I'll give you a couple of days to think about it."

"I'll think about it until I go look at them RV things. If it don't seem right, then all bets are off. Since we got five of us, why don't we play poker this afternoon, instead of dominoes?"

"You as good at poker as you are at dominoes?" Jud asked.

"You'll have to play a few games to find out," Truman answered.

"I'm in if it's poker. What time are we playin'?" Deke asked.

"Right after we get through eatin'. You got enough energy to play after chasin' women all night?" Truman asked.

"It's chasin' them women that has my blood pumpin', Truman. This might be the day that goes down in the history books as the day Deke Sullivan whipped Truman," Deke answered.

"When pigs fly," Truman growled.

"You better be duckin' because there's a possibility they've sprouted wings. Look around the table at who you are having Sunday dinner with. Bet you never thought that was possible, did you?"

"I was right about one thing. All y'all ain't nothing but a bunch of smartass kids," Truman said.

Chapter Twenty

Laden with shopping bags, Fiona climbed the stairs, hoping that Jud would appear anytime and take part of the weight from her. She set all four bags on the floor in front of the credenza and plopped down in a wingback chair and kicked off her boots. Flipping around and throwing her legs over the chair arm, she sighed and wished that Jud were there to massage her aching feet.

She snuggled down into the curve of the chair back and shut her eyes, just to rest them for a couple of minutes. She fell asleep and dreamed of building a huge snowman with Jud. Two big yellow dogs and half a dozen kids, with hair that went from blond to every shade of red, romped in the snow around them.

In the dream, Jud leaned around the snowman and kissed her. She awoke with a start to find that in reality he was leaning around the edge of the chair and she could actually feel the heat from his lips as they came down on hers.

Visions of tangled sheets, his arms around her, and afterglow danced through her head as she wrapped her arms around his neck. Somewhere in the background she could hear Truman fussing about all the stuff Dora June brought home, but nothing mattered except Jud Dawson.

"I've missed you," he said when the kiss ended, and he straightened up.

"Me too," she said softly.

He was dressed in a long-sleeved thermal knit shirt, the three undone buttons at the neck revealing soft brown chest hair and a pair of red and green plaid pajama pants. He held out a hand and she was tempted—Lord help her but she was tempted—to forget what she'd figured out and go with him to the bedroom where the drawer full of glow-in-the-dark condoms awaited.

But she shook her head and pointed to the other chair. "We've got to talk."

He dropped his hand. "Uh-oh. Nothing good has ever come from those four words."

"I don't know. That will be up to you when we get finished. I figured you'd be really mad at me for not returning your calls and texts." She twisted around until she was sitting in the chair with her feet on the floor. "If this is more than casual sex, then you should be storming around in anger, demanding where I've been and what I've been doing."

He combed back his damp hair with his fingers. "Is this where you're going to tell me exactly why you didn't come home last night?"

Fiona shrugged. "Are you mad at me?"

Jud shrugged.

"So you don't even care? Were you just leading me on by saying this is more than sex? You aren't even angry.

God bless, Jud! Dora June was right after all and I never thought I'd say those words, not to you."

Jud's eyes narrowed. "Right about what?"

"That all along you just tell women what they want to hear so you can get them into bed with you."

Jud's jaw worked in anger. When he finally spoke, it was through clenched teeth. "Jesus, woman, I was ready to call out half the country and all the Dawsons to go looking for you."

"Just how many Dawsons is that?" she asked.

"A hell of a lot." He took a breath and settled down, his expression softening. He scooted his chair over and took her hand in his. "Now are you going to tell me what happened to make you run and where you were all night?"

"Is this our first fight?" she asked.

"No, this is a bump in the road. A fight will include some of that storming around you talked about." He scooted his chair closer to hers, picked up her hand, and held it on the arm of his chair.

There was comfort in the touch of his hand but he still had a worried expression on his face. She opened her mouth and told the story, all of it, not leaving out anything from start to finish. With more detail than she'd told her sisters and Dora June, she told him every emotion she'd felt through the whole experience.

"I'm not sure what tomorrow holds but I'm not in a hurry to leave Dry Creek." She squeezed his fingers. "My heart and my mind are at peace with each other and I'm not making five- or even one-year plans anymore. That gets in the way of living, and I'm enjoying the life I've got right here at home." She hesitated. Maybe she'd already said enough but she couldn't stop. "Call it a Christmas miracle or karma or fate kicking me in the butt, but I'm happy and I'm not throwing that away just to prove that I can make a plan work."

"And us?" he asked as he squeezed her hand ever so tenderly.

"Is there an us? Or just booty calls?"

"I'd like for there to be an us," he said.

"Then"—she paused, trying to find the words—"we should slow down."

"What does that mean?" he asked. "Are you saying date without sex?"

She nodded slowly. "I want to know if what I missed was Jud these past two nights or the hot sex."

"That's fair enough."

"So now you talk. And I mean seriously," she said.

"I want there to be an us, Fiona. I want to see where this goes. Knowing that you're happy here and not planning on leaving anytime soon makes me more than just happy. I'm a man and we don't express feelings too well. Living with Truman should teach you that." He paused.

The silence was deafening for a few seconds. Then he went on. "I'm glad you are home and that you found peace in your heart. I'm having trouble here, but..."

She removed her hand from his, cupped his cheeks in her palms, and kissed him. A brand-new feeling joined desire and heat, one that held the promise of a future in the kiss. "I can feel what you feel and that's enough for now."

"I'll gladly move back into the trailer if you want to announce it to the world right now because I sure want to crawl up on the rooftop and tell everyone," he offered.

She shook her head. "Let's keep it under wraps until

Dora June and Truman move out. But I do intend to tell Mama about what happened."

"Then that means I can tell my sister?"

"Of course. Now tell me how in the hell you got Truman to go to the Lucky Penny and to go to dinner at Nadine's today with Blake and Toby." She drew her knees up and wrapped her arms around them.

As Jud embellished the story with facial expressions that were so like Truman's, her laughter seemed to make him give her even more details about the whole day. By the time he wound down the story, her sides ached and she had the hiccups.

"How about a beer to cure those hiccups?" he asked.

"We've still got beer in the cooler? I thought it was all gone. Some boyfriend you are," she said.

"Those are all gone. But Deke brought them to the poker game and Truman said that if Dora June found out and he got into trouble, then he would never play with us again, so I snuck the last two up here in a plastic bag of ice. They're in my room. Shall we have one before we head off to bed?"

A loud hiccup and a nod sent him toward the bathroom. He returned with two icy cold beers, the caps off both, and handed one to her. She tilted it back and let the cold liquid slide down her throat. Lord, that tasted good and it was an instant cure of the hiccups.

Jud did the same as he sat back down. "Fiona, I like that you called me your boyfriend. And FYI, I know for a fact that Truman and Dora June will be gone by Christmas Day. You have to keep this under your hat and not even tell your sisters because if Truman found out I told you, he'd probably shoot me." Jud went on to tell her all about the RV plans.

Fiona hugged herself and giggled. "That is amazing news. You really did turn Scrooge around. So Christmas Day? That sounds like a perfect time for you to announce that I'm your new girlfriend."

"It does, doesn't it?" He set their two empties on the floor and pulled her up into his arms. One brief kiss was all he gave her before he headed off to his bedroom and gently shut the door behind him.

Dammit! She wanted more than a peck on the lips. She wanted the big kahuna, the tsunami, the class-five wild Texas tornado, all of it rolled into one big kiss and then a long bout of amazing sex. What in the hell was she thinking when she said they should go slow?

You are an idiot! she thought as she picked up her boots in one hand and the beer bottles in the other and crossed the landing. Her room looked different, not nearly as confining and more inviting. She tossed the bottles into the trash, making a mental note to get rid of them the next morning and set her boots in the closet where they belonged.

After she got comfortable on the bed, with pillows propped behind her back, she hit the button on her phone to call her mother. Katy answered on the first ring with laughter in her voice.

"Hello, Fiona. I just hung up from an hour-long conversation with Allie. Y'all deserve special things in your Christmas stockings for the way you've turned Truman around. I didn't expect anything but hoped for at least some kind of reconciliation between him and my sons-in-law before I came home. Looks like we're getting a lot more with him talking about a big RV and taking Dora June to see the whole country." Katy stopped for a breath.

"Well, dammit! Do Allie and Lizzy both know? I

wanted to tell you the story. I laughed until I got the hiccups at the way Jud told it."

Katy's tone changed and suddenly Fiona could hear the sound of the ocean in the background. "Blake and Toby can't keep a secret one bit better than Jud can, evidently. Now, I want to know your story. Lizzy just had the highlights. I want the details. What is going on in your heart, Fiona Deann Logan?"

"You just triple named me. Am I in trouble?"

"No, but I want you to know that I'm serious and I want the whole story," Katy said.

"Jud and I are dating, but we don't want to tell anyone until after Dora June and Truman are gone or they'll think it's improper for us to live together in this house. Do you have a problem with that?"

All Fiona could hear were the waves coming into shore for several seconds. "Mama, are you still there? Please don't faint or die of a heart attack."

"I'm still here. Took a minute to process what you just said. I wasn't expecting that right here at the first of the conversation. Can't say I'm surprised, but it still shocked me," Katy said breathlessly.

"Do you want him to move out into his travel trailer?"

"You are both grown adults. What you do or how you handle this relationship has nothing to do with where you sleep at night. Now that that's out of the way, tell me why you thought you had to run away and not let anyone know where you were for a whole night?"

Fiona repeated the whole story, even adding in how every song on the radio seemed to be talking straight to her, from the first one that made her leave to the last one that told her to go home.

"I'm wiping tears from my cheeks," Katy said at the end with a sniffle. "My biggest prayer has been answered. Not that you would come home. Not that you'd find someone to date. But that you'd finally find yourself and happiness."

"And now you've got me crying. I never can let anyone weep alone," Fiona said.

"I can't wait to come home."

"Are you homesick?" Fiona asked.

"Not for Dry Creek but for you girls. I'm really settling in to a life with no responsibilities and liking it. I didn't know how tense I was until I started to relax but I wouldn't want to live here forever. Texas is where my heart and soul is."

"Mama, there won't be a problem with me staying here at the house and working in the back room at the store for a long time, will there?" Fiona asked softly.

"Not at all but I've got some things I want to talk to you about when I get home. It's not something to discuss on the phone so we'll wait. You just go enjoy your newfound happiness and we'll have a long visit. But don't worry, you are welcome to the back room as long as you want it and I love that you are in the house. Now I'm going inside and having a margarita with the girls. Good night, Fiona, and, darlin', you've given me the best Christmas present in the world tonight."

"I think it's me that got the Christmas miracle this year, Mama. Good night, and have an extra margarita for me." Fiona pushed the END button.

She draped her clothing over the back of a chair and pulled a nightshirt over her head, slid beneath the covers, and wiggled into a comfortable spot. It sure beat the hell out of sleeping in her car the night before.

Chapter Twenty-One

On Monday morning, Allie and Dora June began to gear things up for the ranch party the next Saturday night. The whole town was either talking about the party or the fact that Truman was going to be Santa Claus. Everyone had thought that the Lucky Penny would fail for sure and yet here they were throwing a huge ranch party at the end of their first year. No one would have believed that Truman, of all the men in Dry Creek, could ever have been coerced into doing anything for Christmas, but yet he was bragging about the pillow that Dora June was making for him to wear around his midsection.

The end of the world had to be on the way. Any second the clouds would part, a bright white light would shoot down, and a booming voice would come out of the heavens, calling all the saints and sinners to Judgment Day.

On Tuesday night, Fiona met Jud on the landing. He opened his arms and she walked into them, holding him tightly as she inhaled the sexy scent of soap, shampoo, and what belonged solely to Jud.

"I'll be glad when this party is over," she said.

"Me too. Let's celebrate on Sunday by going to an afternoon movie in Wichita Falls. We'll sit in the dark, hold hands like teenagers, and relax," he whispered into her hair.

"Yes, but only if you promise you won't laugh at me if I snore. I'll be so tired by then, I won't be able to stay awake. And can we stop in and see Granny either before or after the movie?"

"Yes, we can. Truman bought an RV today. The fanciest thing you've ever seen. He's going to have it parked outside the house on Christmas morning and as soon as the leftover potluck is finished at the church that night, he and Dora June will head south for the winter," Jud said.

"Oh. My. God! He was serious. Dora June is going to faint."

"I hope not," Jud chuckled, and then he tipped her chin up for a quick kiss. "He's like a little kid about all this. Tomorrow he and Blake are going to Throckmorton to buy a small car that's listed in the newspaper down there. He's going to sell his truck to Toby but this is all a big hush, hush secret. Not even your sisters know it's a done deal."

"Oh, they know. Blake and Toby don't keep secrets any better than you do," Fiona laughed. "We are planning to buy stuff for their new trailer for their Christmas presents."

* * *

On Thursday, things really moved fast. The rental company with all the tables arrived that evening right after Fiona got off work. In an hour the living room was changed into a lovely party area with small round tables scattered with the flow pattern to the bar and the dining room planned out beautifully. Centerpieces were chunks of mesquite with the Lucky Penny brand burned into the sides. Across the tops of the logs holes had been drilled to hold short tapers that would be lit just before the party started. Silk poinsettias and greenery had been used to give the pieces a Christmas flare and the ribbons matched the sashes on the backs of the chairs.

"Oh my!" Fiona gasped.

"Pretty damn impressive, isn't it?" Lizzy asked from the Christmas tree area, where a big red chair waited for Santa Claus. "Did you see the bar? They decided to set it up in the foyer. The guys had to move out the hall tree and the credenza but it looks like it's going to work very well. I wish Mama were here for the party but to have her come home early would be selfish."

Fiona peeked out into the foyer. "It's all decorated, too."

"Oh, yes. This is the party to attend this year from what everyone says. The Dawson guys did not fall on their faces their first year in business and Truman is Santa Claus. What else could we ask for?"

"That Granny could be here and having a good day." Allie carried Audrey into the room. "Who'd have thought a year ago right now that we'd all be where we are?"

"If you'd have told me I'd be married to anyone other than Mitch, I'd have thought you were crazy," Lizzy said.

"We didn't even know the Dawsons and only heard rumors that a bunch of fool cowboys were interested in the Lucky Penny." Allie handed Audrey off to Fiona and straightened several ornaments on the tree.

"Fool cowboys, huh?" Jud asked.

"Yep." Fiona nodded. "That's exactly what they called you three. Like that old commercial said, 'You've come a long way, baby.' You weren't supposed to last past that hard winter or the hot summer and yet, here you still are."

"And we'll be here next year and the one after that, won't we?" Jud asked, but his eyes were on Fiona.

"Hopefully," she said.

"It looks good. The caterers arrive at eight in the morning and take over the kitchen. I'm shutting the store an hour early to have time to get ready. Why don't y'all girls come over here at four and we'll have the whole upstairs to ourselves." Fiona swayed back and forth with the baby in her arms.

Jud cleared his throat loudly.

"Minus Jud's room. We can do mani/pedis," Fiona said.

"Then we can all make an entrance down the staircase." Lizzy nodded.

"Audrey and I will be here at four on the button," Allie agreed.

* * *

Jud waited patiently at the bottom of the stairs with his two cousins on Friday night. The pungent smell of barbecue floated out from the kitchen. Waiters wearing white shirts and black slacks stood ready behind the dining room table to help guests.

Two pretty blond bartenders were in their place to make whatever drinks anyone ordered. A month ago, Jud would have already had two phone numbers and would have been trying to make up his mind which one to call first. But tonight he wasn't interested in either of their sly glances his way. He was waiting on his girlfriend.

Allie was the first Logan sister to appear at the top of the staircase. Blake sucked air so hard that Jud turned to make sure he wasn't choking to death.

"She's wearing the red velvet dress that she wore when we married," Blake said hoarsely. "She took my breath away in it on Valentine's Day and even more so tonight. I've got the prettiest wife in the whole damn state."

They made quite the pair, with Allie wearing red velvet and Audrey all dolled up in a Christmas plaid taffeta dress. Jud wanted what Blake had at that moment even more than he wanted the Lucky Penny to have oil down beneath the surface. His cousin's eyes never left his wife and daughter. It was as if no one else in the world existed but them and when they reached the foyer, he took Audrey from her, cradled the baby in one arm and slung the other around Allie's shoulders.

"You are stunning," Blake said.

"You look pretty damn good yourself. Shall we go on in to the party? It sounds like we've got some guests already and we'll need to greet each and every one," she said.

Lizzy made her way down the steps, but Toby didn't wait for her to get to the bottom. He bounded up to meet her, kissed her passionately right there in front of the bartenders and Lucy and Herman as they came through the front door, and then hooked her arm into his.

"You are beautiful tonight, Miz Lizzy," Jud said when they were beside him.

"Lucy, darlin', I'm so glad you and Herman are here." Lizzy hugged both Lucy and Herman. "Y'all come on into the party room with us. It sounds like folks are already arriving."

"That green satin looks beautiful on you, Lizzy. You should wear that color more often," Lucy said.

"And you look stunning," Lizzy said. "How'd you ever get Herman out of his overalls and into a suit?"

"I threatened to sit on Truman's lap and tell him what I want for Christmas," Lucy whispered.

"Women!" Herman grumbled as he clamped a hand on Jud's shoulder. "If you don't want to be bossed around, take my advice and run when a woman even looks at the rings in a store window."

"Is that what got you in trouble?"

Herman sighed. "Damn straight and now fifty years later I got to wear this uncomfortable suit to come to your party."

"Looks real good on you," Jud said.

"Ain't wore it since my son got married years ago but it still fits so that's a good thing, I guess. I knew y'all boys would make a go of that ranch. Truman was against you from the beginning but he's comin' around. I can't believe he's goin' to be Santa Claus. All the dirt in Texas wouldn't make me put on that suit," Herman said.

"Herman Hudson, quit hangin' out at the bar and come on in here." Lucy crooked a finger toward him.

"The boss speaks." He grinned.

"Sounds like it," Jud chuckled.

"Does that one belong to you?" one of the bartenders asked, and pointed up the wide staircase.

If Jud would have had to utter a word or die before a firing squad, he would have reached for the blindfold and put it on himself. Fiona wore a black cocktail dress that hugged her body like a glove. A choker of bloodred rubies was wrapped around her long, slender neck and her curly red hair was swept to one side, leaving the other bare for his kisses. Between the short skirt and the high heels, her legs looked a mile long.

"Well?" the bartender asked again.

"Yes, she does," he said when he'd found his voice.

"Well, now, don't you clean up well," Fiona said from the second step.

"This old cowboy suit? Why, I've worn it for years." He picked up her arm and tucked it safely into his. "I should have worn my revolver on my hip. As gorgeous as you are, it's going to be a chore just knocking the cowboys away from you. Please, let me tell everyone we are dating. I can live in a trailer for a week until Dora June and Truman leave."

"Shhh." She put a finger on his lips. "This is all about the ranch tonight. Not about us. We can wait one more week. Smile when we walk through the door. Lizzy is going to snap our picture to send straight to Mama."

He closed his free hand around her finger and kissed it. "You rendered me speechless when I looked up and saw you."

"That may be the most romantic thing anyone has ever said to me. Now, let's go make everyone welcome and show them that the Lucky Penny is a ranch to reckon with."

Chapter Twenty-Two

Within seconds of entering the party, Jud was pulled into a group of high-powered ranchers from around Olney. Two were women, an older one with gray hair and a tall blonde wearing a lovely little dark green lace sheath dress that hugged her slim body, leaving little to the imagination.

Instant jealousy washed over Fiona when the younger woman moved so close to Jud that her breasts, sporting a mile of cleavage, brushed against his arm. He took a step to the side and motioned for Fiona to join them. That helped the green-eyed monster subside but only slightly.

She started that way, but Sharlene caught her arm. "Did you see that hussy making a play for Jud? You'd better go rescue him. She's the one who took Deke out to the car to 'cool off' when we went dancing. That's her grandmother with her and the old gal owns half of the county around Olney."

"What's her name?" Fiona asked.

"Lacy, and her grandma says that she has to be married

in the next year or another grandchild is going to inherit the ranch."

"Why?" Fiona asked.

"Because the grandma is eighty years old and wants to retire. But she wants someone who is settled to run the ranch," Sharlene said.

Fiona nodded and took a few more steps toward Jud, who was looking pretty frantic. She'd only gone a few feet when Mary Jo waylaid her and dragged her into a corner.

"This is a really nice party. I'm glad that the Dawsons are making the Lucky Penny into a ranch," Mary Jo said.

"Thank you," Fiona said.

"But that's not why I grabbed your arm. You need to tell Jud to watch out for that woman over there. She wanted Deke but bombed out there, so she's on the prowl again. I imagine that Jud is the whole reason she and her granny are here. I'd tell him but the way he keeps looking at you, I expect he'll listen to you better," Mary Jo said. "I'm going to the bar. Want me to bring you something?"

"Yes, a glass of red wine would be great. Thank you, Mary Jo," Fiona said.

She finally made it to the group and held out her hand to the older woman. "Hello, I'm Fiona Logan. I don't believe I've met you."

"Yes, you have, darlin'." The older lady smiled. "I knew your grandmother, Irene, and your grandfather very well. But I haven't seen you since you were a little girl. Please let me introduce you to my granddaughter, Lacy. I expect she's about your age."

Fiona turned slowly and flashed her best Southern smile. "I'm Fiona. I hope you're enjoying the party?"

Lacy looked at Jud like she'd gladly have him for a

midnight snack. "Oh, honey, it's a great party, but I can't believe I didn't dance with this good-looking hunk when I met y'all a couple of weeks ago. When does the dancing begin?"

"I'm afraid we don't have room for dancing tonight. Maybe next year we'll plan to hire a band when the sale barn goes up," Fiona said sweetly.

"Wine?" Mary Jo handed Fiona a glass.

Fiona took it and extended her arm toward Lacy. "You don't have anything. Please, take this and I'll get a beer later."

"Thank you," Lacy said.

"Oh, Jud, there are some people over here that you have to talk to. They have a little spread down around Throckmorton and they always have a fall sale. We should go to it next year to get an idea of how to build the new barn on the Lucky Penny." She looped her arm in his.

Just as Lacy was raising the glass to her lips, Fiona stepped on her toe. Wine went everywhere: inside all that cleavage, down the front of her dress, the last drops hitting the tops of her ridiculously high heels. Surprisingly enough, not one drop hit the floor and yet the glass was empty.

"I'm so sorry," Fiona said. "Please come upstairs with me and I'll help you clean this up. We'll get some club soda at the bar. It works wonders."

"It's all right," the grandmother said. "We've got another party this evening in Olney, so we'll just run by the ranch and she can change. It's been wonderful meeting you again, Fiona. Come on over to our place anytime. We'll catch up about Irene. Come along, Lacy. We'll have to hurry."

Lacy set the glass on the nearest table and shot Fiona a dirty look. It was meant to kill Fiona on the spot, drop her like a ton of bricks into nothing but a black dress right there at Jud's toes. But Fiona apologized a dozen more times and invited them to come back to the Lucky Penny anytime.

"Did you do that on purpose?" Jud whispered.

"Would you care if I did?" she asked. "Honey, I know how to pick up bits and pieces of conversation. I was saving your ass." Fiona unhooked her arm from his and went to greet another couple coming into the room.

Blake clamped a hand on Jud's shoulder. "I want you to meet Mark Hutchins. He's got a sale barn that we need to look at before we build one. If all goes well, we can have our ranch sale and party in our own barn in a couple of years."

Jud never let her out of sight the entire time he talked to Blake and Mark about a new barn and joined her as soon as he could wrangle his way out of the conversation. He draped his arm possessively around her shoulder when the rattle of sleigh bells sounded on the stairs.

"Ho, ho, ho!" Truman bellowed in his deepest voice.

Fiona had trouble finding Truman beneath all that belly and gray beard. If it hadn't been for his eyes and those heavy dark brows, she might have thought Herman had decided to play the part after all. "I've got a bag full of presents for boys and girls of all ages, and I'll be right over there in my chair for any of you who want to tell me what you want for Christmas."

Folks were still eating, drinking, and talking but the focus shifted to the kids. Cameras came out and Truman was the center of attention for the next hour. Audrey was the first baby to sit on his lap and he was a little awkward, but when she cooed at him and flashed a toothless grin, he softened right up.

"Never actually thought I'd see this happen," Jud said.

"You've worked some mighty fine magic," Fiona told him.

"Not really. I think he wanted to be like this all along but he didn't know how. Now he does. I hope Dora June was serious about that RV thing. He's so excited that he can't be still. I'll be surprised if he keeps the secret another week." Jud slipped an arm around her waist.

"Mama will be home on Tuesday, so I hope he keeps it until then. I want her to be here when Dora June finds out. It's all because she invited them to stay here that this has happened."

Allie bumped Fiona on the arm. "You and Lizzy are going to have to take care of the last of the party. Audrey is getting fussy. I'm glad that she stayed awake long enough to get her first Santa picture made, but I'm taking her upstairs to my old room to rock her for a while."

Fiona kissed the baby on the forehead. "She's been passed around a lot tonight. Her little bones are probably sore."

At eleven-thirty, Truman gave the last present in his bag to a five-year-old who was so tired that she whined because it was wrapped in red paper instead of green. Lizzy and Toby walked them to the door and the second their taillights disappeared, they turned off the porch lights.

"Great party, darlin'." Toby picked Lizzy up and swirled her around in the foyer.

"Y'all told me an hour," Truman grouched. "I've been sitting here in this chair for three hours and my mouth is dry as bone. I need a drink. Don't you look at me like that, Dora June. I earned it."

"The bartenders left thirty minutes ago with the caterers," Blake said. "I bet I can mix up anything you want. There's a little liquor left."

"I don't want liquor. I want a beer." Truman pulled the beard and hair off in one motion. "But first, Dora June, I want you to get me out of this pillow contraption so I can go to the bathroom."

"I suppose you've earned a beer," Dora June said.

"While they're gone, take what's left of the liquor out to our truck," Lizzy said. "We paid too much for that to have Dora June pour it down the drain."

"Part of it can go upstairs to my room," Jud offered.

"We've got maybe five minutes." Blake nodded.

Several cold beers were on the dining room table with the leftovers when Dora June and Truman returned. He was dressed in his usual overalls, a pair of bedroom slippers, and a flannel shirt. To imagine him as Santa Claus at that point was impossible.

He picked up a beer and carried it to the living room, where he plopped down in a chair and propped his feet up in a second one. "I ain't stayed up this late in years," he said as he tipped back the bottle and took a long gulp.

Dora June sat down across the table from him, propped her feet up, and popped the cork out of a bottle of champagne. "Somebody get us eight glasses from that bar out there. We're going to celebrate success."

Truman spewed beer across the table. "Where did you get that?"

"I took it from the bar when they were setting things up.

We done good, so don't you fuss at me, Truman O'Dell. I don't reckon one glass of this pretty pink stuff will make me drunk," she told him.

"I'll get Allie," Blake stammered.

"Good idea," Lizzy said. "She won't want to miss this."

A few minutes later, Blake carried a sleeping baby, all nestled down into her carrier, into the room. "I see that you've got it poured, Fiona. So a toast." He set the carrier on the floor and picked up a glass in one hand and wrapped the other one around Allie's shoulders. "To a wonderful year. We've made more progress than we thought we would and this party was a big success. Thank you to our wives, to Fiona and to Dora June and Truman for helping us."

"Hear, hear!" Toby raised his glass.

Everyone followed his lead and touched their glasses together.

"Well, now!" Dora June said when she tasted the champagne. "If I'd of known how good that tasted, I would have saved back two bottles."

"Dora June!" Truman gasped.

She picked up his bottle of beer and swallowed twice. "Hmmph," she said. "Mine is better than that stuff. It tastes like yeast bread smells when it's risin'."

"Well, I like yeasty bread," Truman said defensively.

"And I like this pink bubbly stuff," she said.

"To the Lucky Penny. May it continue to prosper." Fiona held up her glass again.

Truman hesitated but he clinked his with the others and finished off the remainder of the champagne in his glass. Dora June poured the last of what was left in the bottle in her glass and sipped at it as she stood.

"I'm going to my room now. Tonight will go down in my book of memories as one of my favorites of all times. Truman, you going with me?" she asked.

He picked up his bottle and followed her, weaving his way through the tables to their bedroom at the end of the foyer.

Blake set his glass on the table. "And we're takin' this baby home. See y'all in church tomorrow morning. Don't forget tomorrow is a potluck. I can't believe Truman has volunteered to play Santa again."

"Me neither. Hey"—Toby lowered his voice—"we should give Dora June and Truman a bottle of champagne for Christmas. We could tuck it into their new RV with a card so they'll find it on their first night."

"I'll take care of buying it if Fiona will hide it," Jud said.

"I'll get a card," Lizzy offered. "But right now, we're going home, too. The rental company said they would be here at three o'clock tomorrow to clean all this up."

"If the church thing isn't finished, y'all can stay and I'll come home to let them in," Fiona offered.

"Then good night to everyone." Allie yawned.

Fiona slid down the back of the door, kicked her shoes off, and stretched out her legs as soon as everyone had left. Jud removed his jacket and hung it on the newel post, pulled off his boots, and sat down beside her.

"That went well, except for Lacy's dress."

"I'd say that went well, too," Fiona said.

Jud took her hand in his and brought it to his lips to kiss each knuckle. "You were the most beautiful woman at the party tonight, darlin'."

She pulled her hand free from his and with a single fluid motion she was sitting in his lap. She laid her head on his chest and listened to his heartbeat. "Thank you," she murmured.

"Tired?" he asked.

"Worn out and we still have the church thing. Oh no! We were supposed to have our first date tomorrow," she groaned.

"How about we watch a movie in my room tomorrow evening? We can take leftovers and cookies up there and have a picnic," he said.

"Will you hold my hand?" she asked.

"And I won't laugh if you snore if you don't laugh at me for the same thing."

"Then it's a date." She yawned.

"Come on, Sleeping Beauty. It's past your bedtime and we both have to be up early."

"Jud, I liked being your girlfriend tonight, too. But what I liked most was the look in your eyes when you watched me walk down the stairs. I felt special."

"You, my darlin', are very special."

They went up the stairs hand in hand.

Fiona stopped in front of her door. "My room is a total mess. I'm going to grab a nightgown and sleep in Mama's bed tonight."

Jud's eyes fluttered shut and his lips came closer and closer. She rolled up on her toes to meet him and wrapped her arms around his neck. The kiss was the perfect ending for the whole evening but it created a deep desire for more.

"Sleep tight, darlin'," he said, and disappeared across the landing.

Chapter Twenty-Three

Fiona overslept on Sunday morning and grabbed a biscuit stuffed with bacon on the way out the back door. Dora June and Truman had left more than an hour before because she had Sunday school class. If Jud hadn't knocked on Fiona's bedroom door as he was leaving, she'd still be asleep.

She'd dashed across the hall to her still messy room, found a bright green skirt that had a matching sweater, and gotten dressed in record time. She'd gone to bed with her hair still swept to one side and it looked like an upside down string mop that had been set out in the sun to dry. She pulled it up into a bun on the back of her head, letting a few curls escape to frame her face. Forget makeup, she didn't have time for that.

Everyone was singing when she slipped in the back door of the church and tiptoed up the aisle to sit at the end of the Logan pew beside Jud. He shared the hymnal with her, but they were on the very last line of the final verse.

The preacher took the pulpit and covered a yawn with

the back of his hand. "Y'all excuse me. If you didn't go to the ranch party at the Lucky Penny last night, you missed a good time. I'll make the sermon short this morning. If you will open your Bibles to the twenty-third Psalms, I'm going to talk about the present. The previous two Psalms talk about the future and the past, but this one tells us what we can expect from the present and that's what's important because it's what we have today."

Work all week, church on Sunday, go see Granny when possible. Fiona asked herself if this was what she wanted out of life as she tuned the preacher out and thought about her own past, present, and future.

Jud laid a hand on the back of the pew and let it fall over her shoulder. A smile tilted the corners of her mouth upward. The past hadn't been so great. A job was a job if it was in a fancy office with a view or if it was in the back room of a little convenience store. The future was as uncertain as Texas weather. This was the present and for right now, she liked her place in it.

"A reminder"—the preacher was winding down when she started to listen again—"we are having our annual Christmas dinner in the fellowship hall today. After we eat, I understand Santa Claus will be ready for pictures and will give out candy and fruit to all the children here today. I'll say our ending prayer and the blessing for today's food at the same time so that y'all can go on and eat as soon you get there."

Everyone's head bowed and the preacher said a very short prayer, which led Fiona to believe that he hadn't had time for a proper breakfast, either. Immediately afterward, there was a mass exodus as the women hurried off to the kitchen, leaving the men folks behind to find their own way in their own time.

"So why aren't you hurrying off to get our donation to the church dinner?" Jud asked.

"Dora June brought our contribution this morning. We had leftover brisket and dozens of cookies from the party last night. Besides, there's enough cooks in the kitchen right now," she answered.

Truth of the matter was, she didn't want to answer a million questions. She'd shared Jud's hymnal, even if only for a few seconds, and he'd put his arm around her. In small-town Texas, those two gestures carried weight and lots of it. Hopefully, everyone would still be talking about Truman, but if they saw her, there wasn't a doubt in her mind that poor old Truman would take a back-seat.

"You look pretty serious." Jud propped a hip on the arm of the first pew and waited for the line to go from the sanctuary through a narrow hallway to the fellowship hall to thin out. "What were you thinking about?"

"Truman deserves the place of honor," she said.

"And that means?" Jud raised an eyebrow.

"What does it mean in your part of Texas if a cowboy shares his hymnbook with a woman and then puts his arm around her in church?" she asked.

"What's that got to do with Truman?" Jud asked.

"Everyone is probably talking about him, but when they see us, he'll go to second place and they're going to bombard me with questions," she answered honestly.

"We could always sneak out the front door, go have Sunday dinner in Seymour and go to a movie after all. We could use the excuse that you needed to see your granny." He took both her hands in his.

"I promised to be there for the rental company. Besides,

if we aren't at the potluck, the rumors will get even worse. We might as well go on and take our medicine."

"Then I say let's give them something to talk about."

Eyebrows shot up when they entered the room holding hands, but everyone was so busy either getting food ready or dishing it up that no one approached Fiona right away. It wasn't until she and Jud sat down at a table with Allie and Blake that anyone said a word. Then it was her oldest sister.

"So it's happening, isn't it?" Allie asked.

"Yes, it is. I'm guilty. I'm having all these carbs when I know they'll go straight to my butt," Fiona answered.

Lizzy leaned around her sister. "You can't run from the truth any more than you could run from your heart."

"What? That my jeans will be too tight after dinner today?" Fiona asked.

"You know exactly what I'm talking about." Lizzy frowned.

"So?" Fiona asked.

"Be careful," Allie whispered.

"I told you the same thing," Fiona reminded her. "I don't believe either of you listened to me. Where is Audrey?"

"You can't change the subject like that, but Dora June is rocking her while I eat and then I'll take over." Allie nodded toward the oversized chairs they'd brought in for Santa Claus and Mrs. Claus.

"How serious?" Allie whispered.

"It was just a hymnbook and we were so damn close together that his arm was pinched," Fiona said.

"And the hand-holding?"

Fiona giggled. "We thought we'd give everyone something to talk about. Looks like it's working."

"Well, dammit!" Lizzy said. "I should have known you'd stir up trouble."

"Me! If you two hadn't already created gossip with your escapades, then no one would even think of throwing me and Jud together."

"Did I hear my name?" Jud asked.

"Of course you did," Fiona said. "I said that you liked sweet potato casserole."

"Yes, I do." He grinned.

After the meal, Santa Claus appeared and everyone was so involved with him that only a few folks noticed when Jud and Fiona left by a side door. The snow had completely stopped and the sun was shining but the north wind bit through her coat and flipped her skirt tail up more than once on the way to her car.

Jud followed her in his truck. Déjà vu all over again so much that she kept her eyes on the road and her hands on the wheel. She did not intend for her mother to come home and find that Fiona had driven her car through a barbed wire fence.

She parked in the front yard of Audrey's Place at the same time the rental company truck backed in beside her, and Jud pulled up on the other side. The timing couldn't have been more perfect. She shut off the engine and had reached for the door handle when Jud opened it for her.

"How about that for getting here at the right minute?" he asked.

She unfastened her seat belt and put her feet out on the ground. "Pretty good, I'd say. I'll get the door open for them and then I'm going up to my room to change and straighten things up enough so I can stand to be in

there. I'm the neat freak in the family. My sisters, especially Lizzy, never put anything away."

"While you are doing that, I will set up our theater," he
said.

"What are we watching?" She opened the door and motioned for the three rental guys to come on inside.

"You have a choice. It's one of those six screen things so
you can pick which one you w. .t." He held the door while
they brought in their dollies to help get things out easier.

"Why only six?"

"Because that's all Josie would let me have. She said
I'd have company and she was out there in the boonies all
alone so I couldn't have all the movies."

"Okay, then, see you in a few."

Fiona changed into yoga pants and an oversized T-shirt,
straightened her room in record time, and then started toward Jud's room when she noticed that he'd set up his
laptop on the credenza in the hall and the two wingback
chairs were pulled up close enough so she and Jud could
see the screen.

Three movie cases were on one side of the computer,
three on the other. Some of the *Fast & Furious* movies took
the right side. On the left, she had a choice of *Something to
Talk About* with Julia Roberts, the first *Lethal Weapon* with
Mel Gibson, and *Shooter* with Mark Wahlberg. She'd seen
them all at least once and some several times but she chose
the Julia Roberts movie.

"I can't believe you even have a chick flick in your
stash," she said.

"It's got a good lesson in it." He slid the DVD drawer
out of the side of the laptop, put the disk in, and started the
movie. "Popcorn or a drink before it starts?"

"Too full still for popcorn. What do we have to drink?"

"Enough Jack for a shot each. Two beers and enough Crown Royal for a Crown and Coke. Your sisters pirated off the rest of it," he said.

"A beer would be great." She settled into one of the chairs and wiggled but couldn't get comfortable. "I've got a better idea about how to watch a movie. Please push these chairs back where they belong."

He went into his room, brought out two beers, set them on the credenza, picked up a chair, and put it where it belonged. She glanced over her shoulder as she headed for her bedroom and watched him pick up the second chair. Muscles straining at the sleeve of his shirt, his stance all powerful—her pulse jacked up at least three notches.

She disappeared into her room and brought out a down comforter and two pillows. She fluffed the comforter out on the floor in front of the laptop, tossed the pillows onto it, and stretched out on her stomach.

He eased down beside her with a groan as the movie started. "And to think that tomorrow night we have to move all that furniture back into the house."

"Poor baby, want me to kiss it and make it all better?" She inched over and kissed him long, hard, and with so much heat that they were both panting when it ended.

"That definitely makes it all better," he said.

Three hours later, the movie had long since finished, the beers were warm and flat, and Fiona was curled up in Jud's arms as they both slept. The rental company had finished and locked the door behind them.

They were sleeping so soundly that neither of them heard Dora June's labored breathing as she climbed the steps. It wasn't until she yelled from the top of the stairs that Fiona set up with a start.

"I was worried about y'all," she giggled like a schoolgirl. "We brought some fried chicken from Wichita Falls. Went on up there to see Irene after the church thing and I talked Truman into wearing his Santa suit. We took the extra candy bags and passed them out to the folks in the home there."

"I could eat some chicken." Fiona stretched and yawned. "We were watching a movie and fell asleep."

"I see that. You might as well pour them beers down the drain, though. They won't be fit to drink. Come on down to the kitchen with us and have some chicken. Your granny was having a good day and we talked about all you girls. And guess what, we drove past that RV place. I know Truman would never do it but sometimes I sure do yearn to see things before I die," she said.

"We'll be right down," Fiona said.

"Are we in trouble?" Jud opened one eye a slit.

"I don't think so. She didn't catch us in a bedroom. And I think she wants an RV so bad that she's got that on her mind."

"It was nice to wake up with you in my arms," he said.

"I thought so, too," she said softly. "It felt right."

Chapter Twenty-Four

Only four shopping days until Christmas and Katy would be home the next day. Suddenly, Fiona realized that she had not bought a single thing for Jud or for her mother. She'd gotten gifts for everyone else, including Truman, but not one thing had caught her eye for the man she'd fallen in love with or her mother.

Love!

She stopped in her tracks going from the back of the store to the checkout counter and gasped. There was no use in running from the truth. She was in love with Jud Dawson and there was no denying it.

The morning coffee drinkers had just left when the store phone rang. She picked up the receiver from the base with one hand and a wet dishcloth with the other.

"This is Fiona," she said.

"Fiona Logan?" a deep masculine voice asked.

"Yes," she said cautiously. The first thought that sent her

heart to her throat was that something had happened to her mother.

"You are a difficult woman to track down."

"Who is this?" she asked bluntly.

"Walton Pierce of Pierce, Davis and Green Law Firm in Pasadena, Texas. You brought your résumé to us almost a year ago and we are interested in interviewing you for a job. Are you still in Houston? If so, we'd like to schedule a meeting before Christmas."

"I left Houston a few weeks ago," she said.

"Then I suppose we'll have to schedule for the week after New Year's. It's our company policy to close the offices from Christmas through New Year's Day. How about January fifth? My secretary will be in touch with you to set up a flight from the city nearest to you and we'll arrange for you to stay at the downtown Westin Hotel while you are here. Any questions?"

"What's the job?" she asked.

"We need an accountant who will oversee three other people in that office. Basically the same job you had before but with a little more responsibility."

She popped herself on the forehead with the back of her hand. Pierce, Davis and Green was her in-law's biggest rival. But why now? Why did Fate put this job in her path right now?

"Interested?" he asked.

"Can I think about it? This has fallen out of the sky, so to speak," she said.

"Of course. I'd expect you to need some time. We'll look forward to seeing you in a couple of weeks. My secretary is out today but she'll be in touch to set up an appointment. Merry Christmas, Miss Logan."

"Merry Christmas to you," Fiona said.

The line went quiet and she set the phone back on the base.

She carried the cloth to the table, wiped it down, and then eased into one chair and used another to prop her feet. She was trying to wrap her mind around the phone call and what it meant to her future. Was the coffee shop experience and the trip to Dry Creek a bump in the road or was it to teach her that she didn't want to work in a big city for a big firm? But Lord have mercy, Pierce, Davis and Green? The biggest firm in Houston had asked for an interview. Walton Pierce had called her personally. That meant volumes.

"Hey," Deke yelled as he entered the store by the back door.

"In here. At the table," she raised her voice to say.

He stopped and drew up a cup of coffee. "I was wondering if you'd go with me to Wichita Falls tonight. I haven't done a damn bit of Christmas shopping." He set his coffee on the table, pulled out a chair, shucked out of his heavy coat, hung it on the back, and then sat down. Removing his hat, he looked at her with pleading hazel eyes. "Say you'll go with me. I don't know how to shop for babies and this is important. It's Audrey's first Christmas."

"Sure. I need to pick up some last-minute things, too." How could life go on like this when she had such a big decision to make?

"Good, I'll tell Blake and Jud."

"What do they have to do with us shopping?"

"They need to get theirs done, too, and we all need a woman's opinion, but I asked first so you have to shop with me before you do them," Deke answered. "What's put a frown on your face? Don't you want to go with Blake and Jud?"

"No, I don't mind at all. But what about Toby?"

Deke shook his head slowly from side to side. "He and Lizzy have everything done. He's so damned organized that it makes the rest of us look bad."

Her cell phone rang and she worked it up out of her hip pocket. The jeans that had been baggy on her three weeks ago were fitting pretty dang snug these days. "Hello, Lizzy, what's goin' on down at your end of the street?"

"Allie needs to do some more shopping, so all us girls are going out for one more night to finish up. Dora June is going with us and we'll stop by and see Granny. Leaving at five on the dot. Be ready," Lizzy said.

"I just promised Deke that I'd go with him," Fiona said.

"That rat! He came by here and I told him I was going to call you; then I had a rush of customers."

"Maybe our paths will cross and we'll take a break and have an Orange Julius together," Fiona suggested.

"I hope not. Allie is shopping for Blake and he'll be with y'all. If you see us, steer those cowboys another way. Oh, and Toby is taking Truman to the RV shop tonight. They are bringing the new toy home and we're keeping it out behind our house until Christmas morning."

"Dora June is going to be speechless," Fiona giggled.

"And that will be the real Christmas miracle."

"Ha! Happy shopping tonight."

"Good luck to you. I wouldn't trade places with you for anything. Customer coming through the door. Bye, now."

Fiona shook a finger at Deke. "You are in trouble."

"I know, but it's worth it. Now what's troubling you?"

Fiona told him about the job interview. "It's a big thing, Deke. It's what I'm trained for and it's the city I love."

"Hard decision you got to make. If you need to talk, holler at me. I'm a good listener," he said.

"I'm in love with Jud," she blurted.

"Well, that ain't no surprise. But I do reckon it makes a difference in your decision about Houston."

"Yes, it sure does."

*　*　*

The mall was crazy that night. Christmas music played over the speakers. Last-minute shoppers raced from store to store. And Fiona found out that shopping with men was a whole different experience than with women. They found what they wanted, got her opinion and bought it, had it wrapped if that was an option, and went on to the next person on their list.

For the most part, they were very practical. Sweaters, new work coats, boots, and wallets, belts—that kind of thing was what they were interested in buying. Two western wear stores pretty much finished their job. Blake did want her to go to Victoria's Secret to pick out something pretty in lingerie for Allie. From the time they entered the store to the time they walked out with a lovely bright red silky nightgown in a gift bag, ten minutes had elapsed.

Jud glanced up from the bench where he and Deke had opted to sit. "Are we all done, then? Can we grab some Chinese food at that place?" He pointed. "My treat since you came with us, Fiona."

Deke whispered something in Jud's ear and Fiona heard her name in the mix of muted words. Jud nodded the whole time and clamped a hand on Deke's shoulder.

Fiona hoped to hell that Deke had not just told him about the interview. She wanted to make up her mind about it before she mentioned it to her mother or to Jud. She fought the urge to pop herself on the forehead. She should have told Deke it was a secret.

"We'll eat first and then, Fiona, we want you to call the girls and go with them for a while," Deke said. "We have to shop for you."

She wanted to wipe her forehead in relief but she held her hands together tightly. "I'll call Lizzy. If they're hungry, maybe they can join us."

"Sounds good," Jud said.

Thank goodness the mall hours had been extended from Monday through Christmas Eve because after they'd eaten and the guys had gone off in a different direction from the ladies, Fiona was completely at a loss.

Where did she shop and what did she buy for Jud?

"Did you see that Santa right back there?" Dora June asked.

"You want to go back and sit on his lap?" Fiona asked.

"No, but my Truman looked better than that. I bet he could get a job being Santa and he'd look better than that guy did," Dora June declared. "That man's eyes were glazed over. I bet he's been drinking. I wouldn't let my kids sit in his lap. Oh, here's the toy store. I want to look for a Raggedy Andy doll for Audrey to go with Ann doll I got her last time."

"Y'all go on. I'm going to sneak into this bookstore," Fiona said.

Nothing took Fiona's eye in the store until she was leaving and noticed a small display at the end of an aisle. A cowboy hat hung on a nail up above stacks of long, narrow booklets titled *Merry Christmas Cowboy*. The tagline said, "Something special for the sexy cowboy in your life."

She picked one up and flipped it open to find a coupon

for each week of the upcoming year and they all had to do with something a cowboy would like. A night of western movies. A picnic in the pasture. Plus there were a few that made her blush but Jud would love it.

Did buying it mean that she was staying in Dry Creek? Or did it mean he'd have to drive or fly to Houston to collect once a week? She wasn't sure but she bought the booklet anyway and meandered on down the mall alone.

A sex toy place caught her eye because of the silk boxer shorts hanging in the window. She chose a pair with a picture of glow-in-the-dark tangled Christmas lights printed on the front. With their past experience with the condoms, he'd think those were funny.

Two presents and neither one of them could be wrapped to go under the tree. Now it was time to get serious and buy something for him that he could unwrap in front of the family. She stopped at a jewelry store and stared at the display in the window. A tie tack caught her eye. Shaped like steer horns, it was something that Jud would really like— and then she glanced over at the wedding bands.

She'd had diamonds the first time around and they hadn't helped things to work. Next time all she wanted was a plain gold band—if there was a next time. An antsy feeling told her that someone was staring at her and she looked up to see the manager of the jewelry store smiling from the other side of the glass.

Then an arm slipped around her waist and Jud was there beside her. Her heart jacked up its speed a few notches and her palms got a little clammy as he pulled her close enough that they were touching from shoulder to thigh.

"I've bought you a couple of private things to be opened when it's just us," he said. "But I can't find anything that looks right, that tells you what is in my heart and yet can be opened in front of the family."

"Me too," she sighed.

"How about that?" He pointed toward a red velvet box with a set of matching gold bands.

"Are you serious?" Fiona asked. "We've barely known each other a month."

Her heart fluttered and her hands trembled. She should panic or run but all she wanted to do grab hold of Jud and never let him go.

"We could put them on a shelf until you're ready," he said. "I'm not going anywhere." He dropped down on one knee right there in front of the jewelry store and held her hands in his. "I think I knew I was in love with you the moment you kicked the crap out of the tires on that old truck you drove into town. And since then all I can think about is you. When I go to sleep, I relive the day we've had. When I wake up, I can't wait to see you again. When we dance, it's like the world disappears. I never want to live a day without you. Fiona Logan, will you marry me?"

It was too soon. She had a decision to make about the Houston job. She couldn't rush into anything. She had to plan things out. She couldn't say yes. It was crazy. It was too fast.

She fell to her knees in front of him, hands still in his, and listened to her heart instead of all the noise in her head.

"Yes," she said, and all the doubts and fears about decisions disappeared into the air along with the Christmas music.

He let go of one hand and tipped her chin up with the back of his forefinger. When his lips met with hers, they were the only two people on the whole planet and she knew she'd made the right decision even if it was impulsive.

"I didn't plan this," he whispered softly.

"Neither did I."

"Let's go in here and buy you an engagement ring. We can wait until summer for a wedding." He straightened up and pulled her to her feet.

"Why?" she asked.

"Because I want everyone in the whole world to know that you're mine," he said.

"No, I mean, why wait until summer? I don't want a long drawn out affair that will drive us both crazy. Lizzy did that when she was engaged to Mitch. It was horrible. That's not for me."

"Spring?" Jud asked.

"We could get a license tomorrow and the preacher could perform the ceremony after the Christmas church service. We can have a reception later with all our families there but Dora June and Truman won't miss the wedding that way."

He picked her up and twirled her around half a dozen times until they were both dizzy with happiness. Everyone near them had stopped to stare, so he yelled, "She said yes!"

The applause echoed off the walls of the mall and several people started a mob humming of the traditional wedding song.

Jud bent her backward in a true Hollywood kiss before he led her into the jewelry store.

"Congratulations." The store manager grinned.

"We need to look at that set of wedding bands in the window," Jud said. "We're getting married this week."

The jeweler held the rings out. "They can be resized by tomorrow afternoon."

Jud slipped the smaller one on Fiona's finger and the larger one on his. They fit perfectly.

Fiona held up her hand, the band shining in the well-lit jewelry store. Saying yes might have been impulsive, but it was right. And when something was a right fit, she wasn't going to argue.

Then the guilt set in—she should tell him about the job offer, right? And yet she could not spoil their moment with that news.

On the way home, the guilt got the better of her and she said, "Jud, I have something I have to tell you."

"That you've reconsidered and want to wait?"

"No, it's more than that."

"You look like you are about to explode. Please don't tell me you've changed your mind about us altogether," Jud said.

"Not about us. I love you, but maybe about Dry Creek," she said, and then told him about the offer.

"I don't give a damn if you go to Timbuktu, Fiona. I'll be there beside you. There are ranches and oil in this whole state, and like I said, I want your beautiful face to be the last thing I see at night and the first thing I see in the morning," he said. "I feel like I've been hunting for you my whole life and now that I've found you, I don't intend to let you go."

"I love you, Jud Dawson," she whispered.

Chapter Twenty-Five

Where had the week gone?

Jud proposed on Monday. Not a single member of the family, Dora June and her mother included, was surprised. Happy for them but not surprised.

On Tuesday morning the secretary from Pierce, Davis and Green called and offered her a plane ticket to and from Houston and a car to take her to an interview and then she could catch a flight back home if she would only come to talk to them before the holidays.

When Fiona checked her mother's flight into Dallas on Wednesday, she saw it would all work out perfectly. Fiona's return flight would get in thirty minutes before Katy arrived from Florida. Besides, there was still a tiny little niggling thought in the back of her mind that wondered what it would be like to be back in the city, carrying a briefcase—and being the supervisor of an accounting department.

She had to go.

She had to know for sure.

But how did she tell Jud?

That evening she carried a heavy heart to his bedroom and leaned on the door frame. "I need to talk."

"They called again, didn't they?" he asked.

"I'm going to go talk to them tomorrow. I've got the perfect story. I'm going to Dallas a little early to pick up Mama at the airport, maybe to do some shopping. One of Herman's granddaughters is going to babysit the store for me."

Jud pulled her into his arms. "Of course you have to go, darlin'. If you get down there and it's what you really want, we'll cross that bridge when we come to it. I love you, Fiona. I would never stand in the way of your dreams."

"I love you, too, Jud, and we can work this out no matter which way the ball falls."

* * *

Flying first class that morning, the sky was literally the limit. During the hour-long flight from Dallas to Houston, she made herself forget all about Dry Creek and concentrate on the day at hand. She wanted to feel the rush of the big city, of wearing a cute little navy blue suit and high-heeled shoes. If she had time, she might even slip into her old hairdresser's place of business on the way out of town and get her hair done.

Excitement built higher and higher when she saw the driver holding a tablet with her name on it. He led her out to a limousine and held the door for her. The firm was surely courting her in high style. Twenty minutes later, she was sitting in an office on one side of a highly polished table with four men and a woman on the other side.

"Ms. Logan, I'm very impressed with your résumé. We

like your work ethic, your dependability, and your dedica-
tion. We do, however, have a few questions. The first one
being why have you dropped out of the market for a year?"
the oldest one of the four men asked.

"I was working in the same firm as my husband. We divorced," she said.

"Well, that clears that up. I'm surprised that you didn't
find a job immediately with another firm. We weren't in the
market for your skills but surely there were other places,"
the lady said.

"I put in several résumés with several companies. I
guess no one was in the market for my skills until now,"
Fiona answered honestly.

"Well, we like what we see and we would like to make
you an offer and introduce you to the other three people in
the department," one of the men said.

"I have a question," Fiona asked. "How long have these
other three been working for you?"

"One has been here twenty years, one eighteen, and the
last one fifteen. The supervisor who left retired after thirty-
five years with us. Folks stay with us when they join the
firm," the woman said proudly.

"Why not promote one of those to this position and hire
someone to fill that place?" Fiona asked.

"We thought new blood might be good and all three of
them will retire in a few years. We don't want to be left in
the same position we are now."

Fiona turned over her hands, palms up, in her lap. In the
left one she put the offer of the new job and thirty years of
future work in this firm with all the perks that came with it.
There would be hard feelings in the ranks because she was
younger than any of the people that she'd be supervising.

But she could overcome that with kindness, fairness, and hard work.

She put family, Dry Creek, and Jud in the right one. An old kitchen table in the back room of the store compared to a lovely office—maybe even with a lovely view, with a gorgeous mahogany desk and comfortable chair. Three clients compared to dozens, maybe hundreds. Cute little power suits or jeans and boots.

The lady was shuffling papers and getting ready to take her to see her office but Fiona's hands were still open. She couldn't make herself rise out of the chair.

Not yet.

Seeing Jud every day or maybe a couple of short weekends a month. Watching Audrey grow up or making an appearance in her life a few times a year. Being with Granny while she was sporadically lucid or never seeing the light in her eyes again.

Jud had said he would follow her to Timbuktu, but was that fair? He loved the Lucky Penny. He was lucky when it came to oil and he was so excited about drilling in a few months.

The left hand slowly closed into a fist and she brought the right one up to rest on the desk. "I'm sorry if I have wasted your time. I do appreciate the expense that you've gone to for this interview, but I'm going to have to refuse your offer."

"The salary is negotiable," Mr. Pierce said quickly.

"It's not the money."

"Then, what?" the secretary asked.

"My heart is in Dry Creek, Texas, and if I can't throw everything into a job, I can't do it," she answered truthfully.

"That's exactly the work ethic we want to see. I'm so sorry that we can't persuade you to join us, but I understand." Mr. Pierce offered his hand.

Fiona stood up and gave it a firm shake. "Thank you again, sir."

She walked out of the office, got into the car, and went back to the airport with no regrets and the lyrics of "Breathe" running through her head.

* * *

Jud met her and Katy at the door, a question on his face as he brushed a kiss across her lips. "Welcome home to both of you."

"Can I talk to you upstairs in the hall?" she asked.

He took her hand in his and walked beside her up to the second floor. "I wanted to call or text but this had to be your decision and you didn't need me to influence you one way or the other."

When they reached the hall, she kicked off her fancy shoes and wrapped her arms around his neck, drew his face down for a long, lingering kiss. "I love you, Jud. Let's get married Sunday morning."

"And the job?"

"I turned them down. When I put everything on the balance scale, that just couldn't come up to the benefits and joy I have right here with you," she answered.

"Sunday? That's Christmas Day," he said. "But it's doable if that's what you want."

Her feet left the floor when he picked her up and swung her around. "This is the best Christmas present ever for me."

"Me too," she giggled. "Now let's go tell everyone."

* * *

Fiona awoke Christmas morning and was on her way down the stairs when she met Jud coming back up with two cups of coffee in his hands. He handed her one and drawled, "Merry Christmas and happy wedding day, darlin'."

She took a sip, and then kissed him. "I can't tell you how happy I am."

He turned around and followed her down the stairs. "Fiona, I did a fair amount of fighting with myself, too. That's why I couldn't be really mad at you when you ran away that night."

He stopped at the end of the steps and pointed up to the mistletoe hanging above the doorway into the kitchen. She held her coffee cup out to the side, wrapped the other arm around his neck, and tiptoed to kiss him. It only amazed her slightly that his touch and his kisses made her knees go weak and created a place where there was no time, no world, nothing but the two of them.

"I love you, Jud Dawson, and when we are old and gray and chasing grandkids around the property on the Lucky Penny, your kisses will still make me want to drag you off to the bedroom."

"I hope so," he chuckled. "That's exactly what I'd like to do right now but I hear truck doors slamming, which means the rest of the family is here. And your mama and Dora June have been making a buffet breakfast for everyone for the past hour, so I expect we'd better wait until later."

"Merry Christmas!" Lizzy called out as she and Toby pushed open the door.

"I smell cinnamon." Blake carried Audrey into the house.

"That's bacon," Allie said right behind them. "Mama

always makes her famous oven omelets with bacon on Christmas."

"You are all wrong. It's coffee." Deke brought up the tail end of the parade.

Coats came off and were hung on the hall tree, along with cowboy hats. Boots were kicked off and lined up against the wall before everyone padded in their socks to the dining room.

"Merry Christmas to all y'all!" Dora June and Katy said.

"Breakfast before presents," Katy said. "This is quite a day."

"And I'll never forget my anniversary." Jud kissed Fiona on the top of her head.

"And this morning I'm asking Truman to say grace for us." Katy bowed her head.

Truman pushed back the chair at the end of the table and stood up. "Thank you, God, for this family, for this beautiful Christmas morning, and for all that you have brought into our lives this past month and for this food. Amen."

Jud squeezed Fiona's hand. "I won. He's no longer Scrooge."

"Yes, you did." She smiled up at him.

"He must be hungry for his prayer to be that short."

"More nervous than hungry. Deke has parked the RV out back. He plans to leave right after the wedding. And Mama says that next Saturday there will be a huge reception at the church for us, and all your family has been invited. Allie and Lizzy say there are lots and lots of Dawsons."

He put a finger over her lips. "They will love you because you love me."

"Okay," she said. "But it's not fair that you only had to remember a few names and I'll have to get to know dozens of new faces."

"Dozens?" Jud chuckled. "Try hundreds. I'm just glad that we'll be married or my handsome cousins would steal you from me."

"Not a chance," she said.

* * *

Presents flowed out from under the tree to the sofa, and following tradition, Katy passed them all out before she sat down in a rocking chair. "And now," she said, "you may start opening."

"All at once?" Jud asked.

"That's the way we do it," Fiona answered. "It's noisy but it's so much fun."

Like a little girl, Dora June ripped into her first package and brought out a lovely set of monogrammed towels. The second one produced a set of pots and pans and the third one a set of dishes and cutlery for four.

Truman's first present was a pair of red swimming trunks with bright blue dolphins printed on them. His second was a pair of flip-flops and the third was a digital camera from Deke.

"What on earth does Truman need that for?" Dora June asked. "Y'all are playin' pranks on him, aren't you?"

"He might want to take a few pictures," Deke said. "He can send them straight to your phone and you can send them on to us."

"Well, it will be kiddin' time before long. I expect he could take pictures of the new baby goats." She opened a set of king-sized sheets. "This is a wedding shower. I love it all." Excitement danced around her as she continued to open gifts while everyone else set theirs to the side and watched as Truman handed her a card with a tiny little present on the top.

Dora June's hand went to her heart and her eyes filled with tears. "You bought me a present, Truman?"

"Guess I did," he said with a slight grin. "Open the card first."

Her eyes filled with tears when she read the card. "Oh, Truman, I don't care what the present is. You bought it for me so it's going to be special."

She laid the card to one side and Fiona saw part of the message: *I hope this will make up for all the Christmases that I've been a jackass. All the rest will be special, I promise.*

The whole room went silent as Dora June pulled the ribbon loose from the small package. When she opened the gold box and found keys to a vehicle, she squealed. "Oh, Truman, you've gotten me a new truck, haven't you? But there's two sets of keys. What's the second set for?"

"Yes, I did." He nodded. "And it's sittin' right outside the kitchen door. Want to go see it?"

"Right now?"

"Right now," Deke said. "Do you know how hard it's been to keep this a secret?"

Truman went ahead of her and slung the back door open. Dora June stepped out onto the porch and immediately tears began to flow down her cheeks, landing on her bright blue Christmas sweatshirt. Her palms flew to her cheeks and she kept blinking as if she wasn't sure she was seeing things right.

"Well, don't stand there blubbering, woman." Truman took her hand in his and opened the door of the enormous

RV. "Come on inside and tell me if you like it. I bought one of them crazy-lookin' smart cars and it's on a little trailer on the back so we can get around wherever we stop for the nights."

"Stop for the nights?" Dora June asked.

"Yep. We've got a reservation at a campground in Jacksboro. I figure that's far enough for tonight and then tomorrow we'll be driving south to Florida. From there, you get to choose where we go next. I hope before we die we have spent a few weeks in every state."

Dora June wrapped her arms around Truman's neck and hugged him tightly. "Now I understand the presents."

"Let's go back inside," Katy said softly. "They need to explore their new home for the first time together."

"Are you going to buy me an RV when we're married fifty years?" Fiona asked Jud on the way to the living room.

"No, but I could buy you some goats," he said.

Her eyes widened out. "You didn't? You wouldn't?"

Jud hugged her close to his side. "Don't worry, darlin'. I don't want goats, either. We talked Deke into buying all of Truman's stock. Cattle and goats. Truman gave him a deal on his equipment and all the hay in his barns if he'd take on the goats with the deal."

Paper was scattered everywhere and they were down to only a couple of gifts each when Dora June and Truman came back to the room. They were holding hands and her face was still streaked with tears and be damned if that wasn't a tear in Truman's eye.

"Scrooge is officially dead and Truman is alive," Fiona whispered to Jud.

"I see that," he said softly.

"Now open our presents," Dora June said. "Truman,

you get that camera and take a picture of Audrey with her dolls."

"I don't know how to work that damned thing," he grumbled.

"Like this," Deke said, patiently explaining the basics. "If you can learn how to put a tractor together, you can learn this, Truman."

"I'll give it a try," he said stoically.

All the gifts had been opened, but then Katy held up one present that had been overlooked under the tree. "This one has Jud and Fiona's name on it."

"Who is it from?" Fiona reached out to take it from her mother.

"Me," Katy said.

Fiona tore into it to find a letter and three keys. With a quizzical expression, she started to open the letter but her mother put a hand on her arm.

"I'll explain. The key with the red top is to this house. The one with the blue top is to the store. The one with the fancy stuff is the car keys to my car that I stole from your purse last night because I didn't have time to get another one made."

"But I have keys to all those places," Fiona said.

"These are special keys. They belong to you and Jud, not just to you. I'm giving you Audrey's Place and the twenty acres it sits on with the stipulation that from now on it's not Audrey's Place but part of the Lucky Penny Ranch. I'm giving you the convenience store. Lizzy got the feed store. Allie got the construction business. You get the store. It's a combination wedding gift, welcome-home-to-where-you-belong gift, and Christmas present all in one."

Now it was Fiona's turn to cry. "Mama, I don't ever

know what to say. Thank you isn't nearly enough." She almost bowled Katy over when she hugged her.

"Yes, it is because I'm buying a condo in Wichita Falls in the same complex with Trudy and Janie. I can be near your grandmother so I can see her every day and I've found that I like not having so many responsibilities. It's close enough to y'all that I can visit any time I want and far enough I won't be meddling."

"Jud?" Fiona asked.

"I'm speechless. Thank you, Katy. This is huge," Jud stammered.

"Not really. It's a hell of a lot of work, both here and at the store. You'll earn your living but I've got every confidence that you two are going to be just fine." Katy reached for Jud and made it a three-way hug.

* * *

The preacher took his place behind the pulpit and smiled out over the family and few friends who were attending the small wedding. "It dawned on me this morning that all three of the Logan ladies will be married in the same year, and on or near a holiday. That sure makes it easy for the grooms to remember their anniversary."

He motioned toward the piano player while the chuckles died down. Instead of the traditional wedding song, Fiona had chosen the music from "Breathe." She'd danced to it with Jud and it had been the song in her head as she left her past behind and looked ahead to a bright future with him.

Deke walked Fiona down the aisle, her arm looped in his. Fiona wore a cute little white lace dress that hugged her body and stopped at midthigh, where a white satin garter shined on her leg. Instead of high-heeled shoes, she'd chosen the cowboy boots that she'd worn the night she and Jud had gone dancing. She carried a bouquet of white roses tied up with dark green ribbons.

When she passed the pew where her granny sat with Allie, Blake, and Katy, Fiona stopped and pulled a rose from her bouquet and handed it to Irene. She planted a kiss on Irene's forehead and sent up a silent prayer of thanks that her grandmother was lucid right then.

Deke led her right to where Jud waited and kissed her on the cheek. "Be happy, darlin', and, Jud, you remember who you'll have to deal with if you ever hurt her feelings."

"Never happen." Jud grinned as he took Fiona's hand in his.

"Who gives this woman to be married to this man?" the preacher asked.

"Her family and I do," Deke said.

The first chords of "Amazed" began to play on a CD player. Fiona looked deeply into Jud's eyes all during the song. She'd found her place and now she belonged. Jud had been right when he'd said that maybe what she'd been looking for was someone to put down roots with and she was more than ready to do just that—right there in Dry Creek, Texas.

When the song ended, Fiona took the microphone from the preacher's hand. "Every word in that song is my vow to you, Jud. I can feel how much you love me and it does blow me away. I truly have never been this close to anyone. I can actually hear your thoughts and see your dreams and I'm so glad that I'm spending the rest of my life with you beside me because I'm totally amazed that we have this love."

Jud's lips met hers in a brief kiss as he took the microphone from her. "Darlin' Fiona. I don't even believe in love at first sight, but it happened. And those words sunk into my heart at the bar where we danced that night. I realized that I had the best thing that could ever happen to me in my arms and I wanted you to be there forever and ever."

He gave the microphone to the preacher, who smiled and cleared his throat. "I'm getting used to the Logan ladies doing things their way, so we'll get right into the ceremony." He went on to perform a traditional ceremony, ending with, "And now, Jud Dawson, you may kiss your bride again."

Fiona was breathless when the kiss ended and she was standing upright. She could almost feel the roots growing as she shed her wings that day in front of God and her whole family.

Fiona threw her bouquet toward the back of the church. A pair of hands came up and caught it, but she didn't notice who it was.

The preacher pulled the microphone closer to his mouth so everyone could hear above the noise. "I would like to introduce Mr. and Mrs. Jud and Fiona Dawson for the first time. I'll miss these holiday weddings but there are no more Logan ladies so..."

"Whoa!" Fiona said loudly. "There's still Deke! He's like our little brother so..."

"And I caught the bouquet." Deke held it up.

"And I damn sure ain't married," Granny Irene piped up.

Jud grabbed her hand and the two of them did a fancy swing dance all the way to the back of the church as "Amazed" played for the second time. At the end of the song, Jud scooped her up into his arms and carried her to the fellowship hall.

"We did it our way, didn't we, Mrs. Dawson," he said.

"We did." She pulled his face to hers for a long, lingering passionate kiss.

"Merry Christmas," he drawled.

"Merry cowboy Christmas to me." She grabbed his hand. "And just think, we've got a whole lifetime ahead of us," she said.

* * *

Jud carried Fiona from the pickup and across the yard. She used her brand-new key to unlock the door to their house. It wasn't different than when she'd left it a few hours earlier. The outside lights were still sparkling. The Christmas tree still stood in the corner of the living room. But it felt different because it was now her house and it was part of the Lucky Penny.

He shut the door and locked it without setting her down, then carried her all the way up the stairs and to his bedroom, where he kicked the door shut with the heel of his boot. Then he gently put her feet on the floor and pulled her close to his chest.

"You are really my wife. I've lived in fear that something would happen to make you change your mind. I love you so much," he said.

"Jud Dawson, when I said yes when you proposed, I was more at peace with myself than I've ever been in my life. I love you and our hearts are wrapped up together now and forever."

"Now where are those glow-in-the-dark…" He grinned.

"No need. I made a trip to the doctor in Throckmorton I got a shot that covers all that for three months. We'll talk later about whether I'll take another one or not," she said as she started unfastening the buttons on his shirt, one by one.

"Merry cowboy Christmas to me," he singsonged as he slid the zipper of her dress down slowly, the touch of his hands making her insides quiver...again.

About the Author

Carolyn Brown is a *New York Times* and *USA Today* best-selling romance author and RITA finalist. *Merry Cowboy Christmas* is her eightieth published book. Presently writing both women's fiction and cowboy romance, Brown has also written historical single title, historical series, contemporary single title, and contemporary series. She lives in southern Oklahoma with her husband, a former English teacher, who is not allowed to read her books until they are published. They have three children and enough grandchildren to keep them young.

You can learn more at:
CarolynBrownBooks.com

Fall in Love with Forever Romance

A CHRISTMAS BRIDE
By Hope Ramsay

USA Today bestselling author Hope Ramsay's new contemporary romance series is perfect for fans of Debbie Macomber, Robyn Carr, and Sherryl Woods. Haunted by regrets and grief, widower David Lyndon has a bah-humbug approach to the holidays—until he's shown the spirit of the season by his daughter and her godmother Willow. Paired up to plan a Christmas wedding for friends, David and Willow will discover that the best gift is the promise of a future spent together...

CHRISTMAS COMES TO MAIN STREET
By Olivia Miles

It's beginning to taste a lot like Christmas...or so Kara Hasting hopes. Her new cookie business is off to a promising start, until a sexy stranger makes her doubt herself. Fans of Jill Shalvis, RaeAnne Thayne, and Susan Mallery will love this sweet holiday read.

Fall in Love with Forever Romance

A HIGHLANDER'S CHRISTMAS KISS
By Paula Quinn

In the tradition of Karen Hawkins and Monica McCarty comes the next in Paula Quinn's sinfully sexy MacGregor family series. Temperance Menzie is starting to fall for the mysterious, wounded highlander she's been nursing back to health. But Cailean Grant has a dark secret, and only a Christmas miracle can keep them together.